# The Dressmaker's War

# BOOKS BY MICHELLE VERNAL

BRIDES OF BOLD STREET SERIES
*The Dressmaker's Secret*
*The Dressmaker's Past*
*The Dressmaker's Chance*

THE LITTLE IRISH VILLAGE SERIES
*Christmas in the Little Irish Village*
*New Beginnings in the Little Irish Village*
*A Christmas Miracle in the Little Irish Village*
*Secrets in the Little Irish Village*
*Saving Christmas in the Little Irish Village*

*The Little Irish Farm*

LOVE ON THE ISLE OF WIGHT SERIES
*The Promise*
*The Letter*

THE IRISH GUESTHOUSE ON THE GREEN SERIES
*O'Mara's*
*Moira-Lisa Smile*
*What Goes on Tour*
*Rosi's Regrets*
*Christmas at O'Mara's*
*A Wedding at O'Mara's*

*Maureen's Song*
*The O'Maras in LaLa Land*
*Due in March*
*A Baby at O'Mara's*
*The Housewarming*
*Rainbows over O'Mara's*
*O'Mara's Reunion*
*The O'Maras Go Greek*
*Mat Magic at O'Mara's*
*Matchmaking at O'Mara's*
*Cruising with the O'Mara's*

*When We Say Goodbye*
*Staying at Eleni's*
*The Traveller's Daughter*
*Sweet Home Summer*
*The Cooking School on the Bay*

# The Dressmaker's War

**MICHELLE VERNAL**

*Bookouture*

Published by Bookouture in 2025

An imprint of Storyfire Ltd.
Carmelite House
50 Victoria Embankment
London EC4Y 0DZ

www.bookouture.com

The authorised representative in the EEA is Hachette Ireland
8 Castlecourt Centre
Dublin 15 D15 XTP3
Ireland
(email: info@hbgi.ie)

Copyright © Michelle Vernal, 2025

Michelle Vernal has asserted her right to be identified
as the author of this work.

First published by Michelle Vernal as *The Spring Posy* in 2021.

All rights reserved. No part of this publication may be reproduced, stored in any retrieval system, or transmitted, in any form or by any means, electronic, mechanical, photocopying, recording or otherwise, without the prior written permission of the publishers.

ISBN: 978-1-83618-596-3
eBook ISBN: 978-1-83618-597-0

This book is a work of fiction. Names, characters, businesses, organizations, places and events other than those clearly in the public domain, are either the product of the author's imagination or are used fictitiously. Any resemblance to actual persons, living or dead, events or locales is entirely coincidental.

## GLOSSARY

### COMPENDIUM OF LIVERPUDLIAN WORDS

Antwacky – Old-fashioned or out of dat

Arl fella – Father

Bevvie – Alcoholic drink

Bobby – Policeman

Boss – Describing something you really like

Brassic – No money

Cob on – To feel angry, agitated or irritated

Meff – A derogative term

Ozzy – Hospital

Queen – A woman

# PART ONE

# 1

### 1982

Sabrina peered intently into the bathroom mirror as she did most mornings and wondered whether she looked like her mother. Did she have the same oval-shaped face with milky skin and freckles stamped across an upturned nose? There were so many questions she desperately wanted answered. Why had her mother left her alone as a three-year-old child on Bold Street? Had they been separated by the mysterious timeslip she now knew first-hand existed on Bold Street? Was her mother risking everything like Sabrina was each time she stepped through the portal to another time trying to find her?

'You won't find out by gawping at yourself in the mirror, Sabrina,' she said, sighing and banishing the ghost of her mother before she padded through to the kitchen to make breakfast.

The poppy song that burst out of the radio when she switched it on restored the good mood she'd woken with, and she sang along to it, going through the motions of making the porridge. A silly smile teased her lips as she recalled her cinema date with Adam last night. Not that she could remember much of the film they'd gone to see other than it was called *Cat People*. Adam was the horror buff not her, but he hadn't seen much of it given they'd spent the best part of the film canoodling in the back row as Aunt Evie would say!

Tucking her red-blonde hair behind her ears, she set three bowls out on the worktop. One for herself, one for Aunt Evie and one for Fred. Now spring was here, Fred had returned to Bold Street, spending his nights a few doors down from the flat above Brides of Bold Street where she lived and worked with her aunt Evie.

A surprisingly perky voice called out from the bedroom just off the living room, 'Don't you be using the top of the cream on that vagabond's porridge, Sabrina. I know you, my girl. You're too soft-hearted for your own good.'

Aunt Evie was all-seeing, Sabrina thought, staring at the unopened milk bottle in her hand from which she had indeed planned to scrape the cream. How she'd known this while she was still lying in her bed was a mystery.

'I'm saving that cream for my strawberries,' trilled the voice once more.

Ray Taylor had dropped a punnet of the berries in yesterday as a softener before asking Aunt Evie out – again. He was becoming more persistent on his quest to win Aunt Evie's heart, and how the strawberries had been sourced, given it was only April, was another of life's mysteries. She'd wondered too how he knew they were her aunt's favourite.

A jolt of annoyance passed through Sabrina now as she placed the milk back in the fridge. She'd missed an opportunity yesterday. She should have casually dropped in that she was stepping out with Ray's son while they were both there. The moment she'd opened her mouth to speak, however, Aunt Evie had snatched the punnet out of her hands.

'She'll eat the lot, Ray, with that sweet tooth of hers,' she'd tsked before declining Ray's dinner invitation.

Clearly, the strawberries hadn't been enough of a softener.

Adam had seemed nonplussed when she'd mentioned Aunt

Evie and his dad knowing one another. He'd brushed it off with a throwaway comment as to how his arl fella had had lots of business dealings on Bold Street given he was in the business of property management. She wondered what Adam would say if he knew his dad was trying to woo her aunt and that the pair of them had a shared history. She'd get to the bottom of it one of these days, she determined. Easier said than done, though, as Aunt Evie clammed up whenever she broached the topic.

Sabrina stirred the plopping porridge. 'It's time you were up, Aunt Evie,' Sabrina called out, pouring porridge into two of the waiting bowls. She left hers warming on the stove. 'Your breakfast's on the table.' Her head cocked to one side as she waited for the tell-tale squeaking of the bedsprings. 'And I didn't use the cream, for your information.' She pulled the hand-knitted cosy over the teapot – it would be brewed by the time she got back – then slid her jacket on and flicked her hair out from under the faux-fur collar.

Then came her morning ritual of switching the light in the stairwell on and off three times before she carefully made her way down the stairs with Fred's breakfast. It was an idiosyncrasy of hers – or a compulsion. All Sabrina knew was if she didn't complete the ritual, she was left feeling panicky that something bad would happen. She didn't need a psychiatrist to tell her the root cause of this behaviour because being abandoned by your mother as a small child – or at least thinking that was the case for most of your life – would do that to a girl. She glanced into the workroom to see the gown she'd been hand-stitching lace appliqué onto yesterday was still draped across the table. She didn't linger, traversing the obstacle course of mannequins modelling ready-made gowns and rolls of fabric on the shop floor in the dim light.

The day would be a belter, Sabrina thought as she unlocked the door and stepped outside. Flo would be pleased. It was the first get-together of the Bootle Weight Watchers jogging group this evening – or the Bootle Tootlers, as they were officially called. The name was the brainchild of Bossy Bev, who headed up the weight-loss group, and she was even springing for T-shirts. Flo wasn't best pleased by the name or having to broadcast it by wearing the tee, but she was excited at having been put in charge of the group.

'I've never been in charge of anything before,' she'd told Sabrina excitedly. Then had announced she expected Sabrina to accompany the Bootle Tootlers on their maiden jog around North Park. She'd tasked her friend with bringing up the rear to ensure none of the members dropped by the wayside.

'Or decide to leg it home,' Sabrina had only half joked when she'd finally agreed to take part.

Bold Street was beginning to wake up as she made her way past Esmerelda's Emporium to where she could see the familiar mound in the doorway up ahead. Fred's snores rumbled as she drew nearer, and as she reached the slumbering pile of coats and blankets, she cleared her throat, saying loudly, 'Fred, it's room service.' There was no response, so she turned up the volume. 'Fred, wake up! Your porridge will get cold.'

A woolly hat was the first sign of life emerging, and it was followed by a red-nosed, whiskery Fred, whose rheumy eyes blinked blearily up at her. His expression brightened as he dragged himself up so he was sitting with his back against the wall.

Sabrina beamed. 'Ahright there, Fred.'

He retrieved a bottle with only a few slugs of golden liquor left in it from under the ragtag blanket and coat he'd pulled over himself, eyeing it. 'Better than any fire or electric blanket and cheap at half the price that is, Sabrina, my girl.' His teeth were yellow as he flashed her a grin before being seized by a phlegmy spasm of coughs. When he'd recovered, he stood the bottle out of harm's way.

'I dined like a king last night on a fillet of finest cod,' he told her, gesturing to a grease-sodden sheet of newspaper balled up in the corner.

A fish 'n' chip supper then. Sabrina smiled, amused as he reached up with hands stuffed inside fingerless mittens to take the bowl from her. She watched as he spooned in the oats, scraping the bowl clean and smacking his lips when he'd finished.

'That, my girl, was just what the doctor ordered.'

If he had nothing else, at least he'd had that, Sabrina thought, hesitating. 'Fred, can I ask you something?'

He'd produced a packet of tobacco and was setting about rolling a whippet-thin ciggie. 'Ask away, my girl, ask away.'

She wondered how many young women had a vagabond, as Aunt Evie called Fred, for an agony aunt. It wasn't the first time she'd asked him for advice, and she took a moment to formulate what it was she wanted to say. By the time she'd relayed her dilemma over telling Aunt Evie that her Adam was Ray Taylor's son, Fred had located his matches and was puffing thoughtfully on his ciggie.

'The sins of the father springs to mind, Sabrina.'

'What do you mean?' Adam hadn't done any sinning.

'You're worried your aunt will take an instant dislike to your young man based on her opinion of his father. That she'll assume he's... what did you say her catchphrase is?'

'A wide boy, because Ray Taylor used to be in the Lime Street Boys when he was young, and you're right, I suppose I am.' It was more complicated than that though. Aunt Evie made out she'd no time for the likes of Ray Taylor, yet her face lit up when he paid her one of his ever-increasing visits. She was offhand with him, but it never fazed him. Sabrina also had a feeling that her aunt would view his son as not being good enough for her. She had a saying about apples not falling far from trees she was fond of.

'He's not his father, and no good comes from keeping secrets.'

It was a little cryptic, Sabrina thought, bending to retrieve the bowl. She straightened as Fred added, 'You can't live your life for somebody else.'

There was a wistfulness to his tone, and Sabrina would have loved to have delved deeper, but if she didn't get back upstairs to the flat, she'd have to forego her breakfast!

'Thanks, Fred. I'd best be off. I'll see yer tomorrow.'

She set off back down the street, having resolved to tell her aunt about Adam that morning. What did it matter whether she approved of him or not? She was a grown woman.

But even as she told herself this, she knew she was kidding herself because Aunt Evie's approval did matter. It mattered a lot because if it weren't for her aunt, she'd have had no one to call family at all.

Duran Duran's hit, 'Girl's on Film', was playing on the radio in the workroom out the back of Brides of Bold Street, and Sabrina was humming along. She knew all the words by heart. Her bezzy mate, Flo, was mad on Simon Le Bon, her latest muso crush and Sabrina fancied she'd forget all about Adam's mate Tim Burns if Simon were to rock up and ask her out. The odds of this happening, though, were about the same as Tim giving Linda, his new girlfriend – who bore an uncanny resemblance to Farrah Fawcett – the flick, so to speak. Flo had a face on her like a wet weekend whenever she spied the couple together, which, given the Swan was their local, was often.

Sabrina was finishing where she'd left off yesterday, hand-stitching lace appliqué onto a client's gown. The workroom where she and Aunt Evie worked companionably alongside one another was always a hive of industry even in these lean Thatcherism times. People might have had to tighten their belts under the Iron Lady, but they still got married, and all brides wanted to feel beautiful on their special day. She was fortunate to have apprenticed under the best in the bridal business, Aunt Evie, who'd taught her everything she knew about the process of creating dresses that made dreams come true.

These days, her aunt had loosened her grasp on the reins, and it was Sabrina who was in charge of the bespoke gown designs, pattern making, and cutting out and fitting of the calico toiles. Aunt Evie's eyes weren't what they'd once been, and the delicate needlework required for attaching beading, buttons, lace and other embellishments also fell to Sabrina. Nobody could say Aunt Evie didn't pull her weight though. She still sewed up a storm on the trusty old Singer sewing machine she refused to upgrade.

As Simon continued to belt out the hit song, Sabrina's mind turned to love and how the path to finding your true love was never straightforward. In Flo's case, it was proving especially twisty. There was poor Tony, who went around in the same group as Adam and Tim, who was mad on her friend, but Flo wouldn't entertain the idea of going out with him on a proper date. It was a shame she was digging her heels in because he was a nice fella, even if he did wear trousers that could have been sprayed on. He'd a good job too. By all accounts, he was going places at British Telecom, where he worked in engineering.

Flo could do a lot worse, Sabrina thought, knowing how well she got on with Tony, but she was adamant it was on a friends-only basis. At least she was happy enough to make up a foursome with them when Sabrina met up with Adam at the pub. It would have been awkward otherwise.

The song came to an end, and the pips to signal the news came on. Aunt Evie lifted her foot off the treadle of the old Singer to listen to the dismal broadcast. It was full of unrest in the Middle East, more job losses here in the north of England and race riots in London.

'I'm going to turn the news off from now on.' Evelyn shook her head in a what's-the-world-coming-to manner.

Sabrina paid no attention to her because she threatened that most mornings. She did have a point though. It was never good news.

'Why can't they ever tell us nice things?' Evelyn lamented.

'Like who won the pools and how to beat the crowds in the January sales,' Sabrina added. Then, remembering the promise she'd made herself earlier, she decided there was no time like the present, took a deep breath and adopted a light breezy tone. 'Oh, by the way, Aunt Evie, I almost forgot. You won't believe this. I mean, what are the odds?'

'I'd tell you if I had a clue as to what you were on about, Sabrina.'

It was best she just spit it out. 'My Adam's only Ray Taylor's son.'

Evelyn's teacup rattled in the saucer. 'I thought there was something familiar about him, but I could never put my finger on it.'

If Sabrina had expected fireworks, then she was disappointed as Evelyn nonchalantly picked up where she'd left off, gunning the sewing machine into life once more. Sabrina knew her aunt too well though, and she could almost hear the cogs of her brain whirring as she processed what she'd been told. She was annoyed – she just wasn't letting on.

The bell sounded, signalling a customer was waiting at the counter. Sabrina was glad of the excuse to put some distance between herself and Aunt Evie while she digested what she'd told her. Gathering herself, she set the gown and lace appliqué aside, plastered a smile on her face and walked into the boutique, feeling her aunt's eyes boring holes into her back.

'Good morning.' She beamed at the woman fidgeting at the counter. She looked to be about Sabrina's age, her fiery red hair cut into a cool, Suzy Q shag.

'Hello.' She smiled, and her face transformed from striking to beautiful. 'I'm Alice Waters. I've got an appointment with Sabrina. I spoke to her on the telephone.'

Sabrina had forgotten all about the appointment, but she wouldn't let her know that. 'Of course. I'm Sabrina. It's lovely to meet you, Alice.' She opened the drawer and retrieved her trusty notebook. 'I'll take notes in here,' she explained, but Alice wasn't listening as she gazed about the shop. Sabrina tried to see it through her eyes hoping she approved of her carefully curated decor. Aunt Evie had left it to her when the time came to if not exactly modernise but rather romanticise the shop floor.

She followed Alice's eyes as they travelled over to the rack of ready-made bridal and bridesmaid dresses, then tracked her journey to the rolls of fabric in their varying wedding-day hues that begged to be stroked. The pattern books showcasing the latest wedding trends hot off the catwalks in Paris needed a straighten, she noted, but Alice had moved on to the velvet drapes of the fitting room and the matching pink velvet-covered blanket box used to display the daintiest of satin shoes.

Sabrina's personal favourite was the chandelier centrepiece with its crystal teardrops falling from the ceiling. Although last week it had been the eclectic display of china teacup and saucer sets behind the counter. The display was a result of Aunt Evie's ever-growing collection, which had now spilled over into the shop. They made for a fabulous talking point when the stress and strain of choosing a gown for the most important day of their life became too much for customers.

Alice cleared her throat.

'Right, let's get down to business.' Sabrina jotted down Alice's name on a fresh page in her notebook. 'First things first then, Alice. What date's the wedding?'

'April the twentieth.'

Sabrina blinked, feeling a throbbing at her temples. She stared at Alice, who had the grace to look sheepish.

'I know it's short notice, but I already have the dress. All I want are a few simple tweaks made to it.' She held up a bag Sabrina hadn't noticed in her quick appraisal of her.

'My Mark's in the army, and he's being deployed to Belfast in early May. We want to be married before he goes.'

The way the pink went out of Alice's cheeks at the thought of her fiancé being sent to Northern Ireland didn't escape Sabrina, and she didn't have the heart to crush this young woman's dream of being wed before that happened either. Her attention had been caught too by the flash of green on her engagement finger. 'That ring's gorgeous. Is it antique?'

'It was me nan's mother's. So, yes, I suppose it is.' She held her hand out so Sabrina could inspect the pear-shaped emerald.

'Gorgeous,' Sabrina repeated. 'Was she a redhead too? Because it's perfect with your colouring.'

Alice nodded. 'She wor, yes.'

'Right, let's see the dress then.' Sabrina smiled, deciding she'd make time for whatever alterations needed doing.

Alice flashed her a hopeful one in return before bending to retrieve the gown. She straightened, holding it up and giving it a shake.

Sabrina gasped as she took in the silk and satin ivory dress. It was a simple design with a crossover neckline, puff sleeves with cuffs and an A-line skirt. It was the simplicity that made it so exquisite. For all that, though, it was dated, and she could see in a flash how it could be brought up to date with a few nips and tucks here and there to ensure Alice was a beautiful spring bride. She instantly wanted to know all about the woman who'd once worn it too. She hoped she'd had a happy life.

'May I?' She gestured to the dress, and Alice nodded.

'Of course.'

Sabrina stepped forward and caressed the silk fabric of the skirt. She visualised a petite young woman full of hopes and dreams for her future standing opposite the man she was about to marry as she promised to love him always. Every wedding dress told its own story.

Alice pushed her shoulders back proudly, pleased by Sabrina's reaction. 'It's beautiful, isn't it?'

'It is. The fabric's like water running through my fingers,' Sabrina affirmed.

'As I said, me nan and her mam before her wore it. Lily Waters was Nan's name. She married me granddad Max back in 1945. They've both passed now, but I've gorra photograph of their wedding day if you'd like to see it?'

'I would like to. Very much so.' Sabrina nodded, thinking how special it was that Alice would have such strong connections to her late grandparents on her wedding day, what with her ring and the dress. It gave her a pang for her own mother and the family history she might never know. 'Here, let me hang it up for you.' She took the dress and carefully slipped it onto a padded hanger before hooking it up on the fitting-room wall.

Alice, meanwhile, had opened the purse resting on her hip, and when Sabrina returned, she held out a small card embellished with creamy roses, framed inside of which was a black-and-white photograph.

Sabrina took it, noting that, despite the frame, the snapshot inside was creased. The wedding party gathered on the steps of a registry office was still plain to see though. The bride, pretty as a picture, looked young, as did her new husband, and she voiced this to Alice.

'They were. Nan was barely eighteen, and me granddad wasn't much older. They knew their own minds though. They were the loves of each other's lives.'

'How romantic,' Sabrina said, her eyes sweeping the rest of the clustered group. The maid of honour looked to be around the same age as the bride. She was a sweet-looking, dark-haired girl dressed in a long dress with a ruffle around the bottom.

'Her maid of honour was called Sarah,' Alice supplied.

'She's lovely,' Sabrina murmured, her gaze alighting on the woman partially visible at the edge of the photo. She could only see half her face, but there was something about her. Something she couldn't put her finger on. The feeling of familiarity didn't make sense, and rather than let it niggle at her, she opened her mouth to ask Alice who she was. But before she could, the words died in her throat as her attention was caught by another member of the wedding party: Aunt Evie, as a young woman, but it was the girl behind her that caught her eye because she looked exactly like Sabrina.

She stared at the photograph unblinkingly for a moment, her breath catching. *It was her* – she was sure of it, but that wasn't what had her feeling as though the floor might turn to quicksand beneath her feet. Instead, it was the image of the man standing next to her.

It was Adam.

# 2

### 1939

Lily Tubb clutched her mam's hand so tightly it hurt. The two plaits she'd twisted her coppery hair into coiled down from beneath the hat she'd wedged on top of her head before leaving the house. She was so pale her freckles were standing out like tiny brown pebbles scattered on a white sand beach, and her eyes were wary.

Lily had always hated her freckles – until her mam had told her they were footprints left by dancing fairies. After hearing that, she fancied they made her special, and she hadn't minded Mickey Kelly calling her Freckle Face so much. Besides, he wasn't in much of a position for name-calling with his nitty hair and grubby knees!

Mam always said she was special because they'd waited so long for her. Her parents had been in their thirties by the time she came along, which seemed positively ancient compared to her friends' parents.

She wanted to dig her worry book out of her coat pocket. Perhaps if she wrote the words, *Leaving Mam – what if I never see her again?* in the notebook, it might help ease her anxiety. Lily was terrified as to what lay ahead and had dreaded this moment that was drawing ever closer—the moment when she'd have to give her mam a final kiss goodbye.

She wasn't ready. It had all happened too quickly. Lily didn't like change at the best of times, and this was anything but the best of times.

She was doing her best to be brave because she knew her mam needed her to be, and besides, tears wouldn't help. They wouldn't change anything. She wished she was older because then she'd be working and wouldn't be able to go. Or, even better, that she had a baby brother or sister, which would mean her mam would be coming with her.

Around her, excited chatter filled the frigid morning air. It mingled with barked instructions and howls from the little ones, who were overwhelmed by what was unfolding. Lily felt sick and knew it was down to fear about what lay ahead and having been woken shortly after five o'clock by her mam.

What a strange thing it had been to make their way to school, where they stood now, in the eerie pre-dawn light – the box containing the gas mask slung over one shoulder, her suitcase clasped in her hand.

She caught sight of Edith. Edith and Sarah were her best friends in the whole world, but there was no sign of Sarah. Sarah had said her mam wouldn't send her and her younger brother, Alfie, away. She refused. *Lucky Sarah*, Lily had thought upon hearing that. She wished Sarah's mam would let her come and stay with them. She loved their home, where Alfie always seemed to be making noise, and Sarah's mam was so easy-going compared to the other mothers, even if it did feel a bit strange calling her Fern instead of Mrs Carter.

Fern was what Mam called eccentric, with her odd ways so out of keeping with social norms. She'd come out with strange things now and again that didn't make sense to Lily, but Sarah would just laugh and say, 'That's Mam. Me dad always says she belongs in a different time.' Lily didn't mind – it made being at

Sarah's house all the more interesting. She waved at Edith but stayed where she was because Edith was talking to her nemesis, Ruth.

Lily loved Edith like a sister, but she didn't like the way her friend couldn't stand being alone, not for a minute, and when Lily or Sarah weren't around, Ruth was the girl she turned to.

Ruth had a strawberry birthmark on her cheek she was terribly self-conscious of, and her face was plain with mousy, lank hair and dishwater eyes to match. She didn't like Lily or Sarah for the simple fact that she wanted to be Edith's friend. Her best friend. Ruth liked to bask in the glow of Edith's blonde prettiness because being pretty meant you got attention and you could get away with all sorts of things you'd get raked over the coals for if you were merely ordinary.

The sight of Ruth hanging off Edith usually annoyed Lily no end, and if these were normal circumstances, she'd go and make her presence known. These weren't normal circumstances, however, and she was reluctant to be parted from her mam.

Ruth's face, she could see now the dark was receding, was alight, and her eyes were dancing. Her tearaway little brothers, Peter and George, were nearby. They were probably looking forward to this, Lily mused.

She knew through Edith that Ruth's parents shouted at each other a lot, especially since her dad had lost his job at the factory where Lily's dad had once worked too. Unlike the late Joe Tubb, Ruth's dad enjoyed a drink. He had a big red nose and spidery veins across his cheeks, and he wasn't very nice when he'd a belly full of it, according to Edith. She'd have felt sorry for Ruth if she wasn't always so deliberately mean toward her and Sarah.

The bruise along Mrs Baldwin's jaw and how she behaved like a cornered animal with her nervous skittishness suggested things at home were a lot worse than Ruth let on to Edith. She'd seen Ruth wince and the sudden tears sprout when she'd put her coat on after school more than once too.

Lily might not like Ruth, but she did know right from wrong, and she'd told her mam and dad when he'd still been with them that she thought Ruth was getting knocked about by her dad. Her dad had blustered that he'd like to go round there and give Clarrie Baldwin a taste of his own medicine, but her mam had told him he'd do no such thing. 'Leave it to Father Ian to sort, Joe,' she'd said. 'It's not our business.'

Edith's mam and dad had said the same thing when she'd told them her suspicions, but Fern, Sarah's mam, was the one who'd gone to the police. Though they'd done about as good a job of sorting Clarrie Baldwin out as Father Ian had, Lily thought, now turning her attention to Edith.

Her friend's small heart-shaped face with its pointy chin was pasty beneath her hat. Lily could see fear mirrored back at her in those deep-set blue eyes, which were framed by thick curling black lashes all the girls envied. Her knuckles were white as she clutched her mam's hand. Elsie, her livewire little sister – her mad mop already springing forth from the bunches her mam had tied them into – was hopping about excitedly.

Lily hoped she managed to get a seat next to them both on the train. She scanned the road, in the direction Sarah and her brother would be coming from if Mrs Carter had changed her mind, but there was no sign of them.

They were on the eve of war with Germany, and Lily understood this was why she and all the other children were leaving their home in Edge Hill. It was to keep them safe from the German air raids because everybody knew it was only a matter of time now before the bombs rained down on Liverpool. They were a prime target given the city's port. It was a frightening thought, but it also didn't seem real.

The build-up to this morning's exodus had been gradual. It had begun with murmurings about the children being sent from the city amongst the mams as they stood on their front doorsteps smoking their ciggies. Lily had thought this was just talk, and the news it was to happen, they *were* to be taken and deposited somewhere deemed safe, had come with barely any warning.

It felt like months since they'd been sent home from school midway through the morning after an announcement had been made that the school was to close until further notice. It hadn't been though. It was only yesterday that they'd been instructed to assemble here at the school gates for six o'clock the following morning.

Lily's mam had been home when she'd burst through the door of their terrace house on Needham Road with this news. She'd left work early, having been issued with a list of what Lily was to take with her. She'd insisted on Lily ticking the items off as she'd packed them in the case, calling out as she went.

'Underwear,' Sylvie Tubb had stated as though she were a surgeon asking for a scalpel.

Tick had gone Lily's pencil.

'Nightgown.'

Tick.

'Slippers.'

Lily had hesitated because her slippers were too small, but money was tight, so she'd ticked it off the list.

'Plimsolls.'

Like the slippers, Lily had outgrown them but knowing her mam would be upset if she thought she was sending her off without the regulatory items, she'd given them a tick. She could live without plimsolls.

'An extra pair of stockings?'

'Don't worry, Mam. I'll manage with the pair I've got on.'

Sylvie had nodded before squinting at the list once more. 'Hankies,' she'd murmured more to herself than to Lily before disappearing out of the room.

Lily had heard a drawer next door opening and closing, and

then her mam had returned with a pile of handkerchiefs. They'd belonged to her dad, and her eyes had smarted as she'd glimpsed the *J* she'd embroidered for his birthday on the plain white one. She'd blinked the tears away in case her mam saw them, but she'd already taken herself off to the bathroom to retrieve the last few things Lily would need. She'd returned waving them at Lily before wrapping her toothbrush, comb and some soap in a facecloth.

Lily had tick, tick, tick, ticked.

'And your coat. Where's your coat?' Sylvie's eyes, the same brownish green as her daughter's, had flitted around the spartan but clean room anxiously. They might not have much coming in these days, and she'd learned how to make Monday's mutton stretch until Thursday, but she'd always prided herself on a clean home. Standards had not slipped there.

'It's hanging up on the hook downstairs, Mam, and there's no point putting it in there.' She'd pointed to the open case at the foot of her bed. 'Because I'll be wearing it in the morning along with my hat.'

'Yes, yes, of course you will.' Sylvie had shaken her head and closed the case, her face wan in the fading afternoon light. She had lines etched into her fair skin that Lily hadn't noticed before, and her hair, once fierier than Lily's own rich mane, had faded and lost its lustre since Lily's dad had died.

The click of the latches had sounded final to Lily's ears, and she'd imagined there to be a mass clicking of suitcase latches all over Liverpool.

Now, as the final few stragglers made their way toward the school, she tugged on her mam's arm. Mrs Price, who taught the weekly hygiene class, was marching about importantly with a clipboard marking children off her list. They were all labelled like parcels with their names clearly pinned to their coats.

'Mmm, what is it, Lily?' came the distracted reply.

'Do you think I'll go to the country? Edith thinks we're all being sent to Wales.'

'I don't know about that. I've heard Skem being mentioned.'

Skelmersdale was the closer of the two destinations, and Lily hoped this was where she'd wind up. It had been a mining town and was surrounded by brickworks. There was a river that ran through it, and a paper mill. She knew this because her teacher had explained how paper was made and mentioned the mill by the River Tawd in Skelmersdale.

'But what I don't understand, Mam,' she said, 'is why I've got to go. We've the shelter, haven't we? And there are lots of girls my age who're staying behind to help their mams. Sarah's not going.'

The ugly sheets of corrugated iron had arrived a few weeks back. They'd been stored in their strip of back garden. That had been the first hint that things were going to change again for Lily and her mam. Their already shaken world had begun to slip and slide once more as the inevitably of war loomed.

The talk of blackouts and rationing to come had reached fever pitch, and then the van had pulled up in the middle of their street to distribute mystery boxes. Instead of dread, there'd been excitement in the air, and the boxes had been ripped open to reveal gas masks.

The men had come five days earlier to put up their Anderson shelter, covering it with the dirt they'd dug up.

'Don't make this more difficult than it already is, Lily. You're making me feel vexed. What Mrs Carter decides to do with her two is her business.'

Lily knew her mam thought Mrs Carter an odd woman. She did come out with strange things now and again, but Lily liked her. She always made her welcome.

'I have to do right by you for your father's sake. He'd have wanted me to keep you safe at all costs, and you're not the only one. Look, they're all going.' Sylvie's arm swept wide to encompass the milling group. 'We talked about this, and you promised me you'd make the best of things.'

Lily didn't think it would help any if she were to mention she'd had her fingers crossed behind her back when she'd made that promise. What was making this all the harder was the knowledge it wasn't compulsory. They didn't have to go. So why couldn't her mam be like Sarah's? Her bottom lip trembled. 'I could find work, Mam. I'm nearly old enough. I'd be better off doing something useful. You know I would, like the socks for the soldiers we've been knitting at Guides. Do you want the poor lads all to have cold feet?'

'I'm sure there'll be a branch you can join in with in Skem.'

Lily tried another tack. 'But, Mam, what use is an education when the world is at war and we need the money?'

'Lily.' Sylvie's tone was sharp. 'Keep your voice down.' Money was a topic that was not to be spoken about in public. 'Your poor dad would turn in his grave at the thought of you not finishing your schooling.'

What was niggling at her, though, was if it wasn't safe for them, the children, to stay in Liverpool, then it wasn't safe for the parents either. She'd already lost her dad. If she lost her mam too, she'd have no one. She'd be an orphan, and the very thought made her breath judder out white on the dewy morning air.

'He's watching over us, you know,' her mam said gently. 'You won't be on your own. He'll be with you.'

Lily had felt him alongside her before, and the sentiment did make her feel a little better.

There was no time to dwell on this, though, because a whistle sounded. This was it. She swallowed hard. Her mam pulled her into an embrace, and she felt her breath hot against her ear.

'You're a good girl, Lily. Do as you're told and remember your manners. It's not forever; this horrid war will be over before we know it, and you'll be home with me where you belong.'

'Mam, I don't want to—'

'Quiet now; you've gorra go. I have to keep you safe.' Sylvie's eyes were dangerously bright as she planted her hands on her daughter's shoulders. 'Now then.' Her voice shook. 'You'll be back home with me before you know it. You'll see.' She turned her daughter around and gave her a gentle push toward the line that was forming. 'G'won with yer.'

Lily could barely see through the haze of tears as she made her way over to the other children who were lining up in readiness to walk to the train station. Edith grabbed her arm and dragged her in behind her. Ruth, her birthmark an angry red this morning, stood in front of Edith, scowling at Lily.

'Me mam put an extra apple and biscuit in me bag for you,' Edith said to Lily, dipping her head toward the brown paper bag she'd a tight hold of. Her knuckles were white. 'We'll be ahright, won't we, Lily?' She glanced at her friend fearfully before checking Elsie hadn't darted off. Her younger sister was waving excitedly over at her mam, eager for the off.

'Course we will,' Lily replied with a stoicism she didn't feel as she blinked away the tears. 'We've got each other, haven't we?' That much was true. Edith was with her, and as annoying as Elsie could be, she was as protective over her as Edith was.

The piercing whistle sounded again, and then they were off with much waving, sniffling and flapping of hankies on the mams' parts.

Lily didn't dare look back, and she wished the sense of anticipation and adventure rife amongst her classmates was infectious. She couldn't help but think the cheeriness of the volunteer marshals with their armbands, clearly displayed as they walked alongside them, seemed forced though. Mind you, her mam always said she was far too sharp for her own good.

That's when she saw the woman in the distance. She always

stood far enough away that she couldn't make out her features, only the red of her hair. She was watching her, as she did from time to time. Lily didn't feel threatened by her, more puzzled. She was her guardian angel, and she'd never told a soul about her for fear she might vanish for good if she did.

By the time they arrived at Edge Hill Station, the sky was blushing pink, and the temperature had risen a notch. They piled onto the platform chaotically despite the warden's best efforts to keep them in line and milled about to wait for the train.

Lily's anxiety was growing with each passing minute, and to try and distract herself, she stared around the station, which was a hive of activity. Finally, her eyes alighted on a child standing far too close to the edge of the platform. What if he was accidentally shoved in the melee when the train pulled into the station?

She wanted to bite her nails with the worry of it all but couldn't as the hand that wasn't carrying the suitcase was entwined with Edith's. Edith, in turn, was desperately trying to keep hold of Elsie, who was beginning to wind up to another level as she became overwrought with excitement.

Lily worried about everything these days and with good reason. Bad things did happen. This was something she'd learned the hard way when her dad hadn't returned from the Meccano factory on Binns Road where he'd worked. It would be a year ago come November.

The thing was, Lily knew your day could start like any other, and then poof, just like that, your world could be upended.

The day her dad had died, she'd arrived home from school set to tell her mam about her day, but she'd been busy talking to Mrs Dixon next door, the sheets she'd pegged out earlier in the basket at her feet. So Lily had pushed past her and made a beeline for the kitchen. The jam-smeared doorstop her mam had left on a plate for her afternoon tea had soon been demolished, and she'd headed out to play with the other girls from their street. She'd ignored her mam calling after her to put a cardigan on or she'd catch her death, far too eager to join in with the game of double Dutch she'd seen getting underway.

Most evenings, she'd see her dad sauntering down their street as she turned the long rope while Margaret and Joan, who possessed the most prowess when it came to skipping, jumped it. Then there he'd be along with the other dads, all eager to get home and have a hot meal placed in front of them. He'd have his lunchbox in one hand, a ciggie in the other and his cap pulled down low.

Lily would drop the rope or abandon the game of hopscotch to run over to walk the last few yards home with him. She'd liked to tell him about her day because he'd liked hearing about it.

The thing Lily had loved most about her dad, though, was how he could always make everything all right. 'The Tubbs are a brave bunch, Lily. It's the Viking blood in us, you see.' Like magic, the scrape on her knee or Ruth's meanness, or the telling off from her teacher for talking in class wouldn't hurt so much.

They'd reach their two-up, two-down home where Lily had been born, and he'd hang his cap up on the hook on the back of their front door.

That day last November, there'd been no sign of her dad, and when she thought back on it, she could remember the smell of fish. It was Friday, and the Moriarty family at number twelve always had fish for tea on Friday. By the time Lily's mam had called her home, darkness had been creeping in, a fine mist chilling the air. She'd stood there on the deserted street shivering for a minute longer in case he should suddenly bowl round the corner, but when her mam had called her in again, her tone had been insistent.

She'd found her in the kitchen making noises about the stew

sticking to the pan. Her smile as she'd told Lily not to worry, he'd be home any minute now, had been overbright, and she'd had lipstick on her teeth.

The knock on the door had come not long after that. Three sharp raps.

The policeman had told them Joe Tubb had been on his way home when he'd stepped out of the way of an oncoming bicycle and into the path of a car. He'd died at the scene.

She'd begun writing in her worry book after that. It helped to write her fears down.

The sudden flurry of activity dispersed the memories of that awful night as the train's whistleblowing signalled its approach. There was no time to think about anything as she was propelled forward. 'You're a Tubb, aren't you, Lily? And the Tubbs are a brave bunch. It's the Viking blood in us,' she whispered to herself as she boarded the train.

Operation Pied Piper had begun.

**3**
---
1982

Sabrina fanned herself with the notebook in which she'd written Alice's name. Her heart was thumping. The photograph Alice had produced sat on the counter between them, and Alice, bewildered by Sabrina's reaction, picked it up, studying it intently.

'How weird. The girl in the back there, she looks just like you,' she said, looking up at Sabrina and then back down at the photograph.

'I know.'

'She must be related to you. I don't know what her name was.' She put the framed, black-and-white snapshot back down on the counter, angling it so Sabrina could see. 'Me nan passed away before I was born, and I never had the chance to get to know her.'

Sabrina caught the wistfulness slide over her face.

'Me granddad's been gone a few years now, but he used to talk about her all the time. So much so I feel as though she wor part of my life. Is this your nan then? Or a great-aunt?' She gestured to the picture. 'What a coincidence, eh?' Her face suddenly lit up. 'Whoever she is might be able to tell me some stories I haven't heard about my nan when she was young! Ooh, I'd love that.'

Sabrina shook her head. 'No, sorry. She's not my nan or a great-aunt.'

Alice's lips puckered. 'Are you sure? I mean, look at her.' She stared hard at the picture and back at Sabrina once more, frowning. 'She has to be related to you. A cousin's mam then? I know it's a small photograph, but it's still plain as day. She could be your twin.'

'I just know, and you wouldn't believe how I know if I told you.'

'Try me,' Alice challenged, raising her chin.

Sabrina hesitated and then decided it was best to say it and be done with it. 'I know the woman in the photo isn't me nan because that girl there' – she jabbed at the picture – 'is me.'

'I don't understand?' Alice frowned and then took a step back, her expression guarded.

'Alice, I'm telling you that girl stood behind your nan is me.'

Alice snatched the frame off the counter. 'Don't talk silly.' She shook her head and put the photograph back in her purse as though the matter was now closed.

'Listen, I promise you I'm not making this up, and believe me, I'm aware of how mad it sounds, but I know it's me because me fella, Adam, he's in the picture too.' She wished she had a photograph of Adam to hand.

Alice's lips twitched from side to side for a second or two, and then with another shake of her head, she strode over to the fitting room to retrieve her dress. 'I think I might have made a mistake coming here.' She didn't hang about, stuffing the dress back into her carry bag, obviously keen to put distance between herself and the shop.

Sabrina sighed; Alice clearly thought she was barmy, but it was suddenly vital that Alice hear her out because she wanted to know more about the couple in the picture – Alice's grandparents. 'Alice, don't go. Please, would you let me explain?' Though if Alice thought she was odd now, then she'd think her barking by the time she'd finished.

Alice wavered, and Sabrina seized on her uncertainty. 'Listen, why don't you let me make you a cup of tea? We can talk out the back in the workroom, and then if you still think I'm round the twist, you can go off about your business and tell everyone about the strange woman who works at Brides of Bold Street.' She gave a small laugh, but it sounded forced.

Alice gave a slow nod.

'C'mon then. I'll introduce you to my aunt Evie, who's beavering away out the back, and make us all a brew,' Sabrina said. She needed a strong cuppa to settle her nerves after the shock of seeing herself and Adam in that old photograph.

Alice followed Sabrina's lead into the workroom and smiled uncertainly at Aunt Evie, whose shop coat was a splash of colour in a sea of cream, white, ivory and oyster fabrics.

'Aunt Evie, this is Alice. Alice has a family heirloom dress to be altered for her wedding in two weeks.'

'Two weeks! You're cutting it fine, me luv. How do you do, Alice?'

'Erm, ahright, I think. Me fella's being deployed to Belfast. It's all happened rather fast, and we want to be wed before he goes, and Sabrina here's told me something dead strange.'

Evelyn tossed a questioning glance at Sabrina.

Sabrina pulled a stool out from under the table and gestured for Alice to have a seat. The bride-to-be perched on the edge of it, clearly poised for flight if things got too weird.

'Alice showed me a photograph of her nan's wedding, Aunt Evie. Alice, would you mind showing it to my aunt?'

Alice dipped her head and undid her purse once more to produce the card containing the picture. Then she handed it to Evelyn, who pushed her glasses back up her nose before inspecting the image inside.

The sharp gasp as the penny dropped was audible over the radio.

'Me nan got wed in the spring of 1945, not long after her eighteenth birthday. The war had just ended.'

'And I'd not long reopened. Lily was one of my first customers,' Evelyn said quietly.

'You knew her?' Alice's brownish-green eyes grew round.

Evelyn's head snapped up. 'Oh yes. I knew Lily. I knew Lily well for a time as it happens. That's me there.' She pointed herself out in the wedding party line-up.

'Lily and I worked together – that's how we met,' Evelyn said, filling in the blanks. 'I had to close the shop after conscription came in. There wasn't much call for bespoke wedding gowns at that time, and there was no fabric to be had anyway. My time was better served sewing parachutes. I heard young Lily hadn't long lost her mam, and I took her under my wing when we both worked at Littlewoods on Hanover Street.'

Sabrina was all ears. Aunt Evie had never talked much about the war years.

'We only worked together a few months before the factory was bombed in the Blitz. After that, I moved to another factory and lost track of Lily until she called in here wanting her mam's wedding dress altered.'

'Like I've done today with Nan's dress.' Alice's cheeks reddened with excitement. 'Granddad told me she worked in a factory during the war and volunteered at the Royal Liverpool of an evening. She got into nursing not long after they married. It was her passion. I can't believe you knew her and were at her and Granddad's wedding.' She shook her head. 'It's like fate brought me here.'

Sabrina and Evelyn exchanged a glance. It wasn't the first time they'd heard that.

'She wor a lovely girl who'd experienced a lot of sorrow for someone so young, but she had her fella. They made a fine pair, and their wedding was a lovely do,' Evelyn said.

Sabrina was still waiting for Aunt Evie to mention who else was in the photograph – was it possible she hadn't spotted them? – but Alice had begun talking once more.

'They were the loves of each other's life, Lily and Max. They got married young but never regretted a second of their life together. Granddad was devastated when he lost her. He never remarried.'

Evelyn's eyes took on a faraway glaze. 'We lived with the threat of death every day during the war. When you don't know if you'll have a tomorrow, you don't waste your time on ifs and buts. Procrastination wasn't in our vocabulary. They were lucky to have the time together they did. I'm a firm believer that you only get one chance at love. True love.'

Sabrina gave her a quizzical glance. She'd never heard her talk like that before. Had Aunt Evie had her chance and missed it?

Alice nodded. 'I can imagine. It's why I don't want to wait to marry Mark. I never met me nan, but I feel as though I know her because Granddad talked about her all the time as if she was still with him. There was a photograph taken on her twenty-first birthday that he kept in a silver frame on the sideboard, and he talked to it all the time. "Shall we have rice pudding or tapioca, Lily, me luv?" that sort of thing. I always half expected her to answer him! I'm wearing the dress on my wedding day because I want my Mark and myself to be every bit as happy as Nan and Granddad were.'

'It's a beautiful sentiment, luv,' Evelyn said.

'I've her ring too.' She held out her hand for Evelyn.

'The emerald suits you as it did Lily.' Evelyn smiled. 'Worra lovely connection.'

Alice gave a sad smile. 'Granddad wanted me to have it, and

I knew I wouldn't find anything else this beautiful. It makes me feel close to Nan. I don't get on well with me mam, you see. She and Dad split up when I was young. It wor me granddad who more or less raised me, and it feels right to wear Nan's ring and dress. I miss him.'

Sabrina nodded, trying to cool her heels. She was getting impatient now, waiting for her aunt's reaction to spotting her in the wedding party.

'Aunt Evie, look there, behind you.'

If Sabrina had expected shock to register on her aunt's face when she spotted Sabrina and Adam captured in the photo, then she was disappointed.

'You already knew Adam and I travelled back to 1945, didn't you!' It was a statement on Sabrina's part, not a question. It was written all over Aunt Evie's face.

'Of course I did. I'm there next to you in the photograph, aren't I.'

'Why didn't you say anything?'

'We've had that conversation, Sabrina. It's not for me to tell you what fate has in store. It was fate that brought Alice into the shop today, just as it will take you and Adam back in time. My having said something would only muddy the waters. Things have to play out as they're supposed to.'

Alice's head was snapping between the two women as she tried to keep up with their conversation. 'Would one of you please explain things to me in a way that makes sense,' she said shortly. 'I haven't got all day either – I'm due in work at two o'clock.'

'You've plenty of time for that brew I promised you then.' Sabrina scooped up the tea tray from earlier and moved toward the stairs. 'I'll be back in a jiffy with a fresh pot.'

. . .

Sabrina was glad of the breathing space making the tea had afforded her, and by the time she carried the rattling tray downstairs, she was feeling calmer. She'd plucked the photograph of herself and Adam that Flo had snapped at the Swan from the corner of her dressing table and tucked it in her pocket as further proof to show Alice.

She found her aunt and Alice sitting in the workroom in silence. The radio was playing 'The Tide Is High' by Blondie, and Sabrina thought fleetingly of Flo with her bleached mop. Debbie Harry had a lot to answer for!

Alice, she noted, setting the tray down, wore an expression of disbelief. Aunt Evie had told her then, she surmised, pouring the tea. She put a teaspoon of sugar in Alice's cup, figuring she could probably do with it whether she took sugar or not.

'You've travelled back in time then?' Alice asked, scepticism lacing her question as Sabrina slid the cup and saucer toward her. 'At least that's what your aunt's told me.'

Sabrina nodded. 'It's true. I have. Twice now, and I wouldn't have believed any of it either if it hadn't happened to me.' Sabrina wished she had a biscuit to dunk. 'Here.' She dug the photo out of her pocket and showed the other girl. 'That's me fella, Adam. He's in your nan and granddad's wedding photo too.'

Alice compared the two, shaking her head bewilderedly.

'What did Aunt Evie tell you, Alice?'

Alice glanced at Evelyn and then replied, 'That there's a portal here on Bold Street that sucks some people to another time. She said it's happened to others; there are documented reports even.' She shook her shaggy red hair again.

'As I said, it's incredible—'

'Ridiculous, more like,' Alice snorted.

Sabrina continued doggedly. 'Worever. I know how it sounds, but you can see the truth for yourself right there in those pictures. So hear me out, Alice, please.'

Alice gave a slight nod, perhaps against her better judgment.

'Ta. From what I've heard and managed to read about the Bold Street timeslip, those affected seem to step into another time and step out of it minutes later. It's happened so quick they wonder if they've imagined it. But I get stuck in worever time the slip takes me back to,' Sabrina said. 'Did you tell her about me mother, Aunt Evie? Because that's where this all started.'

Evelyn shook her head; apparently she'd thought it better to let Alice digest what she'd told her about Bold Street first given that she was struggling as it was to take that on board.

Sabrina carried on. 'Aunt Evie found me lost outside Hudson's Bookshop, only back in 1963 it wasn't a bookshop; it was a dressmaker's, called Cripps. To cut a long story short, nobody came looking for me, so she took me in and raised me. I always thought me mam, for worever reason, had abandoned me here on Bold Street. Or at least I did until me fella, Adam, told me his uncle used to bandy about a tale as to how he'd had a most peculiar encounter with a panicked woman looking for her daughter near Cripps back in 1963.'

'The year you were found?'

'Yes. The woman was bewildered and disorientated, and she was also adamant it was 1983. But strangest of all was how she seemed to vanish into thin air.'

'And you think that woman was your mother?' Alice raised a sceptical brow.

'I do. I think we were separated by the timeslip somehow. I've been looking for her ever since in the hope I'll be pulled back to wherever she is because she must be looking for me too. Only, the first time I went through the slip, I found myself in 1928. The second time, 1962. On both occasions, I was gone for months, but when I finally stepped back through to the present, hardly any time at all had passed since I'd left.'

'You said this woman looking for her daughter in the sixties thought it was 1983?'

'I did.'

'Well, that's only a year away. If what you've told me is true – and to be honest with you, I'm struggling to believe it – then you'll find your mother next year because if she lost you, her child, it will be all over the papers and on the tele.'

'Yes, that's why I didn't think I'd go back through the slip again. But having seen your nan's photograph, I know I must do because I'm there, aren't I? In 1945, and for worever reason, Adam's there with me.'

Alice was quiet as she mulled through what Sabrina and Evelyn had told her.

'What was she like, your nan – according to your granddad, I mean?' Sabrina asked.

Alice drained her tea in one long gulp. 'He always said I took after her. She wor strong-willed and very determined.'

'She wor that ahright,' Evelyn murmured.

Alice looked a little sheepish.

'Both good traits to have in a woman,' Evelyn said, adding, 'You've her glorious hair too.'

Alice smiled. 'It skipped me mam and jumped straight to me.'

'What sort of wedding are you having?' Sabrina asked, moving them back to neutral territory.

'Mark's mam wanted us to have a big do, but I put me foot down. She's not best pleased either, but I want to keep it small.'

'Your nan did too. She wasn't bothered about a big do.'

'No. Nan got married in a registry office, as I will.'

Evelyn nodded. 'Your vows are your vows no matter where you say them.'

'I'd dearly love to alter your dress for you, Alice – if you'd like me to that is,' Sabrina volunteered.

Alice looked from Evelyn to Sabrina, and Sabrina sensed the moment she made her mind up. Despite her scepticism, there was a connection between them all she clearly couldn't ignore.

'I'd like that very much,' she replied.

# 4

## 1939

The train journey from Edge Hill to Ormskirk wasn't a long one. Lily wasn't sure exactly how much time had passed, but she felt sure it hadn't been more than an hour and a half. They'd entertained themselves with sing-songs between munching on the treats Edith's mam had packed. A glimpse out the fingerprint-marred windows revealed buildings and green belt interspersed with the occasional early tinges of yellow, red and orange.

Lily wrote, *Will I see Mam again?* in her worry book then snapped it shut, putting the thought out of her head and joining in with the rousing rendition of 'Michael Finnegan' being sung. Before she knew it, the train had screeched to a halt in the station, and they were disembarking. There was no time for lingering in the leafy surrounds of Ormskirk Station as they were led out to the street and seen onto a waiting coach.

The singing resumed throughout the short journey, but instead of pulling up beside the beach as the day-at-the-seaside atmosphere on the rattling old coach would suggest, they parked outside an uninspiring sooty red building. Lily had seen the signs for Skelmersdale as they'd dipped down into the valley where the town nestled. Her mam had been right – this was where they were headed.

The sky was no longer blue. Instead, the clouds hung heavy and grey overhead as she hesitated on the steps of the coach, shivering. She ignored the nudge in her back from Edith in her reluctance to step down from the coach.

'Don't dilly-dally, children,' Mrs Price warbled, fixing Lily in her sights. She had a sharp tongue did Mrs Price, and Lily didn't want to be on the receiving end of it, so she did as she was told and joined the others in the snaking line waiting to go inside the building.

Once they'd all assembled and a final check to confirm nothing had been left on the coach had been completed, one of the volunteer marshals Lily didn't recognise led them inside. Mrs Price brought up the rear.

They entered a foyer with a cloakroom area and then filed into the hall leading off it. Women of mixed ages, one or two with babies dangling from their hips, were milling about chatting as though this were a cup of tea after church get-together. Lily kept her eyes fixed on the floor, which shone and smelled of wax, and bumped into Ruth as she stopped suddenly.

The other girl spun round and hissed, 'Watch it.'

'No fidgeting, children,' Mrs Price bossed as she fussed around them.

Jimmy O'Malley received a cuff across the back of his head and immediately stopped scratching. The children from Edge Hill formed a group at the far end of the room, and the hum of conversation began to slow, and then it ceased altogether as curious eyes settled upon them.

A child was sniffling, and Lily heard Mrs Price tell Joan Storer she was a big girl now, and as such, she was to stop crying and make her mam proud. Poor Joan cried even harder at the mention of her mam, and Lily's hand snaked out to hold Edith's.

Edith squeezed it hard. She wished Sarah were here with them too.

The frivolity of earlier was forgotten as worry about what would happen next spread amongst the Edge Hill children like the chickenpox had at school the year before.

A stocky woman with short grey hair set in tight curls was marching about self-importantly. She was wearing a dark green cardigan, from under which the collar of a white blouse peeked, along with a dowdy skirt. She was holding a clipboard with a list she was working her way down, ticking the gathered women's names off it. When she was done, she turned her attention toward the children at the top of the hall and nodded toward Mrs Price.

'When Mrs Pinkerton calls your name, you're to step forward,' Mrs Price instructed them.

Mrs Pinkerton made her way to the middle of the hall and cleared her throat before calling out Henry, Ronald and John Fitzwilliam's names. All three boys were beetroot-coloured as they stepped forward.

A woman of middling years with a hard line to her mouth stepped forward. 'These three will eat me out of house and home by the looks of them,' she muttered in a voice designed to carry before inclining her head. 'C'mon then, lads; we can't 'ang about 'ere all day now, can we?'

The waiting children's eyes were wide as the three brothers picked up their cases and followed the woman's purposeful stride from the hall.

One by one, the group thinned out, and when Edith's hand slipped from hers, Lily had to blink back smarting tears. She watched as Edith and Elsie were bustled from the hall by a woman with a maroon hat and matching coat with a swan brooch pinned to the lapel. Her smile was kind. That was something, and Lily scanned the handful of careworn faces left, hoping she too would go home with a woman with a kind smile. She glanced to her side, wondering which of the remaining children she'd be billeted with and crossed her fingers it wouldn't be Ruth.

'Lily Tubb, and Joyce and Yvonne Bunting.'

Lily and Joyce shot each other a quick smile; both girls were pleased with the arrangement. Lily liked Joyce. Yvonne, her younger sister, was a happy soul who was constantly flashing her gappy grin. Lily hadn't realised she'd been holding her breath, and she exhaled in a big puff of relief that she wasn't to be sent off with Ruth.

Her relief was short-lived, however, as a stooped old woman with her head covered in a scarf and wearing a navy coat which she'd buttoned right up to her chin pushed her way forward. She wore wire-framed glasses with a crack in one of the lenses, and Lily watched as she shoved those in her way aside with her walking stick. 'I told yer I could only take one of them.' Her voice was gruff with the throatiness that came from too many harsh winters.

Mrs Pinkerton referred to her clipboard. 'You did volunteer, Mrs Cox, and you're down for three. Your cottage has two bedrooms. We've all got to do our bit for the war effort, you know.'

Mrs Cox stood her ground, giving Mrs Pinkerton a withering stare. 'I said I could take one, and that's that.' She eyeballed Mrs Pinkerton, who looked uncomfortable as she studied the list on her clipboard once more.

A young woman with a plump baby with bright red spots on either cheek called out, 'I'll take them two that looks to be sisters, and the taller lass can go with Mrs Cox. How's that?'

Mrs Cox nodded as though the matter was now settled, and Lily turned panicked eyes to Joyce. There was nothing Joyce could do though, other than stare back at her sympathetically. Even Ruth looked sorry for her. Lily's gaze swung pleadingly to

Mrs Pinkerton, but the woman was already moving down her list.

'Are yer simple, lass? Get yer things.'

This time Lily couldn't help the tear escaping, and brushing it away, she picked up her case and followed the shuffling old woman out the door.

'Welcome to Skem, luv,' the bus conductor said, helping Mrs Cox aboard before clipping Lily's ticket. As he looked down at her, his smile was jolly. Lily, remembering her promise to her mam about her manners, rustled up a nod and smile of thanks, though one foot was still planted on the pavement, the other on the open platform at the bus's rear. Her case was in her hand.

It wasn't too late. She could turn and run back to the hall. She could tell Mrs Price and Mrs Pinkerton that she'd go back home before going off with the witch-like Mrs Cox. She was about to step down and do exactly that when the conductor reached out and pulled her up alongside him. 'Best you take yer seat, luv, if you don't want to go flyin'. I don't want any broken bones on my run.'

The bus slowly chugged away, taking a belch of black exhaust with it; Lily's opportunity to run was gone. She turned back in time to see the last few children being shepherded from the building she'd just left. Mrs Pinkerton was locking the door behind her. She opened her mouth as though to call out, but no sound came, and she jumped on hearing Mrs Cox snap, 'Stop making a holy show of yerself, lass, and sit down.'

'Don't worry, luv, she's all bark and no bite that one.' The conductor winked at her, but Lily couldn't find any reassurance in his words.

She made her way to where Mrs Cox had twisted in her seat, annoyance embedded between scraggly grey brows as she approached. As Lily slid in alongside the old woman, she thudded her stick down between them like a divider.

She smelled unwashed, Lily thought, wrinkling her nose and staring straight ahead, trying to ignore the old woman's wheezing breath that whiffed of onions. Instead, she concentrated on the street they were pootling down. It didn't look all that different to Edge Hill. The rows of two-up, two-down sooty brick houses lined either side of the cobbled street. The smell of coal fires clung to the air despite it being the tail end of summer and not so much as a wisp of smoke coming from the chimneys. Coal was embedded in the very bricks of the buildings, Lily reckoned. It was the same at home. Her eyes alighted on the grocer's, noting the advertisements twinned those in the window of Peterson's near Durning Road, where her mam worked.

She watched a bobby making his way down the pavement nodding his greeting to a woman pushing a pram. She clung to the familiarity of the scene, unaware she was gnawing on her nails until she received the sharp end of Mrs Cox's elbow in her side.

'Dirty habit that – get yer hands out of yer mouth if you don't want worms.'

Hot tears sprang forth as Lily folded her hands on her lap, and all the while, the bus rumbled on, stopping and starting as it disgorged its passengers on the residential streets. Even the conductor had clambered off. Then it was only Lily, Mrs Cox and the driver remaining.

All of a sudden, the houses gave way to woodland and barren fields, and it seemed to Lily that they were at risk of leaving the town behind altogether. The thought made panic swell in her throat, and she worried it might close over. Poor little Katie Wandsworth must have felt like this when she'd had an allergic reaction to the bee sting on her foot the previous summer. The ambulance had come for her, and the talk had been it had arrived not a moment too soon. Ana-something-or-other shock, they'd called it.

The road they'd bumped onto was surrounded by dense foliage. Lily imagined a witch's cottage deep in the woods like in the fairy-tale book she had at home. Where was she going? She swallowed hard.

The bus's brakes screeched as it veered over to the side of the potholed road, and the driver called out. ''Ere we are, Mrs Cox, me luv – home sweet home.'

Mrs Cox made a grumbling noise and nudged Lily, who was scanning both sides of the road hoping she'd see some signs of life, in the ribs. But, instead, there was nothing other than a trio of run-down cottages.

'What are yer waiting for? You heard him. This is us.'

Lily shot up, not wanting to feel the sharp end of her elbow again, then picked up her case and hurried off the bus.

'Are your hands painted on, girl? Can't you see I need help?' Mrs Cox glowered from the platform, and Lily, flushing, put her case down and held her hands out to aid the old harridan down the steps. When she'd safely disembarked, the driver tooted, and then the bus rambled on its way.

Lily watched it go, feeling bereft.

# 5
## 1982

Sabrina had not had a good afternoon. She'd pinned Alice Waters's gown ready to be let out and taken in where necessary before she'd left the boutique. They'd agreed on some additional embellishments to give it a more up-to-date feel and made an appointment for her to come in to try the altered gown on early the following week. It had been hard to keep her mind on the job after what she'd learned. She had a hundred and one other bridal dresses to be stitching or altering, but she'd prioritise Alice given their unexpected link. So she'd waved the client responsible for completely upheaving her day off, knowing she'd done the same to her. Alice's brain would be whirring with all she'd been told too.

The thought of her and Adam having stepped back into 1945 had understandably thrown her into a tailspin, and that was why she'd sewn faux seed pearls onto a gown that was supposed to have sequins around the bodice.

She'd made up her mind to leave things alone where her mother was concerned after her last adventure in time. Or so she'd thought. Now the familiar flames of yearning for answers had been fanned.

It had taken her an age to unpick the sodding pearls, and while Aunt Evie might not have tutted out loud seeing her labouring over them, Sabrina knew her well enough to know she'd be doing so silently.

She was desperate to confide her encounter with Alice today to Adam, but it wasn't the sort of thing you could drop casually into a conversation over the telephone. 'Oh, by the way, Adam, I found out a little while ago that you and I time-travel back to 1945.' No, it would have to keep until she saw him in the flesh, which would be after the Bootle Tootlers' meetup and run she'd promised Flo she'd help out with.

This was why when she barrelled out the door shortly after they'd shut up shop for the day, she was clad in a lilac tracksuit with blindingly white trainers. She'd even picked up a towelling headband like Flo's to prove she was taking her role as the backup Bootle Tootler seriously. Aunt Evie, spying her new shoes as she legged it past her, had called out, 'You'll stop traffic in those.'

'Enjoy *Corrie*,' Sabrina had shouted, pausing to complete her light-switch ritual before haring down the stairs. They were somewhat neon, she thought with a rueful glance at her feet.

Just over half an hour later, Sabrina called out hello, having let herself into the Teesdales' house, which was a second home to her. She followed her nose through to the kitchen, inhaling a savoury aroma.

'Ahright there, luv? You look the part. My word, those trainers are bright.' Mrs Teesdale blinked at the sight of Sabrina's snowy footwear as she looked up from the open cookbook she'd been peering at intently.

'They'll see you coming in those, queen,' Mr Teesdale muttered from behind the newspaper he was rustling as he sat at the kitchen table, a cup of tea half-drunk beside him.

'They're new.' Sabrina stated the obvious, tempted to run outside and rub them in the dirt, so they didn't look quite so glaringly so. 'And that smells gorgeous.' She forgot the shoes, sniffing appreciatively and taking in the chaos of the kitchen worktop. 'What's for dinner then?'

'It's French. Beef bourguignon.' Mrs Teesdale indicated the open cookbook. 'A Julia Child recipe no less. It even has wine in it.'

'Ooh, wine, get you.'

'Waste of good wine that.' Mr Teesdale's head bobbed up over the paper this time. 'What's wrong with plain old British fodder? The French eat snails. Will we be having them for our dinner next?'

'Shut your gob. I know you – you'll be after seconds, and I'm serving it with mashed potatoes, Sabrina. There'll be plenty to go round if you fancy having your dinner here with Flo when you get back from your run. I dare say you'll be hungry by then. I can keep a plate warm for you both.'

'Ta. I won't say no.' She never did when it came to Mrs Teesdale's cooking.

'The potatoes are from my allotment,' Mr Teesdale added.

'Eee, there's no show without Punch, is there?'

Sabrina laughed. She loved Mr and Mrs Teesdale and knew they'd be lost without each other for all their bickering.

'Our Flo's in her room. Although why she's worried about her hair and make-up when she's supposed to be working a sweat up around North Park, I don't know.'

'Ah well, you never know who you might see along the way, that's why.' Sabrina gave them both a grin and then ducked off up the stairs.

A door creaked opened as she reached the landing, and two cheeky faces – Flo's younger sisters – peeked around it. 'We're not allowed out of our room until Mam says,' Shona – or was it Tessa; Sabrina wasn't sure – supplied.

'What did you do?' she asked, poised on the top step,

waiting to hear what the terrible twins' latest misdemeanour was.

'We were playing knock on the door and run away with grumpy old Mr Chiswell next door. It was Shona's idea.' Tessa shot her twin sister a look to say their solitary confinement was all her fault.

'You wanted to play too,' Shona retorted indignantly before adding, 'We reckon he's an evil wizard.'

Sabrina bit back a smile.

'Only Mrs Cummings from over the road saw us running away and told Mam. She went mad and chased us upstairs with the wooden spoon.'

Tessa nodded that this was indeed the case.

'Ah, well, I'm sure you'll be allowed down for your dinner.'

They both pulled a face. 'It's French, and Dad says the French eat snails.'

'Shona, Tessa, get back in that room until I tell you otherwise,' was bellowed up from down below.

The twins' eyes widened, and they slammed the door shut. This time, Sabrina did smile, hearing them scarper across the room to their beds. She gave Flo's door a nudge.

'I told you two to stay out of me room,' Florence snapped. She hadn't looked up from where she was arranging the towelling headband just so in her dressing-table mirror.

'It's me, Flo.'

'Oh, hiya, Sabs. Sorry, those two are driving me potty. They're supposed to be in disgrace in their bedroom; only they keep tiptoeing across the hall and poking their noses in here to see what I'm up to.' Satisfied she was as close to Olivia Newton John's look in the 'Physical' video as she was ever likely to get, Olivia being a natural blonde and all, Florence turned away from the mirror to check out her friend.

'I love the lilac, girl.'

'Ta. Worra about the shoes though?'

Florence frowned as she gave the trainers the once-over. 'They're super white, but a few laps of the park should sort them out after the rain last week.'

Sabrina flopped down on Florence's bed and, raising her eyes, saw Midge Ure from Ultravox staring back down at her. 'That poster's new.'

'It was free with the album. I love "Vienna" me.'

'Me too.'

They both launched into '*Ohhh, Vienna*' and then giggled.

'I don't know that I'd want Midge eyeballing me when I'm trying to go to sleep though, Flo.'

Flo grinned. 'I quite fancy him, to be honest. He's grown on me, but I'd fancy him more if he'd shave that silly little pencilly moustache off. You know, if I squint, I can see a bit of Tim in him. I say good night to him before I go to sleep.'

Sabrina laughed at the image of Flo lying in her bed in her flannelette nighty squinting, saying, 'Night, night, Midge.' She couldn't see the resemblance between Midge and Tim, but if Midge's moody face staring down at her made Flo happy, so be it. 'If you tell me he says good night back to you, you'll have me worried.'

'No, he's the strong silent type.'

Sabrina snorted, making Flo laugh. Then Sabrina remembered everything that had transpired with Alice that day and sobered. She rolled onto her side, propping herself up on her elbow.

Florence stared hard at her friend for a moment. 'Come on then – what's happened? I can tell something has. Is it to do with your mam?'

'Yes, no, well sort of. How can you tell?'

'Sabs, you're me bezzie mate. I know your face better than me own,' Florence stated.

It was the same for her, where Flo was concerned; she could

read her like a book. 'Two things happened today. Firstly, I told Aunt Evie that Adam's Ray Taylor's son.'

'How did she take that?' Florence's expression was grave, but it was hard to take her seriously with that towelling headband. Then Sabrina remembered her own.

'She made that stewed-prune face of hers, and I could tell there were a hundred things she'd like to say, but then this girl, Alice, came in. She wanted her nan's wedding dress altered. Gorgeous it was too. Proper vintage, not at all antwacky. Her nan married in 1945 and she had a photograph of the wedding party outside the church, and—'

'I think I can guess where this is going, and if you're going to tell me you were in the flamin' photograph, I'm going to put my hands over me ears.'

'You'd better put your hands over your ears then.'

'Ah, you said you weren't going to go back again! What I don't understand is why these brides-to-be all seem to find their way to your shop?'

'Boutique, not shop, and I don't know, do I? It's fate. It's not like I have any control over it. And it's not only me in the photo, Flo – Aunt Evie was too. And someone else.'

'Put me out my misery – who?'

'Adam.'

Her brown eyes were like organ stoppers. 'Adam went back with you?'

'He must have because it was him in the photograph.'

'Oh my God, girl, have you told him?'

'I haven't had a chance to. I want to wait until I see him to talk to him about it. Apart from Aunt Evie, who was there anyway and not best pleased, you're the first person I've told.'

Florence massaged her temples. 'Hang on a minute, wasn't the war only just over in 1945?'

Sabrina nodded. 'VE Day was on the eighth of May, 1945. I remember the date because when we learned about the celebrations with the big bonfires burning at school, I thought it sounded great fun – and because of your mam, of course.'

Florence mimicked her mother's voice. 'It's a lucky date to have been born, May the eighth – VE Day.' Mrs Teesdale said this every year on the twins' birthday.

Sabrina grinned, but Florence didn't crack a smile.

'Well, that's settled then – you can't go back. What if you stepped back into the thick of the Blitz? No.' She shook her head, and her bleached-blonde bob swung furiously. 'You can't go, Sabs. Adam or no Adam with you.'

'But you know how it works. If I'm there in the photo with Adam, it means we've already been back. It's already happened, and I can't change the past.'

'Yes, but what we don't know is whether you make it back to us this time. There's no guarantee of that now, is there?' She eyeballed her pal.

It was true, Sabrina thought, and it wasn't something she wanted to dwell on.

'I'd like to see Mystic Lou again and hear what she has to say.'

'Well, I don't want to see her,' Florence blustered. She hadn't been impressed to hear her destiny was entwined with a man with a penchant for wearing tight trousers the last time the two of them had paid the psychic on Bold Street a visit.

'You don't have to have a reading with her, but please come with me. I don't want to go on my own, and I don't think I want to hear what she has to say on my own either.'

Florence had a silent debate with herself.

'Flo, supporting each other is what bezzie mates do.'

Florence's eye's narrowed. 'Sabrina Flooks, is there an underlying threat in your tone? If so, that's blackmail.'

'No, it's not. It's a gentle reminder that I'm supporting you by being your backup jogger this evening, so it—'

Florence held a hand up. 'Ahright, ahright, I'll come with you.'

'One evening next week?'

'One evening next week. Bloody hell, is that the time? Come on, Sabs – we can't keep my ladies waiting.'

Sabrina rolled off the bed and stood up in time to see Florence put something around her neck. Her mouth formed an O as she twigged as to what it was. 'Oh, Flo, no!'

'What?' Florence feigned innocence.

'Tell me that's not a whistle.'

Florence grinned. 'Sabrina, all good coaches have one. It's in the coach rule book.' She gave it a blow for good measure, and with a satisfied grin at its shrill whistle, she thundered off down the stairs.

Sabrina rolled her eyes and followed her.

# 6

## 1939

Mrs Cox, with her limping gait, hobbled the few paces to the cottages, opening the door of the middle one, which could have benefitted from a lick of paint. It squeaked, indicating rusty hinges, and Lily, eyes wide, followed her reluctantly inside. Her eyes frantically tried to adjust to the dim light inside, and the aroma of old fat and ciggies with an underlying hint of damp made her want to gag.

'Born in a barn were yer?'

Lily shut the door, feeling like she'd been sent to prison. It wasn't a gaol she found herself in, however, but a narrow hall, and a glimmer of light shone in from the open kitchen door down the end of it.

Mrs Cox unknotted her headscarf to reveal silvered hair pulled back in a bun. She stuffed the scarf in her coat pocket and then hung her coat on the back of the door. 'You can 'ang your hat and coat on t'other hook.'

Lily took her hat off but hesitated, not wanting to discard her coat. It was chilly in here, but Mrs Cox was glaring at her, and once she'd divested herself of it, the old woman poked her stick at the closed door on her left. 'The sitting room's out of bounds, do you hear me? You're not to go in there under any circumstances.'

'Yes, Mrs Cox.' She was too intent on nodding to wonder why she wasn't allowed over the threshold to the front room.

'Your room's up there.' She lifted the stick and pointed to the stairs. 'The back bedroom. Take yer case up and unpack yer things, then you can come down to the kitchen and start earning your keep.'

Lily hastily retrieved her precious worry book and pen from her coat pocket and hurried up the stairs. The carpet runner was threadbare under her feet and the paper peeling off the wall, she noticed, her stomach clenching at the thought of what she might find at the top of the stairs. Whatever lay ahead, she was desperate for a few minutes on her own to absorb all that had happened since she'd left Edge Hill Station that morning.

The light was dim up here too. The floor was bare on the landing, and the boards creaked beneath her feet as she turned, with her hand still on the rail, to steal a glance in the direction of Mrs Cox's room. But, unfortunately, it was as closed off to her as the sitting room had been, and she wasn't brave enough to sneak a peek.

However, the door to the bathroom was open, so she walked the few short steps toward it and ducked her head inside. There was a yellowed sink with a mirror above it, hanging from a nail; a metal tub with handles on either side sat in the corner of the room. She breathed through her mouth because the tiny space smelled dreadfully of damp and needed to be aired. The window by the tub was closed, and as tempting as it was to fling it open, she didn't dare.

She moved across the landing to the room that was to be hers. She hadn't come from luxury by any means, but her mam kept a clean house, and she steeled herself for what lay beyond the door. Chewing her bottom lip, Lily pushed it open cautiously and stood there with her shoulders tensed as she took stock.

The space was hardly big enough to swing a cat and had a slanted ceiling beneath which a bed was pushed up against the bare walls. Spidering cracks laced the plasterwork, and a cobweb dangled in the corner above the pillow, but to Lily's relief, there was no sign of the spider who'd weaved it.

At least the bed was made up, she thought, eyeing the grey wool blanket folded at the end of it. She wouldn't think about who'd slept under that before her, she decided, shuddering, and she'd have to be careful not to bump her head of a morning too, given the ceiling.

She took a cautious step into the room, and the boards squeaked their protest as they had in the hall.

The only other furnishing in the room was a chest of drawers with a thick layer of dust sitting atop it, a mirror on a stand its only adornment. The room was cold and unlived in, and it too needed airing. As Lily moved forward, dust motes danced into the air, disturbed by her presence, causing her to sneeze several times. She put her worry book and pen down on top of the drawers then made for the small window over the bed, suddenly desperate for a gulp of fresh air.

She placed her case on the bed and felt the springs digging into her knees as she climbed on it. It took a moment or two of wrestling with the window sash before she managed to dislodge it and heft it up. Given its stickiness and the musty odour of the room, she suspected the room had been closed up for a long time.

Lily stuck her head out the window and breathed greedily. Her room overlooked a narrow muddy yard with a gravel path from the kitchen door to the privy at the bottom. The washing line was empty, and a picket fence missing a few palings separated the yard from the field beyond, where Lily could see freshly tilled soil.

The yards on either side were separated by a low fence and were identical in size, but to her right was an overgrown tangle of weeds with an abandoned air. *Like me*, Lily thought glumly. Her eyes cut to the left, where washing snapped on the line. Then to the small shed alongside the privy, also at the bottom of the yard.

She'd best unpack, she thought reluctantly, closing the window and smoothing the wrinkled sheets as she scrambled off the bed and opened her case. Her fingers skipped over the meagre contents and, closing her eyes, she remembered her mam folding them and placing them in the case as she ticked the items off the list they'd been given. At the thought of her mam, a self-pitying tear rolled down her cheek, and she waited until it was about to drip from her chin before swiping it away.

She picked up her worry book, and the pen hovered over the page as she tried to formulate what was worrying her the most. *No kindness*, she began to write and then snapped the book shut. 'This won't do, Lily Tubb. It won't do at all. Pull your socks up, girl. Dad would want you to be brave,' she whispered to herself, and for a moment, she felt him beside her, willing her to be strong. It was of great comfort to feel him watching over her. He wouldn't let any harm come to her.

A sudden thudding on the floor beneath her feet made her jump, and she banged her head on the ceiling. It took her a moment to realise what the source of the noise was. Mrs Cox must be hitting the ceiling with her stick. Her way of telling her to get a move on.

There was no time to rub the sore spot on her head as she hastily put her nightwear and undergarments away in the drawer. She left her toiletries on the bed and then closed the case, placing it on the floor and nudging it under the bed with her foot before hurrying back down the stairs.

'What took you so long?' Mrs Cox, seated at the table, her walking stick in her hand, didn't wait for a response. 'It's not a holiday camp you've come to, girl.' She inclined her head toward the worktop where she'd laid out a turnip, potato, carrot and fatty piece of mutton. 'If you don't get that meat simmering, I won't be able to get my teeth through it.'

Lily was used to helping her mam in the kitchen, and she rolled the sleeves of her dress up, opening a drawer in search of a knife to dice the meat when Mrs Cox brought her up short.

'Wash yer hands, yer dirty madam. I know what you lot from the city are like. Slovenly, the lot of yer,' she wheezed before it turned into a phlegmy hack.

Lily wanted to throw the turnip at the old cow but willed herself to ignore her as she gave her shaking hands a good scrub with the soap before running them under the cold tap.

'And when you've got that stew on, you can give the privy a good going over for yer sins.'

Lily stared out the window in horror at the innocuous wooden building she'd spied from upstairs. It was clear to her that Mrs Cox wanted her here as a lackey and nothing else. The words she'd written in her worry book sprang to mind. *No kindness*. The best thing she could do was give the old cow no cause for complaint by setting about whatever chores she was given quietly. They'd been told in the hall earlier that they'd be attending a local school. At least that would be a reprieve, and she'd see Edith and all the other familiar faces from home.

*You're not afraid of hard work, Lily Tubb*, she told herself as she dried her hands on a cloth draped over the oven door, then picked up the knife and sawed into the tough old meat. *You'll show that witch what you're made of for Dad's sake. You can do this, girl. You're a Tubb, and the Tubbs are a brave bunch. It's the Viking blood in us, don't you know.*

# 7

## 1982

Sabrina looked down at her chest where the words 'Bootle Tootlers' were emblazoned in black against the cheap yellow stretchy fabric that left little to the imagination. It was a good job it wasn't cold, she thought mutinously, or their headlights would all be on full beam. So much for not wearing the T-shirt. She'd almost got away with it too.

Flo had remembered the shirts Bossy Bev had organised at the last minute, racing back up the stairs of the Teesdale home just as they'd reached the front door. She'd called Sabrina back up to her room, insisting she put her shirt on, insisting that as Sabrina wasn't an actual member of the Bootle Weight Watchers branch, she was fortunate to have been allocated one. In the end, Sabrina couldn't be bothered arguing. She'd slipped it over her head, and she and Flo had laughed at one another in the one-size-fits-all, too-small shirts before doing a couple of Charlie's Angels poses in the mirror.

The twins had giggled their heads off upon spying them in their matching tops, and made buzzing bumblebee noises as they breezed back down the stairs. Flo had stuck her head around the kitchen door on their way out to tell her mam to sort them out. Her dad had also chuckled at their expense, and Mrs Teesdale had rushed outside after them to take a photograph. She'd wanted to test out her newfangled camera that spat the picture out before they made their way to the park.

Now, as Sabrina stood on the path by the Marsh Lane entrance to North Park where Flo had arranged to meet up with the rest of the Bootle Tootlers, she wished she'd put up more of a fight. The yellow clashed dreadfully with the lilac tracksuit bottoms. At least the odds of seeing anyone she knew here were slim, she thought, wincing as Flo blew her whistle.

Chit-chat in the gathered group ground to a halt.

The members who hadn't telephoned Flo earlier to say they were sick and unfortunately couldn't make it stood to attention. There were ten women in total, ranging in age from Sabrina's and Flo's twenty-two years through to sixty plus, all proudly squeezed into their new yellow T-shirts. Down below, some were clad like she and Flo were in tracksuit bottoms, two or three had braved shorts, and one, for some unknown reason, had wriggled into Spandex like the Nolan sisters.

Sabrina hoped they all had a decent bra on, given how well blessed the majority of the Bootle Tootlers, Flo included, were. She didn't like to butt in, though, as their team leader checked nobody had any pre-existing medical conditions or injuries she should know about.

Sabrina didn't know what Flo thought she'd do if they did because she wasn't a nurse, and their first aid training was limited to knowing how to wrap a bandage around each other's ankles, which they'd learned back in their Guiding days. She held her breath, waiting to see if anyone would raise a hand, but all hands remained firmly by their sides; that was something at least.

It was a balmy evening by early April standards, and with the clocks having gone forward an hour, Sabrina reckoned they had a good few hours of light left before darkness descended.

Plenty of time to do the loop Flo had in mind, she thought as her pal launched into a warm-up routine.

Florence, seeing Sabrina standing about daydreaming, glared over at her, and she quickly followed suit, raising her left arm over her head and bending at the waist to her right before repeating it on the other side. Hands-on-hip lunges swiftly followed the side bends, and heads swivelled at the sound of breaking wind, but no one in the group owned up to it. Once they were sufficiently loosened up, Flo announced, 'Right then, ladies, before we head off, I'd like to invite each of you to share what your motivation is for turning up this evening and to take this opportunity to congratulate each of you for doing so. Sabrina, would you like to start?'

No, she flamin' well would not, she thought, scowling at Florence, but as the Bootle Tootlers turned their attention to her, she cast about for something to say. 'Erm, hi.' She gave a little wave. 'I'm Flo's— I mean Florence's bezzie mate, so I'm here to help out, erm, in that capacity.'

'Sabrina's our backup runner. She'll be keeping an eye on you all, making sure nobody decides to pack it in halfway round,' Florence informed them. 'And she's also here because...'

She'd bloody kill Flo later, Sabrina decided, not knowing how she'd get on if she had to manhandle any of these women should they decide they'd had enough halfway round. She realised they were all waiting for her to answer, and she blurted, 'I'm also here because my favourite jeans – they're Calvin Klein's, you know, like the ones Brooke Shields wears – they're getting a little snug around my middle.'

There were nods of understanding and a smattering of applause, and to her surprise, Sabrina felt better for having owned up. They *were* getting tight. It was the fish 'n' chip suppers she and Adam were partial to, and a gentle jog wasn't going to do her any harm whatsoever. She smiled shyly.

Florence thanked her for being brave and sharing, then

continued around the group until, finally, it was time to get the show on the road.

She put her mouth to the whistle and blew, which saw a man wrestling with his dog, who was determined to hare toward her. Then she was off!

Her arms were pumping and her stride bouncy. Florence was settling into an achievable pace as they jogged past the Vauxhall dealership set back on their left, the trees splitting the park in two up ahead.

The mood was jolly for a while. Some of the Bootle Tootlers waved out to dog walkers and fellow runners or chatted amongst themselves. As they pounded on down the park's gently winding path through the trees to where there was talk of a fancy leisure centre being built, however, the chatter dried up, replaced by gasping and panting. Sabrina was beginning to feel it too and knew her face was glowing red with exertion. Not an attractive combination with the yellow shirt. Bossy Bev hadn't splurged on the tees because the fabric felt sweaty and clingy.

That was when she saw them.

Adam, Tony and Tim. They were sitting astride their motorbikes on the Hornby Street side of the park, ribbing one another and laughing. She wished the ground would swallow her up at the same time she burned with the need to tell him everything she'd learned since meeting Alice earlier. Under any other circumstances, her heart would sing at the sight of Adam, but today, in her yellow-and-lilac ensemble, the poor lad would be blinded. But perhaps they wouldn't notice them. She kept her head down hopefully but realised there was fat chance of that given they looked like a swarm of plump bumblebees.

Florence hadn't seen them, Sabrina realised as her friend jogged on, oblivious to the fellas nudging each other across the way. A cheer went up from the direction of the motorbikes, followed by a wolf whistle as piercing as one of Florence's efforts. It all happened quickly after that.

Florence, shocked at seeing Tim and the other two lads, tripped over her own feet and went head over heels. Janice, directly behind her, wasn't able to stop in time, and neither was Gina, and so on it went, like skittles being bowled. The only woman who remained standing was Sabrina because she'd already stopped and was watching the carnage unfold in what felt like slow motion.

A hand shot up from the pile of bodies a split second later, and a voice from the depths called out, 'I'm ahright.'

Sabrina began plucking the Bootle Tootlers off her friend one by one. Then, finally, she looked up to see Adam and Tony running over. Tim was still sat on his bike, roaring with laughter, though Adam and Tony were doing their best to look serious as they raced toward them.

'Florence, girl, give me your hand,' Tony said as he reached them. 'I'm in charge of first aid at werk; you'll be ahright.'

Florence did so, and Tony helped her to her feet. 'That was quite a tumble you took. Do you need me to check you over?' He smiled at her eagerly, and the tenderness beneath his sandy shock of hair was there for all to see. All except Florence, who pulled her hand away and shook herself down like a dog at the beach.

'I don't, ta very much.'

Sabrina could tell by her tone that the last thing she wanted was Tony feeling her up on the pretence of checking for broken bones. She watched her friend's eyes snake over to where Tim was still in fits of laughter and knew exactly what she was thinking. Why hadn't he been the chivalrous one getting off his Triumph to come to her rescue?

*Life's not fair like that Flo*, Sabrina mentally communicated.

Florence, however, had turned her attention back to the well-meaning Tony and was giving him a weak smile. Then, seeing the rest of the group sorting themselves out, she asked, 'Ladies, do we have any injuries?'

The women had made a speedy recovery and were busy checking out Tony's jeans, which, as usual, he could have been sewn into. How he got in and out of the things was one of life's mysteries.

'Ladies?' Florence asked again, irritation flaring.

Janice dragged her eyes away. 'What? Oh right, no injuries, ta – you wor a soft landing.' There was a murmuring of agreement.

Sabrina couldn't help the grin that crept across her face as she caught Adam's eye and saw him doing his best not to crack up at the unfolding scene. Then, remembering they were responsible for the tumble the Tootlers had taken, she demanded, 'What are you lads doing here?'

'We were headed to the Swan for a pint, but Tony here suggested we come down and give you some moral support first. Flo was telling him about the running group the other night at the pub. Didn't you hear us cheering you on?' He rubbed his ear. 'Tony was yelling right in my ear.'

'I heard the wolf whistle.'

'That was me.' His grin was sheepish.

'Then I don't mind at all.'

They stood smiling at one another as though they were the only two people in the entire park, and Sabrina wondered what he'd say when she told them they were going on a big adventure – an unimaginable adventure for that matter. Then Florence, seemingly having recovered her equilibrium, nudged Sabrina, breaking their trance.

'Time to get this show on the road. I want to put some distance between myself and Tim because look at him. He's bent double on his bike. He'll be dining out on this for weeks.' A glum note had crept into her voice.

Sabrina wasn't looking at Tim though. 'Tony's proving popular,' she said with a wink.

Florence swung back to the group. 'Look at them all. You'd

think he was a cheeseburger the way they're undressing him with their eyes.'

Sabrina giggled. 'Easier than trying to get him out of those jeans in real life.'

Adam, catching what she'd said, laughed too, but Florence wasn't amused. 'This lot would be far better served putting their energy into the rest of the circuit.' She clapped her hands. 'Ladies!'

All eyes slowly turned Florence's way.

'You can't stand about chatting; that's not going to burn the calories.' She blew her whistle extra loudly and hobbled off.

'I better go with them,' Sabrina said, reluctant to leave Adam without telling him everything bubbling up inside her.

'I like the T-shirt, by the way.' He grinned, not looking at her eyes. 'Fits you well that does, sweetheart.'

'Cheeky sod.' She swatted him away, laughing, glad of the distraction because now wasn't the time or place to bring up their foray into the past.

'Meet us down the Swan after?'

Sabrina nodded. 'I've got something to tell you. It's important.'

Adam's expression was panicked, and she slapped his arm gently. 'I'm not preggers! I'll tell you later.'

'That's not fair, Sabrina; don't leave me hanging.' A lock of dark hair fell into his eyes, and Sabrina reached up and pushed it aside. She breathed in the scent of leather from his jacket and spice from the aftershave she'd bought him. It had made her feel properly grown-up buying her man aftershave.

'I'll tell you at the Swan, and it's nothing to worry about.' That wasn't entirely true, but the group was getting away from her.

'At least give us a kiss.'

That she could do. She stood on her tiptoes and planted a quick kiss on his soft lips before charging after the others. She was well aware he was watching her backside, and when she turned to see him staring after her, she gave him a wink before picking up her pace.

The rest of the loop went without incident, with the group rejuvenated after their halfway break. As they drew close to their starting point, they saw a woman loitering with a flag. She looked as though she was going to wave cars in at the end of a race, and as they neared the start of the path, she began flapping her flag in earnest.

Sabrina heard the word go round the tootlers; it was Bev, the team leader at their Weight Watchers branch.

'Well done, girls,' Bev trilled, abandoning the flag to give them a clap. She had a box at her feet and bent down, grabbing the little cans of branded baked beans inside and passing them out. 'A freebie for your efforts,' she said, beaming.

She paused when she reached Sabrina, obviously on the fence about whether she could give a non-member a can of Weight Watchers beans. But, in the end, she decided to spring for it, and Sabrina took hers with a thank-you.

'Who's he?' Janice asked as she spied a man with a cigarette dangling between his fingers. He was leaning against a battered brown Ford Cortina with a camera slung around his neck. It was apparent he was watching them all.

Bev beckoned him over. 'We're ready, Steve. That's Steve from the *Bootle Times;* he's come to take a group shot of us all. Come on, ladies – gather round, and if you could all hold your beans up when he takes a photograph...'

Steve ground out his cigarette and strolled over.

'I don't know why she's got to be in it,' Florence whispered, eyeballing Bev as she got into line next to Sabrina. 'It's not as if she ran around the park.'

'She's after a free plug.' Sabrina whispered back, holding up her beans and waiting for the nod to say cheese. She wasn't happy about this; they'd look like poor excuses for Page 3 girls in their yellow T-shirts. She whispered as much to Flo.

Florence laughed, adding, 'With a penchant for baked beans.'

Bossy Bev shot them a look, and they quietened down, but once the flash had popped, Sabrina elbowed Florence and said, 'You owe me big time, Florence Teesdale.'

'A pint at the Swan do it?'

'You're on.'

# 8

### 1939

'We'd better enjoy this,' Edith stated as she unwrapped her cheese sandwiches. 'The ration books arrived yesterday, and Aunty Em said it won't be long until we're all having things like carrot sandwiches for our lunches.' She pulled a face at the thought of the obscure sandwich filling.

Lily was so hungry she wouldn't care what was squished between the two slices of bread, and she was grateful to her friend for sharing with her.

Edith and Elsie had been fortunate. Mr and Mrs Timbs, whose home they'd been billeted to, had welcomed them. The kindly couple had suggested they call them Aunty Em and Uncle Pete, and as for their two children, Bess and Lionel, they were of a similar age to Edith and Elsie and, as such, had been excited at the thought of extra playmates.

Lily couldn't help but feel envious, and she missed her friend Sarah and calling in at her house, which was always in a state of bedlam thanks to young Alfie and where she'd always been made welcome. Most of all, though, she missed her mam. The past three weeks had been the most miserable of her life, with the only respite being here at school.

Mrs Cox – or the old witch as she now thought of her – worked her to the bone. Lily was quite sure she'd keep her home from school if she felt she could get away with it. She was the unpaid help who was constantly reminded that she had to earn her keep. The old witch had a way of thumping that stick of hers down. It made Lily flinch and loath to do anything other than as she'd been told.

It wasn't even as if she got a decent meal at the end of the day as a reward for her hard work. By the time the old witch had doled out most of the meat in the stews for herself, Lily would be left with nothing more than a bowl of vegetable broth.

Breakfast was a piece of yesterday's bread eaten dry and was only handed to her once Lily had taken down the card from the windows she'd put up the night before to comply with the blackout. The only room she didn't see to was the sitting room, which she presumed the old witch sorted herself.

Her ritual was to stuff the bread down and get on her way, eager to escape out the front door of a morning to pedal to school on the trusty old bicycle that a stroke of luck had seen come her way.

The stew and the bread weren't enough, and hunger gnawed at her constantly. She'd felt faint in assembly this morning, and the ground had swayed beneath her. She'd had to lean on Edith until she'd managed to steady herself.

The only kindness she'd been shown since arriving at the cottage was from Mr Mitchell next door. It was him that had given her the bicycle to use, without which she'd have struggled to make it to school on time each day.

He'd seen Lily in the backyard hanging out the washing on the first Saturday morning after she'd arrived. The old witch had informed her Saturday would be wash day from hereon in. When she'd that done, she could see to the windows with newspaper and vinegar, she'd sniped, buttoning her coat up.

Lily tried not to mind too much, but it did seem unfair that she was to spend all of Saturday doing chores. She knew Edith and Elsie were off for a picnic with the Timbs family, making the most of autumn before winter came calling. They'd been excited leaving school the day before, chattering on about there being the possibility of a cake filled with buttercream.

The old witch had taken herself into town, and Lily had heard the bus moaning to a stop as she'd sorted the pile of laundry dumped on the kitchen floor. She hadn't minded. She'd been grateful to be left on her own without the caustic, constant complaining in her ear. A sigh of relief had escaped her lips as the bus had rumbled on its way, and her shoulders had relaxed, knowing she was gone.

Lily had set to with the washboard and the lemon soap like she'd seen her mam do, and by the time she'd stepped out the back door, the sky had been blue. The sun had dried up the remnants of the damp morning, and a fresh breeze had blown in. It was what her mam would have called a good drying day, Lily had thought with a pang, beginning to peg out the washing. She'd spent the early part of the morning scrubbing the sheets and other sundries on the washboard in the metal tub, and her hands had been red and chafed. Still, there was satisfaction in watching the sheets billowing, she'd thought, gingerly picking up a pair of the old witch's undergarments between her index finger and thumb.

Mr Mitchell next door had leaned on the fence, his cap pulled down low, and a pipe sticking out the corner of his mouth to call out a cheery greeting as she'd pegged the smalls to the line before introducing himself to her. There'd been a tinge of satisfaction at the thought of the old witch's holey undergarments on display for her neighbour to see.

She'd been glad to pause in her task to chat to the old man, eager for company, and had instantly taken a liking to his dancing blue eyes. Eyes were the window to a person's soul, she'd read once, and she reckoned that was true. You could tell a lot about a person by looking into their eyes. The old witch's were the colour of pale tea with not so much as a glimmer of warmth in them.

Lily had breathed in deeply as Mr Mitchell had puffed away on his pipe because she liked the smell of pipe tobacco. Her dad had smoked a pipe, and it was comforting to inhale the pungent, spicy-sweet smell. It brought back happy memories.

'How's she treating you, lass?' he'd asked, taking the pipe out of his mouth to tamp it down with his yellowed forefinger.

Lily had been taught not to tell tales, but she'd also been taught to tell the truth, so she'd hesitated, uncertain as to what to say.

Mr Mitchell hadn't looked up from his task as he'd said, 'I thought as much. She's a hard woman, lass, because life's dealt her a bad hand.'

Lily thought it must have been a truly terrible hand to make her so cruel.

'I worked with her husband, Ernie, at the paper mill These 'ere were the factory cottages back in the day.' He'd made a sweeping gesture at the row of cottages. 'Ernie, now he was a good man, and she wor different back then.'

'What changed her then?' Lily had asked, keen to hear more and happy to abandon the washing a while longer.

'He died, leaving her to struggle alone raising their three young lads. It wor an accident at the mill.' He'd shaken his head. 'Terrible thing. He tripped and fell through a trapdoor onto the machinery below. Torn to pieces.'

Lily's eyes had widened in horror, but he hadn't finished.

'Then she waved her boys off one by one to fight in the Great War, and not one of 'em came home. Three sons she lost in that fight, and now here we are at war again.' He'd pondered the sadness of it all for a moment then added, 'Sent her mad for a while, and she weren't ever the same again after that. It wor enough to turn any woman bitter all that loss.'

Lily had felt a frisson of pity for the old witch, but it didn't make the way she treated her all right.

'My dad died in an accident a year back. He was hit by a car on his way home from work.'

'Eee, lass, I'm sorry to hear that, I am.'

They had both fallen silent as a tractor rumbled past in the field behind the yards. Then Mr Mitchell had waved out to the farmer. 'His sons have enlisted, and he'll be called up any day now too. That farm of his will be turned over to the Women's Land Army soon. Mark me words, it's land girls will be toiling those fields any day now.'

Lily couldn't imagine women driving tractors and the like. 'Do you live alone?' she'd asked.

'I do since my Gladys passed a few years back. Me son and daughter are married with families of their own now. Although they'll be deployed to France any day now, mark me words.' He'd puffed away again on the pipe.

Lily had watched the smoke curling upward. 'Does anybody live in the other cottage?' she'd asked, pointing in the direction of the empty yard behind her.

'That wor old Bill's place. I worked with him an' all. He's been gone a year now. The place has been left to go to wrack and ruin. No children, you see, and it's a right shame. He could have fed all of Skem with the vegetable patch he kept out the back there. It was his pride and joy, but it's a wilderness now. Sally, his wife, well, she'd be turning in her grave if she could see the state of the place. The mice will be making themselves right at home, mark me words, lass.'

Lily had grimaced at the mention of mice – and his penchant for saying *mark my words* – but she wasn't surprised to hear the cottage was empty.

They'd chatted on companionably enough, and then Lily had remembered what had been worrying at her. 'Mr Mitchell,

I'm to go to school on Monday, but I don't know how to get there. Can you tell me the quickest way, please?'

Mr Mitchell had explained the route she'd need to take, and Lily's face had grown longer and longer. 'It will take me forever to walk there.' She hadn't thought it likely the old witch would give her money for the bus or let her off getting the dinner ready before she left in the morning to ensure she'd time to get there on foot.

An expression of pity had passed over his face, and then he'd brightened. 'Wait 'ere; I've had a thought, lass.'

Lily had watched as he'd shuffled over to the shed and returned after a minute or two, looking pleased with himself, bumping a bicycle over the patchy grass.

'It wor me son's. He won't be needing it.'

Lily had stared over the fence at the bike in delight, and then her face had fallen. 'But I don't know how to ride one.'

'Well then, lass, it's high time you learned, in't it?'

She'd hung the last of the washing out then met Mr Mitchell on the road outside his cottage. 'There's nothing to it, lass; you've just got to get on it and pedal for all you're worth.'

Lily had looked at him doubtfully, but she'd swung a leg over and hoisted herself onto the seat, then placed her feet on the pedals. Mr Mitchell had instructed her to pedal while he kept a firm hand on the bicycle, shouting instructions at her to avoid the potholes as he'd pushed her along. She hadn't realised he'd let go until the bike had begun to wobble madly, and over she'd gone, winding up in a heap on the side road.

'Any broken bones, lass?' Mr Mitchell had shouted down the empty road.

Lily had taken stock, relieved she hadn't torn her stockings before picking herself up. The only injury had been to her pride, and she'd wheeled the bike slowly back toward the cottages. 'Can we try again, Mr Mitchell?' she'd asked when she'd drawn level with him. 'Me mam says I'm a quick learner. I'm sure I'll get it this time.'

He'd smiled broadly on hearing this and revealed a missing tooth Lily hadn't noticed before. 'I'd well believe it, lass. C'mon then – on you get.'

Lily had taken a deep breath and, with a frown of concentration, waited for Mr Mitchell to give the word. This time after he'd let go, beyond a few hairy moments, she'd managed to keep the bike upright, growing bolder as she pedalled along, enjoying a sense of jubilation as the wind rushed past her ears.

She'd cycled back to a round of applause from Mr Mitchell, and they'd agreed between them to keep the bike down the side of his cottage. She could come and get it each morning and leave it there of an afternoon. It was unsaid but understood that Mrs Cox didn't need to know about the arrangement.

Lily had leaned the bike up against the cottage's stone wall as they'd agreed she should, and she'd been about to venture back inside the old witch's cottage, knowing there'd be hell to pay if she hadn't managed to clean the windows with the newspaper and vinegar, when she'd frozen. Her spine had tingled, her scalp pricking with the sensation of being watched. Mr Mitchell had taken himself off inside, and his door was shut, and there was no sign of anyone on the road, so her eyes had turned warily toward what had been old Bill's cottage. She'd thought she'd seen the raggedy net curtain twitch but couldn't be sure, and, spooked, she'd hurried inside, closing the door firmly behind her.

'Here.' Edith brought her back to the here and now, handing her the piece of sandwich she'd broken off.

'Ta, Edie.' Lily tried not to snatch it from her.

'Lily, look at your hands!' Edith recoiled in her seat as though she might catch something.

Lily flushed. They were scaly and red, scratched until they'd bled in places between her fingers. 'It's from having them in cold water all the time. I try not to scratch, but it itches like mad.'

Edith shook her head and opened her mouth to say something but shut it again upon seeing her friend's closed expression.

Lily didn't want to pursue the conversation; she was too hungry, but still, she did her best not to eat the bread and cheese too quickly. She knew she'd feel fuller if she ate slower. Her eyes flicked over Elsie seated at the table alongside them. She was stuffing her sandwich in like she hadn't eaten in a week, although she was well fed at the Timbs house by all accounts. It was less about hunger and more about running off outside to play with her new friend, Lily surmised, noticing her jiggling about on the seat like she had ants in her pants.

'You'll get a tap on the shoulder from Miss over there if you're not careful, Elsie,' Edith warned. Her little sister had got a smack on the back of her hand the other day. She didn't need another one. All three pairs of eyes flitted over to Miss Ellis, who cut a lean, stern figure prowling the room.

Elsie settled down in her seat and took a daintier bite before lisping. 'Tell us about the ghostie next door, Lily.'

Lily managed a grin. Elsie loved this tale, not that there was much to tell other than Lily had seen the curtain fall in the empty cottage next door more than once. She was sure she'd heard footsteps through the wall too. It was unsettling, but Lily was too busy scrubbing to feel frightened most of the time. Once more, she relayed this to Elsie, who listened while she finished her lunch at a more sedate pace before scampering off.

'Will you come outside today?' Edith asked hopefully, brushing the crumbs from her skirt.

Lily knew Ruth would keep her company but suspected her friend would rather Lily did.

'I can't, Edie. You know I've got to wash up the teachers'

lunch things,' Lily said, getting up from the seat. 'Thank you for sharing with me.'

Edith, who Lily knew had had a decent breakfast of porridge and toast, was indignant at her friend's circumstances. 'It isn't right, Lily – you not getting fed properly by the old witch. She's getting money for your keep, you know.'

Lily flushed. 'Shush.' She gazed about, but most of the children had disappeared outside, eager to stretch their legs before the afternoon classes began. Lily had admitted to Edith the reason she'd volunteered to clear up after the teachers was to eat their leftovers, and it wasn't something she was proud of. It also rankled that Ruth would pounce on Edie as soon as she made her way into the asphalted play area. She'd link her arm through hers with that superior air of hers.

Things were worse than she'd told Edith. She was too embarrassed to mention she'd been charged with emptying the old witch's chamber pot of a morning. This morning she'd taken the loathsome thing down the stairs, and its yellowed contents had sloshed on her dress. She'd done her best to sponge it off but still felt tainted. She knew it was in her head, but she couldn't get that acrid smell out of her nostrils and had been terrified arriving at school this morning that she might smell of wee.

'You've got to say something,' Edith urged. 'I told Aunty Em how awful she is—'

'Edith, you promised!'

Edith was unrepentant. 'She said you should speak to Mrs Young.'

Mrs Young was the rather formidable headmistress, and she wasn't young. She was at least as old as the old witch, and Lily had no intention of confiding in her as to how horrid her living circumstances were because she knew she wouldn't find sympathy there either.

She pulled a face. 'I don't want to make things worse. What if she were to have a word with the old witch? She'd make my life even more miserable then. Besides, I promised Mam I'd make the best of it. I'd send her a letter if I'd money for a stamp.'

Edith tilted her head to the side for a moment, saying, 'I know. I heard there's to be a Wednesday night youth club meeting for us Edge Hill kids. The vicar's cycling out here to see us so he can take messages back to our mams and dads. You could tell Father Ian. Your mam's sure to make things right when she hears how bad it is for you.'

Lily felt a surge of hope and determined she'd get away next Wednesday night even if she had to climb out her window and shimmy down the drainpipe.

# 9
## 1982

Sabrina and Florence had said goodbye to the Bootle Tootlers and ducked back to Flo's. Both girls were starving after their run. Mrs Teesdale had left their dinner warming in the oven as promised, and they'd agreed between them that French fare was tasty as they'd wolfed down the beef bourguignon and mashed potato.

Florence, uncaring that the buttery mashed spud was breaking her Weight Watchers programme, mumbled through a mouthful, 'I deserve this after what happened tonight.'

Sabrina wasn't sure whether she was talking about the tumble she'd taken or the fact they were all going to be in the local paper.

Florence raced upstairs to get changed once she'd all but licked her plate clean while Sabrina washed up. She could hear the television playing in the front room and was about to pop through to tell Mr and Mrs Teesdale how they'd got on when Florence reappeared. She was wearing a new maroon rara skirt, tights and flat shoes, which she'd teamed with a high-collared, ruffled blouse. Her fringe had been re-gelled and was suitably spiky. Fresh make-up, too, had been applied.

'Wow. You look fab, girl. I love the skirt,' Sabrina gushed. She'd yet to splurge on one of the new miniskirts hitting the high-street shops, but seeing Flo modelling one now, she wished she had.

'It's not too much, is it? I know we're only off to the Swan, but I wanted to wear it, being new and all.' Florence glanced down. 'Do me legs look like tree stumps?'

Sabrina laughed. 'No and no.' She knew why Flo had gone to town, and it had everything to do with Tim having seen them in all their yellow T-shirt glory at the park – she wanted to knock him out and replace the memory of her going head over heels with an updated and much-improved one. She'd given up on trying to get through to her friend where Tim was concerned. Flo was going to have to learn the hard way.

Florence, happy she didn't look as though she should be standing alongside the oaks in the park, shouted out a 'we're off' to her mam and dad. Then, pulling Sabrina along behind her, said, 'Come on – if we get cornered by them, we'll never get out of here, and Dad will only go on about the length of me skirt.'

Sabrina, equally eager, hurried out the door after her.

They got the bus from Marsh Lane back to Bold Street, and Sabrina let them into the flat, determined not to mess about getting ready. The sooner she got down to the Swan and told Adam what she'd learned today, the better. However, Aunt Evie, who was settled in her armchair, had other ideas.

She had slippers on her feet, a cup of tea on the side table next to her and was leaning forward in her seat, telling the Sharon Gaskell character on *Coronation Street* off for being cheeky to poor Rita.

By the looks of things, Sabrina mused, Aunt Evie was taking her annoyance at Sabrina out on Sharon. And there was no chance of slinking past unnoticed in her yellow T-shirt because Aunt Evie had already turned her gaze from the screen to greet the girls, blinking behind her thick lenses at the sight of Sabrina squeezed into her Bootle Tootler T-shirt.

'I'm surprised you didn't cause an accident wearing that,' she said curtly, then she turned her attention to Florence. 'You're looking swish tonight, Florence. I like that blouse on you. It's very chaste being done up to the neck like that, but a word of advice.'

Florence raised an eyebrow, waiting.

'Don't be bending over to tie your laces in that skirt.'

She grinned. 'I won't, Aunt Evie.'

Sabrina bristled as she plucked at her T-shirt. 'It wasn't just me wearing this. We all were, Flo included. Tell her, Flo.'

'We were, Aunt Evie. I think Bossy Bev – she's the head honcho at the Bootle branch of Weight Watchers where I go – scrimped getting them made because some of the girls have already ripped the seams of theirs. They get awful whiffy quick too.'

Sabrina frowned, hoping she wasn't implying she smelled.

Evelyn's mouth twitched, and Sabrina thought perhaps she'd forgotten she was annoyed over her Adam Taylor revelation, but then it flatlined again. *No such luck*. She couldn't stand it when her aunt was out of sorts with her, and given she didn't have a good reason to be, Sabrina launched into a speech. 'I'm sorry you disapprove of me going out with Adam, Aunt Evie, but I love him. I won't stop seeing him because you, for worever reason, have a problem with his dad. Adam's not his father; he's his own man, and it's not fair you lumping them together.'

Evelyn opened her mouth to interrupt, but Sabrina wasn't stopping.

'And as for him and me going back to 1945, you know full well there's nothing I can do about that. The past has already happened.' Her heart was thumping hard, but she was pleased she'd said her piece.

Florence fidgeted nervously at her side, obviously unsure where to put herself.

Evelyn shook her head, causing the grey curls she had shampooed and set every week to bounce. 'There's no need to take that tone with me, Sabrina, me girl,' she huffed back. 'I worry that's all – and not without good reason, might I add. And you've got it all wrong,' she added. 'It's not that I dislike Ray. He can't be trusted when it comes to women is all. He's a heartbreaker.'

Sabrina and Florence exchanged a glance.

'Not that he's ever broken my heart, before you go jumping to conclusions, either of you. I wouldn't let him. Just remember, Sabrina, Adam's his son, and the apple—'

'Doesn't fall far from the tree. I know, I know.'

'And I worry for you disappearing off into time.'

Sabrina softened, knowing Aunt Evie's concerns came from a place of love. 'I know you do, but this time I'll have Adam with me, and he's a lovely lad, Aunt Evie. He'll look after me. Give him a chance. Please.'

'He is lovely,' Florence confirmed. 'And he adores Sabs. Thinks the sun shines out of her.'

Sabrina flashed Florence a grateful glance.

'Well, someone has to, I s'pose,' Evelyn muttered, looking from Florence and back to Sabrina.

'Good grief, that T-shirt!' She began to chortle, and Sabrina exhaled, feeling the tension in the air dissipate.

'This is the last time I'm wearing this shirt, Flo,' Sabrina huffed, taking herself off to her bedroom to get changed, glad things seemed to have been smoothed over with Aunt Evie – even if it had been at her expense.

She reappeared in record time wearing a sweater she knew Adam liked and her Calvin Klein's. 'I think these feel a little looser already,' she announced happily to Florence, who'd taken up residence on the sofa.

'Let me watch the end of this, Sabs; it's all happening tonight.'

Sabrina frowned. She was in a hurry to get to the pub, but she was a closet *Corrie* fan herself and settled in next to Florence, not rising to the bait when Evelyn mentioned a little bird had told her she and Florence were future cover girls. However, she did elbow Flo and mutter, 'You better not have told her you'll get her a copy of the *Bootle Times*.' She knew by her friend's silence that she'd done just that, and when the familiar tune signalling the end of the long-running soap opera began to play, she hauled her friend out of her seat. 'C'mon, Judas – the pub will be shut by the time we get down there.'

'Night, Aunt Evie,' Florence sang, picking up her shoulder bag from where she'd tossed it on the table.

'Don't forget the newspaper next time you come, Florence.'

'I won't.'

Sabrina glowered at them both then leaned down to give her aunt's soft powdered cheek a kiss. She was pleased they'd made peace, and she caught the faint whiff of the Woodbine ciggie she'd have allowed herself after her tea.

'Good night, luv,' Evelyn said, reaching up to pat her arm instead. 'Behave yourselves,' she added. 'Making the papers once in one evening is enough, do you hear me?' But her tongue was firmly in her cheek.

Sabrina and Florence left Evelyn for her evening in front of the tele, and Flo waited patiently for Sabrina to flick the lights three times. Then, once Sabrina was satisfied all was as it should be, they took to the stairs. The back door beside the workroom disgorged them onto Wood Street, where, a little further up, the Swan waited.

It was getting dusky dark now, and linking arms, they clip-clopped their way over the well-worn cobbles to the pub they called their local, giggling about Bossy Bev and the cans of baked beans. They could see the light beaming from inside the pub each time the door opened and closed, revealing the row of motorbikes lined up outside, which signalled Adam and his mates were inside. An old Led Zeppelin number was thumping and drifting down the quiet street, filling them both with anticipation of a good night ahead. Or at least Sabrina hoped it would be a good night. She'd no idea how Adam would react when she told him what she'd found out today.

The door opened as they reached the pub, and a lad who hadn't realised flares had gone out at the start of the decade held it open for them to pass through, giving them both an approving once-over.

Not forgetting her promise to Sabrina earlier, Florence made her way to the bar to get the bevvies in. At the same time, Sabrina scanned the heaving pub for Adam. She spotted him, Tim (his new girlfriend Linda of the Farrah flick hanging off him), Tony and a few of the other lads they went round with taking up several tables near the jukebox. A haze of cigarette smoke floated overhead, and their helmets sat in a pile on another table.

The silly smile she got whenever she spied Adam played across her lips, and Sabrina fluffed her hair before making her way toward him. Sometimes she could pinch herself that they'd wound up dating. It didn't seem all that long ago that her eyes had first alighted on him walking into the Swan with Tim Burns. She remembered how gorgeous she'd thought he was with his dark eyes and blue-black hair curling at the collar of his shirt. He'd worn his battered leather jacket and jeans well, and she'd been smitten at first sight.

Adam put his pint down, an identical silly smile spreading across his face as he saw Sabrina. He got up from the table to greet her with a kiss, and if he noticed she was a little more passionate than usual given they were in public, he didn't comment. She was filled with a need to cling to him, suddenly frightened as to how he might react upon hearing he would find himself alongside her in a Liverpool neither of them recognised in a time when it had ravaged by war. Would he regret ever having met her?

'Gerra room, you two,' a lad called Lenny called out as someone else way-hay-hayed.

Adam grinned over at them and told them they were jealous when they broke apart, and Sabrina reached up and wiped the lipstick off his mouth. 'Not your shade,' she said with feigned light-heartedness.

'Ta.' He winked and then took a step back to appraise her. 'You look gorgeous, girl. Although I did like you in the yellow.'

'I know what you liked, and it wasn't the colour,' she said, brushing past him to squish in at the table. She sat on the edge of the seat with her back to the wall. Behind her hung a black-and-white print of Liverpool of old. Adam pulled a chair round next to her before resting his hand territorially on her leg. Tony was already up scanning the pub for a spare seat for Florence.

Sabrina knew she should just come out with it, but the words were stuck in her throat, so instead she looked to the bar to see how Flo was getting on with the bevvies. Her bezzie mate was chatting away with Mickey, the bartender, whose polished head and gold tooth shone each time they caught the light. It was a few minutes before she made her way toward the table with a face on her like she'd trod in dog poo. She'd obviously spied Linda.

Sabrina would have liked to have kicked Tim under the table upon seeing him whisper in Linda's ear, making her toss her blonde hair and laugh before they both turned to look at Flo.

Florence had seen the exchange and was doing her best not to spill the pints she was carrying. Her face flushed pink, knowing she was being talked about, but she held her hands steady.

'I hear you've taken up jogging, girl,' Linda said, a sly look on her over-made-up face as Florence set the glasses down on the table. Tim dragged on his ciggie and exhaled lazily, waiting to see what Florence's reaction would be.

'Yeah.'

'Not good for your health from what I hear,' she tittered and then took the cigarette from Tim's hand and puffed on it deeply.

'Neither's that,' Florence retorted, pointing to the cigarette. 'And jogging won't give you a mouth like a cat's arse either.'

Sabrina snorted into her pint glass, and Flo, head held high, sat down, turning her back on Tim and Linda.

'Well said, Flo,' Sabrina whispered, leaning close to her friend, feeling proud of her. Tony and Adam were laughing, and Sabrina was pleased Florence had missed the flash of admiration that had passed over Tim's face at her snappy comeback. She didn't need any encouragement where he was concerned.

'I put your favourite song on the jukebox,' Tony said to Florence, edging his seat closer to hers.

Flo inched hers away as 'De Do Do Do, De Da Da Da' by the Police came on.

Sabrina would have to get Adam to have a quiet word with Tony about behaving like an eager puppy. If he was going to win Flo over, he would do far better to try an uninterested—she couldn't think of the right sort of dog and realised Flo was talking to her and the others.

'Mickey says Georgie Best's upstairs at the Steering Wheel.'

A conversation buzzed as to who'd seen who venturing up to the exclusive club. But, of course, it was closed to the likes of them, though the girls had on occasion managed to wangle their way in there.

Having finished sulking over Flo getting one up on her, Linda studied her polished red fingernails, feigning boredom and told them she didn't know what the big deal was. She'd been to the Steering Wheel loads of times, and if you'd seen one celeb, then you'd seen them all. Tim butted in at that point to inform them that Linda had dated several footballers, and Sabrina nudged Flo with her foot, sensing another remark about to slide from her friend's lips. She didn't want a full-on catfight to pull apart.

She needn't have worried, though, because as Devo's 'Whip It' came blaring out, Linda squealed and began wiggling in her seat as though she'd filled her pants. 'Timmy, come and dance with me.' She stood up, all fitted top and skintight jeans as she pouted at him until he got up from his seat, running a hand through his dirty blonde hair.

'Timmy?' Florence mouthed at Sabrina incredulously before accepting Tony's offer to dance.

Sabrina knew she'd only agreed so she could accidentally on purpose stand on Linda's foot. The four of them moved to the area reserved for those who fancied dancing.

Adam squeezed Sabrina's knee. 'Come on then – what did you have to tell me?' he asked over the music.

Sabrina, put on the spot, swivelled to face him. 'You won't believe this...'

And Adam's mouth fell open as Sabrina told him all about Alice's visit to the shop and what had come to light as a result.

# 10

### 1939

Lily was on her hands and knees, giving the kitchen floor a scrub. With its busy pattern, the worn linoleum hid many sins, and the water in the bucket was almost black. She'd washed up after their meal and stuck the blackout cardboard to the windows in all but the sitting room. Her irritated hands were burning, but she intended to finish the task the old witch had set her.

She wanted to give her no cause for complaint because she had a plan. She'd formulated it carefully and had written it all down in her worry book because it made her feel braver. She'd fallen into the habit of writing in her worry book each evening before she put her light out. The pages were filling up rapidly.

It was Wednesday evening, and from seven o'clock, the youth group would be gathering. They were to meet at the centre where she and her fellow schoolmates had been taken when they'd arrived in Skem. Lily was determined to get back there tonight to speak to Father Ian about sending word to her mam as to how unhappy she was.

She didn't think she could stand it much longer. She was beginning to suspect the old witch was quite potty.

Once she'd finished the floor, she was going to feign a headache and take herself off to bed. The old witch liked to sit in the front room Lily wasn't supposed to venture into after dinner, and she was determined she wouldn't hear her sneak back down the stairs. Nor was it likely she'd check to see how she was, and her plan was to duck past the front windows. Then she'd sneak round the corner of Mr Mitchell's cottage to collect the bicycle and get on her way.

Lily had leaned with her ear to the door of the sitting room the other night before heading up to bed. Her curiosity had been piqued because she could hear the old witch talking to someone in there. Her tone was unfamiliar and soft, and she'd thought it odd given she hadn't heard anyone knock at the front door.

What the old witch did for the hours she shut herself away in the room had been a mystery until Saturday – then Lily had used her absence to investigate what secrets the space held for herself.

She didn't know what she'd expected to find. Still, surveying the front room, she had been disappointed nonetheless to find it was rather ordinary and, like the rest of the cottage, it smelled of damp. The odour was insidious, akin to dirty socks.

The only point of difference was how clean it was compared to the state the rest of the cottage had been in when she'd first arrived. The old witch was determined Lily should give the place a top and tailing while she was here. It wasn't something Lily would have begrudged had any kindness been sent her way – she wasn't frightened of hard work.

In the sitting room, however, the hearth had been swept, the carpet, although threadbare in places, was spotless, and there was no sheen of dust coating the sparse furnishings. Instead, there was a shrine-like feel to the space.

Net curtains yellowed by age hung in the window facing

the road outside, and pale green drapes patterned with roses hung from the pelmet above the frame. Lily had spied the blackout cardboard laid out on the floor in the corner, ready to be put back up that evening. With its fading green leaf swirls, although beginning to peel in corners, the wallpaper gave the room a cheery feel. It would be a cosy space in which to while away the evening, she'd thought as her eyes had swept over the furniture.

A chair was covered in the same fabric as the curtains near the fireplace, and there was another plain green armchair with a white embroidered antimacassar draped over the back. A rug separated the space on either side of the fire between them. An oak sideboard was the only other piece of furniture in the room. It had spindly turned legs, and sitting upon lace doilies on top of it was a pile of envelopes and a cluster of photographs.

On the wall above the sideboard were four identical oval frames. With curiosity outweighing caution, Lily had moved closer to inspect them. The first image her eyes had alighted upon was of a couple in their wedding finery. She'd thought their outfits were odd, staring up at the sepia photograph inside the oval frame.

It had been hard to equate the young, serious bride standing formally next to a stern, moustached groom with the nasty bite to whose care she'd been given over, but it had to be the old witch. It had made her feel strange to think of her husband on his wedding day, so unaware of the horrible death fate had in store for him. She'd felt a chill dance up her spine, and she'd glanced back over her shoulder, even though she'd known she'd hear the door if the old witch came back.

A young man in uniform with carefully combed hair had been depicted in the next frame, matching the other two hanging on the wall alongside it.

Her sons. All of whom had died in the Great War.

Her fingers had touched upon the pile of opened envelopes

on the sideboard, and she'd picked the top one up, carefully sliding the letter out.

*Dear mam*, she'd read before placing it back in the envelope. The cluster of photographs alongside them were grainy shots of the Cox boys as younger lads perched formally in a photographer's studio.

Lily's breath had caught as it dawned on her who it was she'd heard the old witch talking to.

The ghosts of her husband and sons.

She talked to the photographs and read and reread the letters she'd been sent from her boys while they'd fought for their country. She dwelled in her memories.

It was terrible what had happened to her family. Still, Lily found it hard to rustle up sympathy given the way she'd been treated. She'd done nothing to deserve it, and she'd backed out of the room, putting what she'd seen from her mind.

Now, as she continued swirling the rag around on the floor, she heard the familiar thudding plunk of the old witch's walking stick as she made her way toward the kitchen. She put extra elbow grease into her cleaning.

'I'm nearly finished, Mrs Cox,' she said without looking up from her task.

'Not until it's been polished with the wax too. Did your mam not teach you anything?' Her voice was as coarse as her words were sharp.

Lily could hear the clock ticking. Time was marching on. She needed to be on her way – and soon. Panic swelled. 'Please, Mrs Cox, could I do that tomorrow? I've a terrible headache. I think I'm sickening for something.' It wasn't a lie. Her head was beginning to pound.

Mrs Cox kept her distance, leaning heavily on her stick.

'Your cheeks are flushed. I can't be picking anything up.' She wheezed a sigh. 'Yer to have it finished before you leave in the morning, do ye hear me? I won't have a job half-finished.'

'Yes, Mrs Cox. Thank you.' Lily nodded gratefully, feeling the fear that she'd be too late to make her way into town abate.

The old witch didn't say anything but made a harrumphing sound before turning and shuffling back to the sitting room.

As soon as Lily had painted herself into the corner, so to speak, with the wet rag, she got to her feet and brushed herself off before heading upstairs. The deliberate thump of her bedroom door closing was loud enough to reverberate downstairs but not so loud as to earn her a telling-off. Next, she stuffed the pillow under the covers to make it look like she was in bed before unlatching the window in case the old witch decided to lock the front door. There was always a first time for everything, and she wasn't leaving anything to chance. How she'd clamber up to the second storey, she didn't know, but where there was a will, there was a way.

Then, satisfied she'd done what she needed to do, she let herself out of her bedroom, quietly closing the door behind her this time.

She stood poised for a few seconds at the top of the stairs, listening out. But all was quiet, and so she gingerly put a foot on each step, testing it out before putting her full weight down. She could hear the old witch murmuring quietly in the sitting room and held her breath as the floor creaked under her feet, waiting. The one-sided conversation didn't falter. Satisfied she could make her escape, Lily unearthed her coat from beneath the old witch's and shrugged into it. Then she opened the front door and pulled it gently behind her.

The evening air was considerably cooler than the day had been, and she shivered, despite her coat, as she took a moment to survey the street. It wasn't dark yet, and even though she wasn't visible thanks to the curtains being drawn over the blackout paper in the windows, she ducked down and made her way past Mr Mitchell's cottage and around the corner.

The bike was where she'd left it, but as she wheeled it up to the road, she noticed it was hard to push, and one of the tyres was making a thwumping sound. She glanced down at it, and her heart sank. The tyre was as flat as a pancake.

She moved across to the other side of the road a little way down from the cottages as she tried to think of what she could do. Mr Mitchell would have a pump, but he wasn't home. She'd seen him go out earlier and had no idea when he'd be back. Tears of frustration welled.

'Where are you off to?'

The male voice behind her made her yelp with fright, and her hand flew to her chest as she spun round, eyes wide with fear. A young lad stood there.

'Shush.' She held her finger to her lips and gazed toward the cottages, holding her breath as she waited to see if the door she'd not long exited through would be flung open. She counted to ten slowly and then relaxed.

'Sorry. I didn't mean to startle you,' the boy whispered.

He looked to be the same age as herself, Lily deduced.

'I'm Max. Max Waters.' He held his hand up in a conciliatory manner, and she noticed a hole in the elbow of his blue sweater. His shirt hung out the bottom of it, and his shorts looked too big for him. Hand-me-downs from an older brother, no doubt. She could see the piece of string he'd tied around his waist to hold them up dangling down. His knees were grazed,. She moved back to his face. He had a cap on, and the face beneath the peak was grubby, but there was a liveliness to it too.

'Well, you did,' she said, in no mood for chit-chat. Where had this Max come from? The road had been empty when she'd stepped outside. Had he been lurking in the woods? And if so, that could only mean he was up to no good. Was he planning to rob Mr Mitchell or the old witch?

'Your tyre's flat.'

'Obviously,' Lily retorted, careful to keep her voice down.

Max didn't seem bothered by her tart tone. 'Where were you off to anyway?'

'None of your business. And where did you come from?' She squared up to him.

'None of your business,' he flicked back, quick as a flash.

They eyed one another, his blue eyes refusing to budge from Lily's brownish-green ones until Lily sighed. There was no harm in telling him what she'd had planned, she supposed.

'I'm Lily Tubb. I was billeted there to the cottage in the middle.' She pointed across the way, and this time, she whispered, so Max had to lean in to hear what she said. 'There's only the old witch who lives there and me. I'm off to a youth group in town because I need to tell our vicar how awful she is. Father Ian's cycling up from Edge Hill where I come from to see us kids tonight and take any messages back to our mams.'

'An old witch, aye?'

'An old witch,' she confirmed. 'Who thinks I'm asleep in bed because if she knew what I'd planned, she'd have stopped me going out.'

'How old are yer?'

'Twelve, but I'll be thirteen in a few months.' Lily placed a hand on her hip. 'I answered your question; now it's your turn.'

Max nodded. 'Fair enough. I turn fourteen soon. I'm due to start work at the paper mill, only I'll be long gone before then. I go to the empty cottage sometimes when I've had enough of things at home. I don't do anything wrong,' he added hastily, seeing Lily's wary frown. 'I like being on my own is all, and nobody can find me there.'

'How do you get in?' she asked, understanding now that there was no ghost in the cottage next door, only a boy who didn't belong there.

'There's a window down the side I climb in. There's a lot of shouting goes on in my house. I like the peace and quiet in the cottage, that's all. It's full of mice, though, you know, so I'm not alone. Not really.'

Lily pulled a face at the mention of mice. Then another question occurred to her. 'How did you know the cottage was empty?'

'Everybody knows everything about everybody in Skem.'

'Have you lived here all your life then?'

'I have, but I want to move to my brother and his wife's flat. They're not far from Edge Hill themselves.'

'Why?'

He shrugged. 'I don't like it much here.'

'Me either.'

A silence swelled between them. All that could be heard was the running water of the River Tawd off in the distance and the rustle of leaves beside them.

'I could take you into town. I've gorra bike – it's how I get here. I hide it in the bushes up the road, so nobody sees me going in and out of the cottage.'

Hope flared on Lily's face, and Max grinned a slightly crooked smile.

'G'won – put that back.' He inclined his head to her bicycle. 'And I'll meet you back here with it in a few minutes.'

Lily watched him run back up the road for a second, and then she wheeled the bike back to its hiding place. She'd have to get up at the crack of dawn tomorrow to get the floor waxed and leave enough time to ask Mr Mitchell if he'd pump the tyre up for her so she could get to school.

She waited under the whispering leaves, and true to his word, Max pedalled up alongside her in no time at all.

'Hop up on the handlebars,' he said, placing his feet on the ground to hold his bike steady.

Lily smiled. The road was full of potholes, and if he were to go down one, she might go flying. Cuts and bruises would be hard to explain come the morning.

'What's so funny?' Max was bemused.

'Nothing. I'm not sure getting on there's a good idea is all.'

'Then why are you smiling?'

'It's something I do when I'm nervous or scared; I can't help it.'

'Oh right. I stutter when I feel like that.'

Most people didn't understand, and Lily felt a kinship with this strange lad, but still, she hesitated.

'Listen, Lily, I know this road like the back of me hand. You'll be safe as houses with me, I promise.'

She had two choices. She could hop on or go back to the cottage, and the latter wasn't an option. So she jumped on and held on for dear life.

# 11

―――――

1982

'How are you, Florence? I didn't hear you come in,' Evelyn said, appearing in the shop, where Sabrina stood at the till, tallying up. She'd turned the radio off in the workroom, and without the steady thrumming of the Singer, the shop was suddenly quiet. Both her hands were in the pockets of Friday's lilac shop coat and her glasses had slipped down her nose.

'I'm brill given it's Friday, Aunt Evie, and I have to say you're looking spring-like. The lilac looks well on you.'

'Thank you, Florence.' Evelyn preened.

Sabrina knew Friday's coat was one of her aunt's favourites. Apparently, she'd once read that lilac symbolised living in the moment and opening yourself up to new experiences, among other things. Sabrina had tried not to snort when she said that was how she lived her life.

'I'll get Sabrina wearing one, one of these days.' She fixed her wily gaze on Sabrina, who closed the till with a flick of her hip, finished now with the tallying up.

'Here she goes, Flo.' Then Sabrina adopted a bold tone. 'I can carry my pinking shears, a tape measure and the kitchen sink in these pockets, I'll have you know.'

Florence giggled and then sobered as she found herself on the receiving end of Evelyn Flooks's stare overtop of her glasses.

'Mock me as you may, Sabrina Flooks, but did I spend half my morning looking for the scissors and the pins?' She didn't wait for an answer. 'No, I did not. I knew where everything I needed was.'

Sabrina rolled her eyes. 'Come on, Flo. We'll get on our way.' She stuck her hand in her pocket and produced her packet of Opal Fruits.

'Gie's one.' Florence held her palm out, and Sabrina dropped the orange-wrapped sweet into it before peeling one open for herself.

'Where are you two off to then?' Evelyn pushed her glasses back up her nose.

Sabrina paused mid-chew, jumping in before Florence could land them in it. 'We're off to see a film. I don't know what's showing, but something's bound to take our fancy.'

Florence's cheeks reddened at Sabrina's fib, but she didn't say a word, smiling and nodding as though the cat had suddenly got her tongue.

Sabrina held her breath. Not much slipped past Aunt Evie, and Florence looked like a guilty beetroot shifting from foot to foot. Her friend had never been able to get away with fibbing because she wore her heart on her sleeve.

Sabrina didn't like not being truthful with her aunt either, but needs must, and she'd made her feelings about the clairvoyant a few doors down clear whenever she heard her name. The words *Worra lorra rubbish* sprang to mind from the last time she and Florence had paid her a visit. But her disparaging remarks aside, Sabrina didn't want her worrying about what she might be told tonight. While Aunt Evie might disapprove of Mystic Lou, she'd still like to know all the ins and outs of their visit.

Evelyn, however, seemed to have her mind on heading

upstairs – no doubt for a cigarette – not Florence, and she shooed the girls out the door, telling them to get on their way and enjoy their film.

'What was all that about?' Florence asked once the door was shut behind them.

'I don't want Aunt Evie grilling me about our visit to Mystic Lou because she'll only fret regardless of what she has to say. Alice Waters called in today for a final fitting. She took her dress home with her.' With the alterations having been made, her grandmother's dress – now Alice's – had fitted her like a glove, and she'd looked a picture in it.

'The girl who showed you the wedding photograph of her grandparents? The one you, Adam and Aunt Evie were in.'

Sabrina nodded. 'She's swinging between thinking I'm completely mad and wanting it to be true. She said she'll call in again even though there's no need now she's got her dress.'

Florence's attention was caught by the front window of Esmerelda's Emporium. 'Eee, look, girl, Esmerelda's changing her window display.'

The two girls came to a halt outside the emporium to watch the spectacle of Esmerelda wrestling with a mannequin. She was decked out in fuchsia pink with a matching turban and fingernails. Her requisite Silk Cut cigarette was firmly in place in the long black holder dangling between her fingers.

'She'll burn that dress if she's not careful,' Florence said, watching the glowing tip get dangerously close to the batik-print minidress. Esmerelda was attempting to pull it down to a decent length over the mannequin's legs.

'No, she won't. She's an expert,' Sabrina assured her pal, and indeed she was right.

The show was over, and the girls were set to carry on when the woman herself appeared in her emporium's doorway. She had her arm posed at an angle, and her cigarette was nearly burned down as it smouldered away in its holder. 'You two are just the girls I want to see.'

'We are?' they chimed.

'You are,' Esmerelda confirmed, batting heavily made-up eyes. It never ceased to amaze Sabrina how she managed to find the exact shade of lipstick to match her outfit, which was guaranteed to be outrageous and flamboyant. Behind her, the tantalising whiff of joss sticks hinted at the exotic goods to be found inside the emporium. 'I need fashion models.'

The words 'fashion' and 'models' had a transforming effect on Sabrina and Florence. They instantly straightened, as if they'd books balancing on their heads for deportment lessons, and sucked their stomachs in.

'U-us?' Florence finally stammered.

'Yes, you two. I've a fabulous array of summer garments on the way as we speak, and I want to showcase them by holding a fashion show here in the emporium in a month.'

Sabrina's first thought was, how on earth would Esmerelda find room for a runway? You had to pick your way through her treasure trove of incense, candles, love potions and other bizarre items to get to the counter as it was.

Esmerelda produced a portable ashtray from the voluminous folds of her caftan then flicked the ash from her cigarette into it before inhaling what was left of it. She exhaled upward and leaned toward them. 'The show will be an intimate soirée for my best clients on a Friday evening. We'll rearrange the shop floor so the runway can be down the middle and guests can be seated around the edges of it. I'll expect it to be all hands on deck, and I can offer you a silk scarf by way of payment. Are you up to the job?'

Florence, her eyes resembling milk chocolate buttons, spoke up for both of them. 'We are.'

'And do you have friends you could recruit? Because I'll be needing more than two models.'

'We do,' Florence replied again. Apparently, she wasn't going to miss her modelling spotlight moment for anything, so she'd rally up someone or other.

Esmerelda held out a vein-lined hand, which they both solemnly shook before saying good night to her.

'I can't believe it, Sabs! Me and you, we're going to be models!' Florence linked her arm through her pal's as they opened the door leading to the staircase which would take them up to Mystic Lou's rooms. Sabrina gave her mate an indulgent grin, but her mind was on what the psychic upstairs would have to say.

## 12

### 1939

The wind whistled past Lily's ears as she perched on the handlebars of Max's bicycle. His hands were on either side of her, steering them in a straight line toward town.

Under any other circumstances, she'd have been embarrassed by their close proximity. Still, these weren't normal circumstances, and she'd been too worried about falling off her precarious perch to be anything but grateful Max was holding the bike steady.

It had taken a good few minutes to stop clenching her jaw and trust Max at his word because he did know this road well. They hadn't gone over a single bump.

They heard the low purr of an engine long before the slotted covers over the headlights, deflecting the light downward, alerted them to the car's approach.

Max slowed the bike and then came to a stop, and Lily jumped down as they melded into the trees. Neither of them wanted to be questioned about what they were doing out here. They watched the car glide past then, once it was a safe distance down the road, carried on their way.

Aside from the car, there were no signs of life until they

reached the town, and in an unspoken agreement, they were silent as they sailed along the cobbled streets. The houses were a long line of rectangles with stark chimney pots on either side of them. A bored dog's bark was the only alert to their presence.

'Nearly there,' Max called out softly, swerving and muttering under his breath as a cat suddenly streaked out in front of the bike. He managed to keep it upright, but Lily's heart pounded at the near miss, and her jaw tightened once more. Her heart was banging, and she was grateful they weren't far off now.

The cars idling slowly home were few and far between, and a dustbin lid rattling echoed loudly in the still night. They didn't encounter anyone, except a man whose face was hidden by a hat as he mooched down the street, until they reached the community centre. It looked like a grey box in the dim light. Not so much as a chink of light showed from its windows. The thumps of children running about emanated from inside though.

How could it only be a month since they'd arrived here from Liverpool by bus? It felt like a lifetime, Lily thought, jumping down from the handlebars and rubbing her backside surreptitiously through her coat.

The air was growing damp with fog, and she didn't see the young couple until they were almost upon her. They had their arms linked, and the man was clutching an open newspaper parcel of chips. The woman giggled over something he'd said.

Lily's mouth watered at the salty, greasy smell, and her legs felt weak. Her mind flew back to sitting with her dad, watching the boats navigate the busy port of Liverpool. Squalling seagulls had circled above them as they'd munched on a parcel of fish 'n' chips. The memory was so vivid she could taste the hot vinegar-soaked chips with their crispy exterior and floury middle, and her stomach rumbled as she gazed after them longingly. She flushed as Max coughed, wondering if he'd heard it.

'I'll wait for you here, shall I?' He was still seated on the bike with his feet planted on the ground.

Lily couldn't read his expression, but she'd understood what he'd said. 'Don't be silly. You'll get drilled if anyone sees you loitering about. Come in with me. There'll be too many kids running around for anyone to notice you're not one of us Edge Hill lot,' she urged.

She was desperate for him to venture in with her because he might get tired of waiting and go home if he were to stay out here.

'There's sure to be supper,' she added, hoping it would be enough of a sweetener to sway him because she didn't want to walk back on her own in the dark.

It worked, and from the way he leaped at the offer, she sensed that, like her, he knew what it was to go to bed hungry, only it wasn't an experience that was new to him like it was her.

The thought of telling Father Ian of her treatment buoyed her, and she fidgeted, eager to get inside. At the same time, Max clambered off the bike and wheeled it to rest against the side of the building. Then they followed the thumping clues, letting the sound lead them to the main doors. These opened up into the semi-darkness of the foyer, but there was a sliver of light under another door.

Lily shed her coat and hat, hanging them up along with all the others in the cloakroom area, then pushed the door to the hall open. It was hot and stuffy and smelled of bodies, and she and Max stood blinking against the light. The curtains covering the windows on the outside wall were firmly closed. Once their eyes had adjusted to the light, they saw a handful of children charging about in a game of tag.

A harassed Father Ian was trying without success to rein them in, but his attempts only seemed to excite them further, as though it were part of the game. Over in the far corner of the hall, a much more sedate game of ludo was underway with four earnest faces bent over the board. A group of little girls were drawing away at a table, and a bunch of lads were spinning a top for all it was worth.

The older children milled about awkwardly. They were too old for games and too young for much else. All, however, were eager for the supper that was being laid out on a trestle table.

A matronly woman shooting disapproving looks at the mayhem unfolding was setting down a tray of triangle-shaped sandwiches with meat paste squishing out the sides. At the sight of the butterfly cakes with their whipped buttercream icing, Lily's mouth watered. As for the sandwiches, she planned on stuffing as many as she could get away with taking into her pockets. They'd do nicely for lunch tomorrow.

'Lily!' Edith came rushing over, a beret on her head and her blonde plait draped over her shoulder. Her cheeks were pink with pleasure at the sight of her friend. Ruth, who she'd been chatting to, stood back, glowering at the sight of Lily and Max.

Edith's gaze swung quizzically from him to Lily once she'd let her friend go.

'Edith, this is my new friend, Max. He brought me here on his bike.' Lily enjoyed the incredulous look that passed over Edith's and Ruth's faces.

Max gave Edith a nod, and she said a shy hello.

She wasn't ordinarily shy, and her coy reaction didn't escape Lily's attention.

Her blue eyes widened as Lily filled her friend in on the adventure she'd had getting here. She felt very grown-up compared to the other children in the room all of a sudden, and if Ruth's face could have turned green, she was sure it would have.

Max hadn't begun acting foolishly like most boys did when they were in Edith's presence, and Lily was pleased. It would have been a let-down if he had. She'd also noticed that the face she'd pegged as lively was, under the bright lights of the hall, handsome. Now that he'd taken his cap off, she could see his mid-brown hair, and his eyes were an unusual ice blue. The contrast was arresting. It was his eyes she liked best – and that lopsided grin, she decided, sneaking him a surreptitious sidelong glance.

He had a way about him that Lily recognised because she'd seen it in her reflection that morning when she'd told herself to hold her head high because she was a Tubb. It was how he carried himself. His posture whispered of courage.

Yes, she loved Edith dearly, but she was glad he wasn't swooning all over her.

Edith, who took the reaction others had to her prettiness for granted, seemed a little taken aback at the lack of attention as she toyed with the hem of her sweater uncertainly. She chattered about the picnic with the Timbses, going on about having seen a swan with its cygnets.

Ruth had edged over closer to listen to her story, and there was no chance of anyone else getting a word in.

Edith was trying to impress Max, Lily realised, but it wasn't working because his attention kept drifting toward the lads engrossed in their game of whip and top. He waited politely for a break in her monologue and then took himself over there to show them how it was done.

Edith stared blatantly after him, and Lily was stabbed by annoyance. He was *her* friend. She was the one who'd brought him here, and this was one occasion she wouldn't let Edith take over.

Lily tried to shake off the unfamiliar pique with her friend. She needed to focus on what she'd come here for, and she cast about for Father Ian. He'd collared Elsie, she saw, who had been the one leading the charge where the game of tag was concerned. The sight of her blonde head bowed but by no means cowed by the telling-off she was receiving made her smile. Beside her, Edith sighed heavily, well used to the sight of her little sister in bother.

Now would be as good a time as any to have a word with him, Lily decided, and told Edith her plan.

∽

Ruth listened in on Lily's story with disbelief. What did Lily have to go running to the vicar about? She had to do a few chores and didn't think there was enough meat in her stew. Well, bully for her. Where Ruth and her brothers were concerned, being sent to Skelmersdale was the best thing that had ever happened to them.

She knew Lily had lost her dad, and it had been sad what happened to him, but she still had her mam. Ruth would give anything to have a mam that put her and her brothers first the way Lily's mam did her. She didn't know how lucky she was, and she'd no clue what hardship was.

Lying in bed with your brothers squeezed in beside you with your hands covering their ears, so they didn't have to listen to the sound of their father's roaring and their mam's sobbing night after night – that was hardship. Her blood boiled as she watched Lily make her way importantly over to the vicar. She'd better not spoil things for the rest of them with her whining.

∽

By the time Lily reached their young parish vicar, he'd let Elsie go on the promise she'd behave. She bit her bottom lip uncertainly, unused to having one-on-one conversations with a male adult.

An exasperated expression on his freckled face, Father Ian ran a hand through his dark hair upon seeing Lily standing there. 'Lily Tubb, how are you getting on then?' he asked, affixing his piercing gaze on her.

The tears that sprang forth took her by surprise, and Father Ian, clearly not used to dealing with weepy young ladies, took a step backward. He sought help, but Mrs Hamilton – who was in charge of the supper – had her back to him and was shooing away a little boy. The cheeky lad had been trying his luck at getting in early with the sandwiches.

'Homesick, are you?' Father Ian finally offered up, and his tone was sympathetic.

Lily nodded and wiped the tears away with the back of her hand.

Noticing the state of her hands, Father Ian winced. 'That looks nasty. Have you something to put on it?'

'No.' She'd scratched the dermatitis rash to the point of weeping.

'You mustn't scratch at it, or you'll get an infection. I'd get your billet mother to take you to the doctor or at least the chemist.'

'She won't take me,' Lily murmured.

'I'm sure she will.' Father Ian pinched the tip of his nose. It was a habit of his he didn't seem to be aware of.

'No,' she said louder. 'She won't, Father Ian. She isn't kind.'

'Now, now, Lily. You're not the only one missing your mam, but in times like this, we've all got to make sacrifices. It's not safe for you in Liverpool. You're better off here.'

If Lily had been of a different temperament, she'd have stamped her foot. But as it was, she had to clamp her mouth shut to stop the 'shurrup' that was poised on the tip of her tongue. From what Lily had heard, there hadn't been so much as a sniff from a German plane. Liverpool was still standing, but she'd fade away if she had to stay put in Skelmersdale.

'Please listen, Father Ian.' She tried to stay calm and quell the rising panic that he wouldn't do anything to help her.

'I am listening. Tobias Finch, how many times! Stop running. This isn't a racetrack.'

'I'm not being fed properly, and I'm being treated like a skivvy.' Lily noted his lashes were transparent as he finally gave her his full attention. 'I said, I'm not being fed properly. I feel faint at school of a morning, and she works me to the bone. That's what caused this.' She held out her hands. She wouldn't tell him about the chamber pot. She'd never tell anyone about that.

Father Ian rubbed his chin, frowning, and Lily noticed even the backs of his hands were freckled. 'You're not being given enough to eat, you say?'

Lily nodded. 'Please, will you tell me mam? I've written a note for her, and I'd be ever so grateful if you'd pass it on to her. She'll send for me when she reads it and finds out how bad things are for me here.'

'You're not exaggerating, Lily? I know it's hard to be away from your home, but your mam wants to keep you safe. She can't be with you all the time now, can she? And here you can go to school. I could perhaps have a word with Mrs Pinkerton to see if there's somewhere a tad more suitable you could be moved to.'

'I don't want to go somewhere else; I want to go home. Please won't you give me mam the note?'

Father Ian took the note and gave her a nod as little Mary Smith tugged at his trousers.

'Father Ian, can I show you the picture I've drawn for me mam and dad?'

He smiled down at the little girl, who was missing her two front teeth. 'Of course, Mary.'

He turned back to Lily. 'I'll pass it on.'

He gave her a smile she was sure was meant to be reassuring but did little to comfort her.

She'd said her piece and given him her note. Now she could only hope and pray extra hard that she'd be sent home.

She felt a tap on her shoulder and turned, expecting to see Edith. But, instead, it was Max, and his expression was grave. 'They don't listen properly, do they? Adults, I mean. They only hear what they want to hear. They're supposed to help us, and they say that's what they're here for, but then they don't do anything.'

Lily didn't know what to say, but she hoped with all her heart that on this occasion Max was wrong and that Father Ian had listened. She didn't know what she'd do if he hadn't.

∼

Lily didn't see Ruth have a quiet word in Father Ian's ear about how Lily was prone to storytelling – on account of her being an only child, you see, Ruth explained to the young minister. She was an attention-seeker. Everybody knew that.

∼

Before he journeyed home that evening, Father Ian balled up the folded note and tossed it in the bin, having decided poor Lily's mam had enough on her plate without worrying unnecessarily about her daughter.

# 13

---

1982

Sabrina threw her jeans-clad leg over the back of Adam's pride and joy, his 1970 Triumph Bonneville. She scooted up so her body was pressed hard against his back and wrapped her arms around his waist. She could feel the juddering of the engine beneath her as Adam, with his booted feet on either side of the bike, holding it steady, let it turn over at a fast idle.

He reached down and squeezed her gloved hands. She'd learned the hard way that it could be cold riding pillion and never forgot to wear her gloves when they ventured out, even when the sun was shining like it was this afternoon. Gloves and sunglasses. She'd no wish to look like Alice Cooper when they arrived at Blackpool, ta very much. Been there, done that!

'Ahright?' His voice was muffled behind his helmet, as was hers as she shouted back, 'Yeah.'

He waited for a break in the Saturday afternoon match traffic before pulling away from the kerb outside Brides of Bold Street, where the closed sign was displayed in the window.

It had been a chaotically busy morning with a steady troop of brides-to-be, bridesmaids and mothers of the bride piling in the door. Sabrina would have been worried if it had been any other way, given the time of year.

Aunt Evie had left half an hour before, all wrapped up in her red-and-white Liverpool colours to catch the number 17 bus to Anfield, as she did every Saturday. She never erred from her routines – Wednesday evenings, she put the world to rights with Esmerelda, and Friday nights were reserved for bingo with the long-suffering Ida. Her football season ticket was her one luxury. She never missed a match, come rain or shine, and it was on a Saturday that she smoked most of her ciggie allowance for the week.

Sabrina hadn't elaborated on her plans with Adam because she knew her aunt would worry about her going all that way on the back of his bike. Aside from that, she'd a cob on because it was Ida who'd taken home the rolled beef roast from their Friday night bingo. There'd been mutterings of foul play and cheating on and off for the best part of the morning. How you could cheat at bingo was beyond Sabrina, but she knew better than to make mention of that.

Adam steered the bike deftly around the traffic, making the lights ahead of the cars jammed up behind one another. They roared through Bootle, Crosby and Formby, following the A565 through to Southport. Sabrina loosened her grip around his middle as they blatted along. She was far more relaxed on the back of the bike these days, although she'd never go so far as to call herself a biker girl.

Her mind was full of the story Mystic Lou, the fortune teller whose premises were upstairs a few doors down from Brides of Bold Street, had imparted to her the night before. She'd tell him everything once they reached Blackpool. It had been Adam's idea that they visit the popular seaside resort, and she'd leaped at the chance to forget about her encounter with Alice Waters. For a few hours at any rate. Adam had said it would do them both good to go and have fun, to take their minds off Bold Street and its timeslip portal. After all, he'd elaborated, whatever would happen, would happen. They couldn't change it. What they had to do, he'd added, was 'live life to the fullest in the present.'

He was right, and as such, Sabrina fully intended to let her hair down. Today she wouldn't think about finding her mother. She might even go up the Tower, despite being dubious when it came to heights, and she was definitely bringing a stick of rock home. She'd promised Flo one too. But, unfortunately, they wouldn't see the famous illuminations today because the lights wouldn't come on until September.

She hadn't been to Blackpool in years. The last time had been as a teenager with the Teesdale family. She smiled as the wind whipped cold against her cheeks, recalling how she and Flo had spent the best part of the day trying to shake off her mam, dad, brother and the twins because they were cramping their style.

They'd failed miserably as Mrs Teesdale had been determined they wouldn't be left to their own devices. 'It's a family day, girls,' she'd said more than once. Sabrina and Flo had heard the unspoken message that they weren't to be parading up and down the prom, showing off to the local lads in the boob tubes they'd worn under their jackets.

Shona had thrown up on one of the faster rides, and Tessa had nearly been abducted by a donkey with a mind of its own on the beach's wet sands. In one of the penny arcades, they'd lost Flo's older brother, Gerard, and spent a good hour searching for him. Dinner had been vinegar-soaked fish 'n' chips, after which they'd watched the famous Blackpool lights come on. They'd all been open-mouthed by the magic of the illuminated spectacle. The day had been rounded off with a ginormous piece of candied rock to suck on the way home.

A perfect family day out.

Sabrina cherished those times with the Teesdales because

being around the boisterous family made her feel normal. She loved Aunt Evie with all her heart and knew she'd done her best by her, but it had always been just the two of them. She was torn between her aunt and loyalty to a mam she barely remembered, and she longed to know whether she had siblings. She had so many unanswered questions.

Adam slowed his speed, and they put-putted down terraced residential streets, the paint flaking from the houses' front doors thanks to the salt air. They weren't far from the Golden Mile – as the stretch between the North and South Piers was known – when he spied a narrow parking spot beside a green Ford with a sticker in the window saying 'I Love Jesus', and he nosed the bike in deftly.

Sabrina clambered off the Triumph and stretched before removing her helmet. She gave her hair a surreptitious fluff then pushed her sunglasses up onto her head. Adam waited, hand outstretched, while Sabrina discarded her gloves and shoved them into the pocket of her bomber jacket. Then she took his hand, and they meandered down the sloping street toward the promenade.

'The last time I was here was for a stag night.' Adam grinned, regaling Sabrina with a story as to how the poor groom had wound up minus his eyebrows thanks to Tim.

'Well, he better not do anything like that to you on your stag night.' She coloured, hoping Adam hadn't taken her comment to mean she was assuming they might one day get married. A girl could dream though, and Adam didn't loosen his grip on her hand.

They reached the road and waited until it was clear before crossing over to the promenade, where a stream of people in all shapes and sizes were wandering. Laughter and chatter overrode the thrum of vehicles passing by loaded with day trippers and early holidaymakers. Sabrina paused for a minute to inhale the fresh air, which carried a whiff of seaside fodder.

*The Dressmaker's War*

The sand was a golden-brown expanse with the Irish Sea in the distance. She watched the white horses dancing as the waves rolled in, leaving a wet arc behind as they were sucked back out.

The sun might be out, but it wasn't warm enough for lazing on a striped deckchair, not with the stiff breeze whipping down the promenade, she thought, glad of her jacket. However, hardy children were still playing in the sand, being watched over by parents rubbing goose-pimply arms. They were probably wishing they hadn't been lulled into a false sense of summer having come early.

A red kite flew high, a bright stain against the blue sky, and the wind carried the sound of the penny slot machines cashing out from the arcades. The atmosphere was festive and relaxed. It was contagious, and Sabrina felt as though she were on her holidays. Not that she'd had much experience of such things.

'What do you want to do?' Adam asked as she began to walk once more, her step light as she kept pace with him.

'I want to go up the Tower. I wasn't brave enough last time. What about you?' They sidestepped a large family with a tot in a pushchair hidden behind an enormous pink frothy swirl of candyfloss.

'The *Doctor Who* exhibition.'

She should have guessed what with Adam being a fan of all things sci-fi. He nudged her and inclined his head toward the beach. 'I reckon you could get away with looking like you're under sixteen if you fancy it.'

Sabrina looked toward the soft damp sands upon which colourfully bedecked donkeys were parading children up and down. She grinned. 'No, ta. You can't trust them.' She told him what had happened to Tessa on her last visit to Blackpool. 'It took off at a canter with her. They can move when they want to, you know. I wouldn't mind one of them though.' She pointed to the ice cream van down on the sand.

'Your wish is my command.'

True to his word, Adam returned with two 99s – ice cream cones with chocolate Flakes in them – a few minutes later.

'My favourite, ta.' Sabrina took hers, licking the bottom of the ice cream before it melted and ran down the cone. They walked the short distance to Central Pier, perched on its mesh of stork legs, and made their way through the excited rabble before nabbing a spare seat from which to watch the world go by. A seagull perched nearby on the rails, surveying the scene with disdain. Sabrina enjoyed what was left of her cone as the waves rolled in beneath them.

'I used to sit here with me mam and dad when I was a kid, eating ice cream. We came to Blackpool every year. Never missed,' Adam said, biting the bottom of his cone and sucking the remainder of his ice cream through it.

Sabrina watched him, amused, but didn't say anything. He didn't often talk about his childhood, and she wanted to hear what else he'd say.

'They were good times. We had a lorra laughs on those days out. It's the place, I think. It's not real, is it? You come here to have fun and forget about all the other stuff at home. Me mam always seemed' – he frowned, searching for the word – 'I dunno, carefree I suppose when we were here. I liked seeing her like that.'

'Tell me about her. What wor she like?' Sabrina wanted a sense of the woman she'd been.

'She wor lovely, me mam. You'd have liked her, and she'd have liked you.'

She hoped so. She hoped Mrs Taylor would have approved of her and not seen her as a stray whose mam had abandoned her. She looked at Adam from under her lashes, seeing a tenderness had settled on his face. 'What did she like? You know, what interested her?'

'What made her tick, you mean?'

'Yeah.'

His arm had snaked across the back of the white iron fretwork, and his hand rested on Sabrina's shoulder. 'Well, she loved music. All kinds of music and dancing. When I got older and came here, I'd bring a mate, and me mam would make the arl fella take her dancing at the Tower Ballroom. She loved that she did. She'd gush about the polished mahogany floor and the frescoed ceiling all the way home, in between complaining about how many times me dad had trod on her toes.'

Sabrina laughed, and he flashed her a smile.

'She wor always making things too. Dad would tell her she could go and buy worever she wanted for the house, but it wasn't about that. She liked the satisfaction of knowing she'd made it.' His face was animated now with memories. 'She'd turn her hand to anything. She re-covered all the furniture one year, and I remember her going through a macramé phase. We had that many hanging macramé plant holders. Dad said it wor like livin' in the flamin' botanical gardens.' He laughed, staring out beyond the people strolling past, lost in his memories. 'She spent more time hammering away or painting or worever in the garage than he ever did.'

Sabrina sensed a shift in his mood, and she glanced at his face, watching his smile fade.

'I don't think she should have married me dad. I think they only got wed because she wor expecting me.'

He'd told her his dad had taken a back step when his mam had been dying. The reality of it was something he'd been unable to cope with, and her care had fallen to Adam. There was resentment wedged between father and son as a result.

'I heard her talking to her sister, Aunty Jean, once. She told her she always thought his heart belonged to someone else.'

Sabrina felt clammy. 'He was having an affair, you mean?'

Adam made a disparaging noise. 'Knowing the arl fella, I think he had plenty of those, but no. I don't think that's what she meant. I think she meant he loved someone else – properly loved them, I mean – and that's worse, isn't it?'

Sabrina nodded slowly, unsure what to say. She couldn't shake the thought the woman Ray Taylor had loved was Aunt Evie. How would Adam react if she told him her suspicions? Would it taint the way he felt about her? It was best to say nothing. She'd no evidence her suspicions were correct anyway, and it wasn't worth risking the best thing that had ever happened to her on a feeling.

'Come on,' Adam said, shaking her out of her reverie as he stood up. Her shoulder felt bare without his hand resting on it. He shoved his hands in the pockets of his leather jacket, a closed book once more. 'Let's go up that Tower.'

Sabrina followed after him, feeling instead like the sun shining down on her day had disappeared behind a cloud.

## 14

1939

It had been two long, dreary days since Lily had pleaded with Father Ian to get word to her mam, and nothing had changed. Well, that wasn't entirely true, she thought, pedalling down the long stretch of road. Today had been different insomuch as she was annoyed with Edith over the way she'd been drilling her about Max whenever she had the opportunity.

'How old is he, Lily?'

'Nearly fourteen.'

'Where does he live?'

A shrug.

And so on.

Lily had thought hard about it, and she couldn't recall ever having felt properly annoyed with Edith before. She wished Sarah were here to talk to. Lily hadn't even taken the sandwich half Edith offered her today, preferring to act the martyr and go hungry. She'd regretted that choice all afternoon as she'd sat at her desk with her arms wrapped around her tummy, trying to ward off the hunger pangs.

It seemed unfair that Edith should set her sights on Max. She thought herself worldly at times did Edith, especially since she'd started her courses. She was too young to be thinking about a boyfriend though, and Max was *her* friend, not Edith's. She'd met him first. She didn't know why she felt so protective of him because the feelings were all new to her.

He'd pedalled back to the cottages with her after the youth group had disbanded the night before last. Thrillingly, he'd shown her how he stole in and out of the abandoned house with no one noticing. He'd dared her to go inside with him, and Lily, not wanting him to think her a scaredy-cat, not even when mice were involved, had shimmied in the window after him.

She'd wondered as to what sort of a family he had if his mam didn't notice he wasn't home.

Max might not have been a ghost, but the cottage felt full of them, and she'd sat down on the floor, pulling her legs up under her chin and wrapping her arms protectively around them. It had been freezing, and Lily had shivered inside her coat before turning her head to rest her cheek on her knees. She'd watched Max's shadowy shape as he'd produced a match and lit a stubby candle in a holder, careful to keep it low to the ground.

'What if someone sees the flickering light?' Lily had asked.

'Pull the curtains,' Max had suggested, shrugging. 'And so what if they do? The place is empty. It isn't as if there's anything to rob. They'd probably think it was down to a ghost.'

He'd laughed softly as Lily, dragging the curtains together, had relayed how she'd thought the strange noises she'd heard coming from the place were thanks to a ghost.

'Your hair's like fire,' he'd said, suddenly staring at her copper plaits.

'It's the Viking blood in me,' Lily had replied without thinking, although the red hair came from her mam's side. She'd found herself telling him about her dad and what had happened to him.

'Everything changes when yer dad dies,' Max had said when she'd finished talking.

Lily had nodded. It was true.

'Just be sure if your mam decides to marry again, she picks a good'un.'

'Oh, she won't marry again,' Lily had said. Her mam would remain a widow.

'People marry for all sorts of reasons, you know. It can be because they're lonely or because they need food putting on the table. Me mam needed food putting on the table, but he – me stepdad – barely manages that. His wages are all but spent at the pub each week. I can't wait to leave.'

'Your brother's near Edge Hill?' Lily had asked, remembering what he'd told her earlier.

'Yeah, Toxteth.'

He'd been easy to talk to, and Lily had opened up to him in a way she hadn't been able to her friends. They'd whispered back and forth until, yawning, she'd fancied it must be at least midnight. Then, finally, she'd got to her feet, brushing herself off and told Max she had to go. He'd blown the candle out and clambered out the window after her, then watched in the shadows as she'd let herself silently back into the cottage. She'd been terrified she'd be rumbled, but it had made her feel a little better knowing he was outside.

She needn't have worried. The cottage had been in darkness, the only sound that of the old witch's grumbling snores drifting out from under her closed bedroom door. As she'd climbed the stairs, Lily had wished her bedroom overlooked the street so she could watch Max cycle away.

Now her mind returned to Edith. It was unfair too that today she'd go home with Elsie to a house where there was laughter, kindness and, most of all, enough to eat. Yet Lily would suffer at the hands of the old witch for yet another night. She'd written all this down in her worry book first thing this morning but hadn't felt any better afterwards.

The sense of trepidation she felt each afternoon as she

made her way back to the cottage intensified with every turn of the wheels.

Lily was lost in her thoughts, and the grass verge was nearly upon her, she realised, blinking and managing to swerve in the nick of time. *Stay on the road, Lily Tubb*, she told herself, knowing coming a cropper wouldn't help matters.

She prided herself on being a level-headed sort of a girl who could focus on whatever she set her mind to. Lately, though, she found it impossible to concentrate on anything. It was hard to pay attention when she was permanently hungry. It was a constant gripe that had only been staved off by the supper at the community hall and the secret sandwiches she'd stashed in her coat pockets the other night. She still had crumbs in them.

You couldn't stockpile food in your belly though, and now it was empty once more. Lily had been told off more than once today for not getting on with her work. How could Miss Lewis possibly understand how hard it was to do your sums when all you could think about was steak-and-kidney pudding and the like?

Adults, she'd realised in her brief time in Skelmersdale – though it felt like a lifetime – only saw what they wanted to see. Her hands were evidence that something wasn't right, and she flexed them now as they cramped holding the handlebars of the bike. Her skin was openly weeping, and she'd seen Mrs Lewis's lip curl with distaste, but she hadn't asked her if she was all right. Was this why Ruth's dad got away with the way he treated his family? And Max, too, had hinted at hardship on the home front.

It wasn't right. It was the adults' job to see what was going on. Her eyes watered both from the cold and frustration. She resolved on that empty stretch of road to never ignore what was right in front of her eyes when she was a grown-up.

It had been freezing that morning, and the chill had barely lifted. Her cheeks felt icy, and she knew they'd be stained red from the cold. The temperature had been positively freezing first thing. If she wasn't sent home or, at the very least, moved from the old witch's, then she could add being chilled to the bone to her woes. She didn't relish the thought of weathering winter in the stone cottage.

The condensation had run in rivulets down her bedroom window when she'd opened the curtains, reluctant to leave her bed first thing. The inside of the curtain was blackened with mould specks, and she'd traced 'Lily Tubb was here' with her finger onto the pane. She'd been consumed by an irrational fear she'd be forgotten about. Inside her worry book, she'd written with stiff fingers, *I might be forgotten if something happens to Mam.*

A motorcar puttered past, and she jolted. She hadn't heard its approach, and the bike wobbled for a precarious second, but again, she managed to straighten the wheel and steady the bike. She'd fully expected a knock on the classroom door at any minute these last couple of days. She'd pictured an indignant Mrs Pinkerton appearing, demanding Lily Tubb be excused. She had the scene set clear in her mind. She'd be bustled into a motorcar and driven back to the cottage to fetch her things. She'd toss her meagre belongings in her case, hearing the old witch being berated for her shameful neglect beneath her.

Oh yes, she'd thought. She'd close those suitcase latches with satisfaction and walk down the stairs with her head held high.

Lily had two versions of this particular scenario. In one, Mrs Pinkerton went so far as to call the old witch a traitor to her country in its time of need. Even she'd fancied this was a little far-fetched though. So, in the end, she'd settled on the old witch being told her behaviour equated to abuse and that she was lucky she wasn't being prosecuted.

She had no scenario for what she'd do if Mrs Pinkerton didn't come.

Her mind had drifted to Father Ian. Had he passed her message on? Then, drawing near the cottages, she braked and hopped off, pushing the bike the final few yards to its hiding place down the side of Mr Mitchell's.

There was no sign of the old man, and if she wasn't rescued and taken home in the interim, perhaps she'd see him the following morning when she tended to the washing. Lily stood beside the cottages a few seconds longer, hoping to see another car because perhaps it would be Mrs Pinkerton come to take her home. The road, however, was deserted apart from a stoat. It zipped out of the woods on one side, disappearing into the foliage on the other.

Lily's sigh was dredged up from the bottom of her belly as she let herself in the door of the cottage. The smell of onions, carrots and the fatty meat she'd diced and put in the pot earlier hit her. Despite the unappetising aroma, her stomach rumbled loudly. She shrugged out of her coat and hung it on the back of the door over top of the old witch's. Then she made to retrieve her notebook from her coat pocket. But it wasn't there. It must have slipped her mind to bring it down with her when she'd left for school.

The door to the front room was shut, and the house was silent. Lily didn't think about what she did next. It was as if she were on automatic pilot as her legs carried her through to the kitchen.

Retrieving the soup spoon, she lifted the pot's lid, plunged it into the steaming stew and filled it up. Then she carried it over to the sink, careful not to spill a precious drop, and blew on it until she was satisfied she wouldn't scald her mouth.

The blow when it came saw the spoon fall from her hand, and Lily coughed and spluttered orange flecks of carrot and stock into the sink.

'Steal from me, would yer!'

Lily's eyes were streaming, and she tried to catch her breath as she got her coughing under control. Her shoulder hurt where she'd been struck by the old witch's walking stick. Rubbing it, she turned round. 'I'm s-sorry, Mrs Cox. It was wrong, I know, but I was so hungry.' It was then she saw what she had in her hand. Her worry book.

The old witch waved it at her. 'And the lies in 'ere about me. You're a wicked girl you are.' Spittle oozed from her mouth.

Lily stared at her, horrified. She was like a rabid dog.

'Wicked, I say.'

Something inside Lily snapped. 'I'm not wicked. It's you who's wicked. You're a wicked, evil old witch,' she spat back, her heart thudding as adrenaline surged. 'And you've no right to treat me the way you have. Or read my private things!' She snatched her worry book back. 'You'll get your comeuppance – you'll see.'

'Threaten me, would yer, girl?' Mrs Cox snarled. She raised the stick and brought it down on Lily's shoulder before she could dodge it, with surprising force for someone so frail.

Lily crumpled this time, and the blows began to rain down on her back. She crouched with her hands over her head, her worry book hidden beneath her.

'That's enough!' Max's voice sounded. 'Stop hitting her.'

Mercifully, the blows ceased as there was a moment of silence, then Mrs Cox, wonder in her voice, said, 'Billy? Is that my Billy come home at last? Oh, I've missed you, son. Are yer brothers with you?'

Lily squinted up in time to see the old witch reach out her hand to pat Max's cheek. He sidestepped her and then took the walking stick from her. Her eyes were cloudy as she stared at him, seeing someone from the past. All the fight had gone out of her.

Lily clambered to her feet. She hurt all over, but she'd mend.

'Get yer things,' Max said calmly. 'You can't stay here.'

The old witch was murmuring to herself now, her hands clutched in front of her, lost in another time.

Lily didn't hang about. Instead, she fled up the stairs and grabbed her case, flinging the few things she had into it.

Max was standing in the kitchen doorway when she ventured back down, keeping guard. After shrugging back into her coat, she pulled her hat down low on her head. Finally, Lily put the worry book back in her pocket where it belonged. Then she and Max stepped outside. He took her case while she retrieved the bike from down the side of the cottages. Then he fetched his own.

As they pedalled off, Lily heard the old witch's plaintive cry, 'Don't go, Billy. I've missed yer, son.'

She didn't look back.


Lily would dream about Skelmersdale from time to time. But, unfortunately, they were never good dreams, and she'd wake in a sweat thinking she was still in that room, upstairs in the cottage. The blood would thunder through her veins, and it would take her a few seconds to realise she was safe back in her own bedroom. Her mam had promised no matter what happened, she wouldn't send her away again. They'd weather this war together.

She'd been home with her mam for two months now, and Christmas was around the corner. As for the war, not a single bomb had fallen on Britain – unlike the snow. Plenty of that had been dumped. In fact, it was the coldest winter in years people were saying as mist puffed from their mouths, and they huddled inside their coats, trudging through the wet, white drifts.

Sarah had been pleased to have her friend home, saying she'd felt like the child left behind in the Pied Piper story with only Alfie for company. Lily had been delighted to see Sarah too. She'd confided everything that had happened to her in Skem, even the part about the chamber pot.

She'd seen the redheaded woman only once – her guardian angel. She'd been at the end of the road watching, waiting for her to leave school one afternoon. Lily had raised her hand and waved. To her surprise, the woman had waved back before hurrying away.

Her mam said she should put her experiences in Skem behind her, and Lily did her best not to feel angry over having been sent away in the first place. She was old enough to know that there was no certainty as to when the Germans would strike, but that month of mistreatment at the hands of the old witch seemed like such a terrible waste of time now. The only good thing that had come from it was meeting Max, although she wondered now if she'd ever see or hear from him again.

Most of the other children who'd been evacuated were now home too. Edith and Elsie had returned, as had Ruth and her brothers, though Edith had told Lily on the quiet that Ruth would have preferred to stay in Skem.

Edith and Ruth seemed to have forged a tighter bond in Lily's absence, which perturbed Lily. She didn't trust the other girl, although she did feel sorry for her. Knowing the sort of home she'd been returned to, Lily had thought her mam must be a selfish woman to put up with her husband and allow her children to be treated like so. She'd voiced this opinion to her mam, who'd told her that until she'd walked a mile in another woman's shoes, she'd no place commenting. That had told her!

Despite the blanketing of snow, life carried on much as it always had. Lily knew for the other children their time away had been relegated to an uninspiring holiday. School had reopened. Guides, where she was off to now, had been up and running again for the last three weeks.

Things had changed in subtle ways for Lily though. She'd started her courses – or the curse, as Edith called it – for one thing. She'd had it twice now, and it made her feel as though she'd joined a particular club.

Her mam was different too. She was working more, having increased her hours at Peterson's Grocers while Lily was away. Mrs Peterson was bedridden, although Lily didn't know what ailed her – her mam had been annoyingly vague. Whatever it was meant Mr Peterson needed Sylvie Tubb in the shop more. All the supplies arrived loose these days and had to be packaged up, which in itself was a full-time job. Some evenings she didn't get home until after eight, complaining her feet were killing her.

Her increased hours meant more responsibility for Lily. It was up to her to light the fire and get the dinner on. All of which she was perfectly capable of. She missed not arriving home to a warm house each afternoon, but the extra money meant they had plenty of coal for the fire.

It hadn't escaped Lily's attention that her mam was taking more trouble over her appearance these days either. She'd even taken to wearing lipstick when she went to work, and the melancholy air that had hovered over her like a pea-souper since her dad died had dissipated.

Instinct told Lily not to delve too deeply into these changes because she might not like what she uncovered. She enjoyed seeing her mam happier though.

She hadn't mentioned any of this to Edith because she always read far too much into everything. It was a funny thing, but since she'd met Max, she'd stopped telling Edith lots of things.

She hadn't told her that she missed Max – pined for him in fact – because Lily knew it would sound silly given she hardly knew him. She had told Sarah though, on one of those many quiet afternoons of late where a lonely evening had loomed. Instead of sitting by herself waiting for Mam to come home, Lily would take herself off to the Carters' house. Fern Carter always made her welcome, and there was comfort in listening to her wholehearted conviction that Britain would win the war and enjoy peace once more. Lily would get the uncanny sense of her knowing something they didn't when she'd add, 'We'll get through this and rebuild – life will carry on.'

So it was when Sarah's little brother was out of earshot and Fern was listening to the radio that she'd told her friend that Max had become her knight in shining armour. If it wasn't for him, who knows what might have happened that awful day when she'd helped herself to the stew.

Lily trudged through the sleety snow, her mind flitting back to the moment she'd pedalled away from the cottage. She'd been oblivious to the throbbing pain where the stick had landed on her back as she'd made her escape, wanting to get far away from the cottage.

With Max leading the charge, her suitcase dangling from his front handlebars, they'd cycled to the police station in town. He'd seen her inside the building, which was just as well because she didn't know if she'd have been brave enough to say her piece to the po-faced constable on the front desk otherwise.

Mrs Pinkerton had been called down to the station. A kerfuffle had ensued after that, culminating in a red-faced Mrs Pinkerton driving her back to Edge Hill. Her face had been even redder by the time her mam had finished with her. The words *disgraceful*, *I trusted you* and *shame on you* had been hurled at her. Then Lily had been shepherded inside and the door shut firmly in Mrs Pinkerton's face.

Lily had turned around before she left the station to look for Max, to thank him, but he'd gone. There was so much she'd wanted to say to him, but she knew the words would have come out in a jumble. He'd made her feel safe when he'd stepped in that evening and confronted Mrs Cox, and she hadn't felt safe since her dad died. Perhaps it was just as well he hadn't hung about. She'd have only embarrassed herself and him had she had the opportunity to say her piece.

She'd made up her mind that evening as she lay safe in her own bed with her mam sleeping next door that one day she'd marry Max Waters. She felt certain when she did, she wouldn't need her worry book anymore. She was only a few months away from turning thirteen now, and she knew her own mind right enough.

She hoped Mr Mitchell had got his bike back too and didn't think badly of her leaving without saying goodbye. She'd jotted this concern down in her worry book.

Now she turned onto Edge Lane with her head held high, the way she always did when she wore her Guiding uniform. So what if it couldn't be seen beneath her coat? The wide-brimmed hat gave the game away, and she had her promise badge pinned to her coat collar. She'd attach it to her tie when she got to the hall. The uniform gave her a sense of pride – even more so now their hard-earned skills were being put to use for the war effort.

She'd taken the vow at the age of ten when she'd graduated from Brownies to Guides, and Lily took her pledge to do her duty to God and the king, to help other people at all times and obey the Guide law very seriously.

The thrill of receiving a new badge was as fresh now as it had been when she'd got her first badge for handwork and raced home eager to tell her mam and dad. She had a slew of them carefully stitched onto the arms of her blue dress these days and was at present working toward her telegraphist badge.

It wasn't going to be easy, but she was determined. First, she'd have to construct her own wireless receiver and be able to send messages in Morse code at a speed of thirty words a minute. She had high hopes that Mrs Ardern might consider her for the role of patrol leader of the Edge Hill troop once she achieved this. She had it on good authority that Juliet Rendell, their current leader, would be moving up to Rangers now she'd done four years with the Guides.

Mrs Ardern, their group leader, was keen for their troop to

pull together for the war effort. The Guides were doing good work, she'd told them, and indeed, they'd spent their first weekend back in operation whitewashing kerbs so people could find their way in the dark during a blackout. On Saturday just been, they'd been out, despite the diabolical weather, collecting funds for the ambulances. Tonight was a session on first aid, and Lily was eager to learn this new skill. She might need it one day.

This was why she didn't mind venturing out into the cold that evening, even though with each footstep, her shoes plunged through wet, dirty snow to the icy pavement below. Her toes would be numb by the time she reached the hall.

The sandbags outside the shops, churches and community buildings she passed each day had become commonplace now. What she still couldn't get used to, however, was the yellow squares painted on the pillar boxes. A pillar box should be red, and that was all there was to it. The yellow paint was special, though, because it would change colour to alert them in the event of a poison gas attack.

They had to take their gas masks everywhere these days, and hers clunked against her side with each step. This was something they'd learned the hard way when Edith had been turned away from the cinema, having left hers at home. It had been disappointing but not as frustrating as it had been for Elsie. She'd howled on account of having dropped her sweet coupon on the way to the cinema. Edith had said she was a big baby and stomped home, and Lily, feeling sorry for her, had shared her small ration with her.

Mam had told her, too, there was a wedding boom going on as couples hurried to be wed before their fellas were called up. The government was encouraging it, saying it was good for morale and family stability. She'd got a faraway look on her face then and said she was glad Lily's father wasn't here in that respect because she didn't think he'd survive a second war. The first had knocked the stuffing out of him and so many others.

Lily's teeth chattered as she was hit by a gust of arctic wind. The light was eerie thanks to the snow, and the sky above her was a heavy, blanketing expanse. She couldn't help but wonder what it would be like when it was full of fighter planes. The thought made her even colder, and she hurried on.

The church hall was already noisy with laughter and conversation when she barrelled in, even though she wasn't late. Groups of girls in matching blue uniforms with belted waists milled about waiting for Mrs Ardern to clap her hands and call them all to order. Coats had been discarded, hung on the back of the chairs lining the edges of the hall.

Lily bravely shrugged out of her own and draped it over the back of one of the chairs, leaving her hat on as she made her way over to Sarah, who was standing a little ways off from Edith. She could see why. Ruth was bending Edith's ear, and Lily wondered what was being said because Edith had become animated. They both looked up, and Lily caught the sly expression that had crept over Ruth's face as she watched her approach.

'Lily!' Edith cried, her blue eyes dancing as she rounded on her. 'Give your hat a shake; you've snow on it.'

Lily did so, waiting to hear what had Edith so excited.

'Listen, you'll never guess who Ruth saw this afternoon?'

It irked Lily to give Ruth the satisfaction of asking who it was that had them both jigging about like so, but curiosity won out. 'Who?' she asked the other girl.

'Max!' Ruth declared. 'Remember the boy from Skem you brought along to the community centre that evening? Sarah, you want to see him. He's a dreamboat.' Ruth pretended to swoon. 'I'm sure I went bright red when he said hello to me. He's living with his brother and his wife not far from here now.'

*In Toxteth*, Lily thought, and of course she remembered him. A hot flush washed over her despite the chilly air.

'I've never seen eyes that blue before. He looks like Gary Cooper, don't you think?' Edith added dreamily.

'You've never even been to a Gary Cooper film,' Lily snapped, unable to help herself. Max was *her* friend. It was her he'd saved, and these two had no place carrying on as though they knew him well.

'I've seen photographs, haven't I?' Edith was equally snippy back, unsure as to why Lily was being terse with her.

Sarah watched the exchange. She knew why Lily had been offhand, but she stayed silent.

Ruth was nodding emphatically, clearly enjoying the wedge she was driving between the two friends. 'I think you're right, Edith,' she said. 'He does have a look of Gary Cooper, and he remembered you alright. His face lit up when I said you were back in Edge Hill!'

Lily was positively burning now, wanting to know whether Ruth had said anything about her to him. If so, what had his reaction been?

Infuriatingly, Ruth didn't say any more, and Lily couldn't help blurting, 'What else did he say?'

Sarah moved closer and took her arm, giving it a supportive squeeze.

Edith and Ruth exchanged a glance, obviously weighing up whether Lily deserved to know the rest of the information Ruth had gleaned, given her snotty attitude.

Edith was the decider. 'G'won – tell her.'

Disappointment flickered over Ruth's face, but it seemed she didn't want to cross Edith. 'He's working in Ogden's, the tobacco factory over in Everton, but he said as soon as his eighteenth birthday rolls around, he's enlisting.'

'Well, he's a few years to wait.' Lily's voice was clipped, but inside she was alive with excitement. Max was working at Ogden's! She'd go see him, she resolved. Thank him properly for what he'd done for her.

She wanted to tell Sarah her plan without Edith and Ruth earwigging, and her fingers itched to write in her worry book, *Will Max choose Edith?* Her friend was making it obvious she'd set her sights on him, and Lily knew how determined Edith could be. So mentally, she wrote, *How will we remain, friends if she steals the boy I'm going to marry one day?*

At least she'd still have Sarah, she thought, her friend loyal by her side.

Though as it happened, Lily would soon have far more to worry about.

# 15

## 1982

Everton Brow was Sabrina and Adam's special place. Or at least it was so far as Sabrina was concerned. This was the spot where they'd exchanged their first kiss. Of course, there'd been lots more kissing since then – and snuggles on the bench overlooking the park. Together, they'd watched the seasons change from autumn to winter and now here they were in spring. She smiled watching him unwrapping the newspaper parcel they'd picked up from Clive's Chippy. His mind wasn't on romantic moments they'd shared but rather his dinner! Typical fella, she thought as her tummy rumbled at the whiff of the deep-fried battered cod they'd ordered.

Adam offered her the first chip, and she helped herself, biting into the crisp exterior to release a little puff of steam before juggling the hot potato middle from cheek to cheek.

There'd been no right moment to mention her visit with Mystic Lou in Blackpool; the timing wasn't right, but Adam's sombre mood had lifted on the ride here.

First things first though – dinner! So she picked up another chip.

The sun was now dipping low in the sky its dying rays had

cast the hillside in a warm light. Adam looked like a Greek god bathed in gold, she thought poetically before picking up her piece of fish and blowing on it.

'Penny for them?' Adam asked, feeling her eyes on him.

'I was thinking this fish looks bloody gorgeous.'

He laughed. 'Fibber.'

Sabrina grinned. 'Don't go getting a big head, but I was thinking you remind me of Adonis in this light.'

'That Greek god fella?'

She giggled and nodded.

'You can have another chip for that.'

The orb on the horizon sank lower.

'Five, four, three, two,' Adam counted, and as he reached 'one', it vanished altogether. The sky was washed with orange and yellow before it turned a more profound, dusky blue.

Sabrina licked greasy, salty fingers and was finally about to tell him about her encounter with Mystic Lou when Adam began talking. Instead, she listened as he told her about an altercation on Friday with the owner of a business in one of the buildings Taylor Holdings leased out.

'There's this fella driving around in a flash Merc and wearing natty suits, but he can't pay the rent.' Adam shook his head.

It wasn't his favourite part of the job; he was all for an easy life. In that respect, he wasn't cut from the same cloth as his father, who took no prisoners when it came to late rent payments. Taylor Holdings, a father and son business, dealt in property, he'd explained to Sabrina not long after they'd first met. This entailed the buying of commercial properties and leasing them out. His father had started the business as a young man, having seized an opportunity that had come his way thanks to his time in the Lime Street Boys. The gang had been notorious in Liverpool back in the day.

Sabrina couldn't for the life of her visualise Ray Taylor as a fast-talking member of gangland Liverpool. But, according to her aunt Evie, who'd known him back then, he'd strutted about the city streets as if he' owned them.

She eyed the last few chips and felt the waistband of her Calvin Klein jeans digging in. She really shouldn't. Then again, hadn't she gone for a run the other night and suffered through a photoshoot while clutching a can of Weight Watchers beans? The things she did for her bezzie mate! The fish 'n' chips were well earned, she told herself, chomping down another handful and enjoying the tang of vinegar as it hit the back of her throat.

'That's Vega that is,' Adam said a little while later after he'd binned the grease-soaked newspaper and sat back down to hold Sabrina's hand. He pointed to the bright star that had, like the flick of a switch, lit up the sky. 'We'll be able to see the summer triangle soon.'

'Since when do you know so much about consonants?'

Adam laughed, and Sabrina watched in fascination as his Adam's apple bobbed up and down. 'Consonants are letters that aren't vowels. You mean constellations, and it's not one of them. It's an asterism.'

'That still sounds like something my English teacher tried to drum into me,' Sabrina said. English hadn't been her strong suit. Instead of analysing *Wuthering Heights*, she'd been staring at the cover, thinking the long-puffed sleeves of the Victorian-era dress Cathy was wearing would work a treat on the wedding gown she was doodling on the back page of her exercise book.

Adam carried on, caught up in the star overhead. 'The summer triangle's made up of Vega, Deneb and Altair.'

Sabrina looked up at the star and then back at Adam's profile. He was constantly surprising her.

'They shine so bright come summer you can see them even when there's light pollution. Each of them is in a different constellation. Lyra the harp, Cygnus the swan and Aquila the eagle.'

'Beautiful,' Sabrina breathed. She was seeing the night sky through new eyes. 'And how do you know all this?'

'I went up the Pex Hill observatory on a school trip when I was a kid, and Mam said I talked about it non-stop for weeks. She bought me a book on the stars for Christmas that year, and I read it cover to cover at least five times. I wanted to be an astronomer after that trip.'

'I never wanted to do anything other than make wedding dresses.'

'You're lucky. By the time I was set to leave school, I'd moved from astronomy to wanting to be a mechanic like Tim. It wor me arl fella who wanted me to go into the family business.'

Sabrina was unsure what to say, so she said nothing, squeezing his hand instead as she decided it was time to tell him about her visit with Mystic Lou.

'Adam, Flo and I went to see the psychic I told you about Mystic Lou.'

'Oh yeah, when?'

'Last night.'

Adam dragged his eyes away from where a carpet of twinkling stars was now appearing as the sky darkened. He turned to look at Sabrina, a question in his coal-black eyes.

'Well, you won't believe what she said.'

'That's what you said when you told me about the girl who came in the shop with the photograph showing us at a wedding in 1945. I'm still trying to wrap my head around that.'

'You got more than you bargained for when you met me, didn't you?' Sabrina said softly.

'You're not wrong there.'

Her heart sank. Did he think she was trouble?

'But I wouldn't change any of it. Now tell me what your Mystic Lou woman had to say.'

Sabrina stepped back into that dimly lit chamber once more as she elaborated.

. . .

The space where Mystic Lou dished out her prophecies was too exotic to be called a room, so Sabrina had settled on the word *chamber*. Flo was waiting outside, as the psychic had said she'd only see one client for a reading at a time, insisting the messages that came through to her could get muddled otherwise.

It was comforting for Sabrina to know her friend was sitting outside in the waiting room, engrossed in the latest copy of *Cosmo*. She'd left her taking notes on an article titled 'Ten Signs He's Into You'.

Mystic Lou was seated at the table covered with a red cloth upon which her pièce de résistance, a crystal ball, sat. The curtains were drawn despite it not being dark outside yet, and the shadows of the flickering tea-light candles danced eerily on the walls. Music was playing softly, and Sabrina fancied the strangely hypnotic sounds might have been the Cocteau Twins.

The poster she'd been transfixed by the last time she'd been here caught her eye briefly. The image of hands clasped around a crystal ball alive with lightning-bolt energy was as startling this time around, she thought before turning her attention to the psychic herself.

If you'd asked Sabrina to draw a picture of what she thought a fortune teller should look like, she'd have drawn Mystic Lou. Black hair hung straight down her back from beneath the red scarf knotted about her head, gold hoop earrings dangled heavily from her ears, and she was wearing a robe with an amber gemstone brooch fastening it.

Sabrina had none of the nerves she'd had fluttering about on her first visit. Instead, she clasped her hands in front of her on the table, leaning toward the psychic – eager to get to the crux of the matter. 'I'm hoping you can tell me about a journey I'm to go on with my boyfriend, Mystic Lou.'

Mystic Lou stared intently at Sabrina. 'You 'ave been through ze timeslips we talked about on your last visit.'

It was a statement, not a question.

'I have, and you were right. I did fall in love with a man with dark hair and eyes – my Adam. And I did go on a journey all the way back to 1928 where I met Jane and Sidney.' She thought back on her adventures where she'd befriended the young maid on Allerton Road who'd fallen in love with her mistress's son. They'd got their happy ever after. She'd been there to witness their autumn wedding.

'I also went back to 1962.' That had been every bit of an adventure as her first journey. She'd even seen John Lennon and, on that occasion, had helped her friend Bernie choose her gown for her winter wedding.

Mystic Lou nodded, appearing unsurprised. She began polishing the crystal ball on its mounted stand until satisfied, then she picked up a candle, lit it and wafted it back and forth over the top of the orb. She then sat back in her chair and stared into the ball.

Sabrina was sure it was only a few seconds as she squirmed anxiously on her seat, but it felt like minutes until Mystic Lou spoke. Her nails were digging into her palms as she listened.

'I see a reunion in a different time.' She ran her palms over the orb. Her eyes focused on the crystal. 'You're caught up in a great celebration, and your boyfriend, the man with the dark hair and eyes, is with you. I'm glad,' she added softly, looking up.

Sabrina bit her bottom lip. It wasn't enough. 'Please, Mystic Lou, could you take another look and see if there's anything else?'

Mystic Lou closed her eyes as if she might be in pain, and Sabrina was uncertain whether she'd even heard her. Her lashes were spidery against her pale skin under the flickering candlelight.

'Mystic Lou?'

'I heard you.' Her eyes snapped open. 'It doesn't work like that. The ball will only show me what it wants me to see.'

'Please.' Sabrina's voice took on a begging note. 'Please, could you try? It's important.'

Mystic Lou rubbed her temples and then sighed. 'Ahright. I'll take another look.'

'Ta.' Sabrina, with all her muscles tensing in anticipation, didn't pick up on the accent slip.

Mystic Lou went through the same ritual as before, her eyes narrowing as she sought to see the secrets the crystal ball might still hold in its murky depths. Finally, after a moment or two, she spoke. 'There's a parade of some sort.' She peered closer, as if she was trying to understand. 'Excitement because it's a momentous occasion, and I see fire, flames dancing. Look for the woman you seek amidst the celebrations.' She blinked and held Sabrina's gaze. 'That's where you'll find her.'

Sabrina was speechless as fear and anticipation fought to take the lead. Finally, she would find her mam!

Mystic Lou wasn't finished, however. 'Be careful. You might not find what you expect.'

But her warning fell on deaf ears.

Now, as the lights of Liverpool twinkled below them, Sabrina waited to hear what Adam would say to the news that going through the timeslip once more would mean she'd find her mother.

'Well, that's it then, isn't it?' he said after an age. 'We've no choice but to go back.'

# 16

## 1940

Grey-faced people hurried past Lily as she huddled in her coat, waiting for the bus in the deepening gloom of evening. Her feet ached from standing on them all day, and the wind was stinging her face. Tendrils of fog were beginning to slither around street corners, and the air she was breathing was damp and filled with the distant smell of smoke. She'd be glad to get home tonight, she thought, shivering.

It had been a strange day. She'd woken with a sense of dread as if having had a bad dream, but she couldn't recall what it had been about. She'd been unable to shake off the feeling something terrible was going to happen all day, and it lingered even now.

Knowing she was in of a Thursday night, Max would sometimes swing by for a cup of tea to warm himself up if he had a window of time, so she hoped he'd call in tonight. She'd like to see him even if it was only for a few minutes to put her mind at rest that he was all right.

He was kept busy most evenings running messages across the city, delivering news of the injured to anxious families. He volunteered to keep watch up the fire tower too. It was a source of great consternation that he wasn't old enough to enlist, unlike his brother, who'd entrusted him with the care of his wife and their baby boy in his absence. The last they'd heard, he was headed for France. Max was desperate to fight for his country.

It worried Lily how fearless he was when it came to the air raids, which had begun with a sudden ferocity on 28 August. They'd kept on coming night after night ever since, or, at least, that's how it felt. She'd spent more nights in the air-raid shelter at the bottom of the garden than she had her own bed these last few months. The sound of the siren was commonplace, as was the drone of planes, followed shortly after by the whistling and whump of bombs. It was terrifying, and the devastation they were faced with come dawn heartbreaking. She wondered if she'd ever get the smell of burning timber from her nostrils.

Lily, too, did her bit. Her time in Skem had changed her. She was braver. She worried less. And, of course, now she had Max to help her stay strong. She'd have liked to have joined the ATS and become a FANY, but at thirteen, she was too young, so, like Max, she'd found another way to serve her country. She and Sarah had no qualms about lying about their ages, having decided to put the first aid they'd learned in the Guides to good use by volunteering at the Royal Liverpool, which meant an evening in was a rare treat. She'd soon stopped being squeamish at the sight of blood, too.

Sarah's mam had wanted her to join her and her younger brother in Wales, having taken them off to a cousin of their father's in mid-August. But Sarah had refused and a terrible row had ensued, which she felt awful about, confiding to Lily that her mam hadn't had a good upbringing and clung to her family as a result.

'Mam never talks about her past, and she's no family other than us. We're it,' Sarah had said, rubbing the goose bumps on her arms and telling her how sometimes she wondered if her mam had second sight because it was as if she'd had forewarning of the terrible air raids that were to come. She'd stood her ground about staying in Liverpool, however. Having shouted herself hoarse that she was too young to stay behind, Fern was marginally mollified when Lily's mam had agreed she could come and stay with them.

Lily no longer felt like a thirteen-year-old girl. For one thing, she'd left school to work at the parachute factory, telling her mam her time would be put to better use helping with the war effort. For another, seeing the folks coming in on stretchers at the hospital while tending to those who'd presented with minor injuries was enough to make anyone grow up overnight. It made her feel world-weary and sometimes sad that lives could be changed forever in a split second, though she knew this first-hand, thanks to losing her dad. Her compassion was wasted in the world of parachute making, one of the nurses had said to her the other night. She should think about nursing. She had a knack for it.

Lily further resolved to join the FANYs as soon as she turned eighteen if the war was still raging. Right now, it was hard to imagine it ever ending.

As the bus belched to a stop and she clambered aboard, she wondered if Mr Peterson would be there for his tea again when she got home. She had mixed feelings about Mr Peterson – unlike her mam, who'd made her feelings quite clear.

He was a big man with a booming laugh that made Lily jump. His hair was thinning, and he had red cheeks and a large nose. To Lily, he was reminiscent of a giant gnome, not handsome like her dad had been, and for the life of her, she couldn't see what her mam saw in him.

Sarah said her mam was lonely, and Mr Peterson was lonely too. Lonely hearts gravitated to each other, she reckoned. Lily was sceptical about how Sarah knew so much about lonely hearts, though she supposed Fern must be lonely too in a strange house in Wales, with Sarah's dad, who was a lovely man, away fighting.

She'd have liked to have asked Edith's opinion on the matter, but they were no longer friends, having fallen out when Lily began stepping out with Max.

She and Ruth had gone about with their noses in the air and their arms linked. Until Ruth, also having lied about her age, left to join the Land Army. Edith, meanwhile at six months older, was working in an office and had left Guiding to join the Sea Rangers.

Lily had been on the same bus as her former friend one evening and had overheard Edith holding court to those seated around her. She'd flashed the special pass needed to enter the dock area and had been full of how she'd learned to ship oars and how choppy the waters were near Pier Head. Edith had giggled and told her audience that the port was full of Allied ships and sailors who'd wave to her and the other girls.

Lily had uncharitably wondered if that had been Edith's primary motivation for joining the Sea Rangers.

At first, Lily had been heartbroken by the falling-out, but then it had dawned on her that if Edith was any sort of a friend, she'd have been happy for her. Especially knowing the sadness she'd suffered losing her dad. Edith was anything but happy where Lily and Max were concerned, though, because Edith was a girl who was used to getting her own way. She was spoiled in the way that beautiful girls sometimes are. And Lily knew, even though she'd never come right out and said it, that she couldn't understand why Max should prefer Lily, with her red hair and freckles, to her.

Thank goodness she still had Sarah.

Max had told her he couldn't be doing with a girl that talked as much as Edith did. Not that she'd passed this on to Edith, of course, but Sarah had laughed when Lily had confided what he'd said. 'He's got a point,' she'd replied, giggling. For her part, she didn't seem perturbed by the end of the friendship.

As for Mr Peterson, he'd come to their house for his dinner three times now. On the first occasion, she'd arrived home to find her mam's boss sitting at the table waiting for his tea. She'd been uncomfortable seeing another man so at ease where her father had once sat. She hadn't had much appetite for the sausage roll served up alongside a plate of veg, and her mam had snapped at her that it was a criminal waste of food when she'd cleared her plate from the table. Nevertheless, the sausage roll had found its way into her lunchbox the next day.

When Mr Peterson had gone home that evening, her mam had announced, 'There's lots to be said for a man who makes you laugh, Lily.' She'd spoken to her as though she were confiding in a friend, adding that she was lonely.

Lily had replied, 'But we've got each other, Mam.'

Her mam had looked at her sadly, like she didn't understand anything at all.

Lily knew her mam was being talked about in the neighbourhood too. She'd overheard snippets between gossipy Mrs Dixon and plump Mrs White as they'd chatted over the fence. Lily had been sitting on the back doorstep out of their line of sight, and she'd blanched upon hearing them tut that Sylvie Tubb's behaviour was disgraceful given poor Mrs Peterson was barely cold in her grave.

She didn't know about disgraceful, but she did know that it would no longer be just her and her mam one of these days. Well, Sarah too, but it wasn't like she'd be living with them forever. She didn't want to think about that, and if she got wind of any plans her mam had to wed Mr Peterson, then she'd find a way to join the FANYs. She wouldn't live under the same roof as him.

The bus stuttered off, and she plucked her hand from her pocket, putting it over her mouth to stifle a yawn. She couldn't remember the last uninterrupted night's sleep she'd had. It was the same for everyone. She hadn't seen her guardian angel for a while either, she thought, stealing a glance at the woman sitting opposite her. She was clutching her purse on her lap and wearing a red tam o'shanter beret from under which brown curls peeked. Lily couldn't help but think that a jauntily placed bow on the hat would have elevated it from nondescript to knock-out.

She noticed hats all the time these days, having had a brief stint working after school in a milliner's, Hats by Jacqueline on Great Charlotte Street. She'd never had any interest in hats before and had only got the job because her mam's cousin, Jeanne, was great pals with Miss Jacqui, as she liked to be called who needed part-time help.

As for Miss Jacqui herself, she was pencil thin and glamorous. She could make something beautiful from a flour sack if need be and was a dab hand at turning the fabric remnants she could get her hands on into works of art. She also ran hot and cold. Some days she'd be a tyrant overseeing Lily as she tidied the workshop, other days sunshine and light eager to fill Lily in on the fine art of millinery. Lily had put it down to the fella she was seeing. He was home on leave at the time, and if she'd heard from him, she was happy. If not, she was a bite.

She'd had a good mind to seek him out herself and tell him to stop messing Miss Jacqui about because he was making her life miserable too! Before she could, though, she'd lost her job. As a thirty-two-year-old woman who was single for all intents and purposes, Miss Jacqui had shut up shop to join the WAAFs after conscription had begun. She'd opted for the air force rather than the Land Army, which she'd confided was because she couldn't stand the thought of dirt under her fingernails.

Lily had been making mental tweaks to every hat she saw ever since. In her short time working for Miss Jacqui, she'd learned that the slightest embellishment could make all the difference.

There was no glamour in her new job, but Lily didn't mind. At least it was useful. She worked at the warehouse Littlewoods had converted on Hanover Street and had been instructed along with the other girls by an expert in the cutting out, sewing, rigging and assembly of parachutes.

Once lit by yellow hissing lights, the streets were dark these days, and sometimes Lily could pinch herself at all that had happened in the space of a year. The sights and sounds she no longer blinked an eye at were ones she could never have dreamed of before the war began in earnest.

This morning, for instance, she'd seen little ones picking through the rubble as she'd made her way toward the factory. When she'd asked them what they were after, a little boy with a grubby face had informed her there were sweets to be had. He'd held up a lemon sherbet jubilantly as proof of this. The rubble was the remains of a grocer's and confectioner's. Mercifully, not Peterson's.

It was the norm, too, to see families with bedding tucked under their arms making their way to the larger shelters once six p.m. rolled around. As were the craters that would appear overnight, the debris-filled streets and the smoking skeletons of houses and buildings. The shock and grief etched into the faces of those who'd lost loved ones. The sky, once black at night, would turn red.

Lily was fortunate; she knew this. The war had yet to touch her or her mam personally. That wasn't to say they hadn't suffered, though, because they had. However, their suffering had come before the war started. Families were suffering everywhere now, and more grieving was to be done with each dropped bomb. There seemed to be no end in sight to it all.

Other things had changed too – being Max's girl for one.

It had been just before last Christmas when she'd decided

to be bold and take herself off to the tobacco factory where he'd not long started work. She'd hung about outside that enormous Victorian building, waiting for him to finish for the day. It had given her a rebellious thrill to think how livid her mam would be if she found out what she was up to.

Her anxiety had increased as the minutes ticked by. What would Max think seeing her there? No matter what anyone said, she knew her mind and she wasn't too young to be courting. She resolved to tell him she'd come by to thank him for his help back in Skem. This was partially true. She did want to say how much she appreciated what he'd done for her. However, she also wanted to see him with a desperate, unfamiliar longing which she would not breathe a word of to him.

As the factory workers had begun to stream out from the building, her worry over what he'd think had morphed into how on earth she'd spot him in the sea of men and women. But he'd spotted her first, and he'd made his way toward her, smiling that slightly lopsided grin, his eyes a flash of colour at the end of a dull day. Her heart had soared.

They'd become firm friends over the ensuing months. Then one evening, as he'd walked her home, having treated her to dinner in a café, which had made her feel ever so grown-up, he'd suddenly come to a halt. 'Lily, can I kiss you?' Later, Max had told her he'd felt if he didn't throw caution to the wind there and then, he never would.

'Erm, yes,' she'd replied, uncertain of what she should do and uncaring of the foot traffic stepping around them.

His soft lips had settled briefly on hers, and then they'd broken apart giggling as an older woman tutted, muttering that the war was no excuse for indecent behaviour and, sure, what did they think they were doing when they were no more than children playacting at being grown-ups.

Lily, once she'd stopped laughing, had gazed into Max's eyes and said, 'Max Waters, I'm going to marry you one day.'

He'd replied, 'I don't doubt it for a minute.'

He'd won her mam over when he'd presented her with a tin of broken biscuits. Goodness knew where he'd got them because they were like gold dust since rationing had begun in earnest. But after that, he couldn't put a foot wrong. Of course, it had helped that when she'd opened the door to him, he'd asked if her sister was home!

Lily, lost in her thoughts, nearly missed her stop and had to call out to the bus driver. He slowed once more, allowing her to jump nimbly down and step onto the pavement. She pulled her coat around her and walked quickly down the foggy street.

A man loomed up in front of her, and she nearly jumped out of her skin in fright.

'Lily Tubb, is that you?' a voice she recognised asked, and a torch was flashed in her face.

Lily, her hand still on her chest, blinked at the sudden light and then peered closer at the man. She could just make out the steel helmet he was wearing – it had a large $W$ on the front of it – and he'd an armband on too, signalling he was an ARP warden. It was Mr Green. She'd taught his daughter when she'd had a brief stint helping home-school some of the local children shortly before starting work for Miss Jacqui.

'It is, Mr Green.'

'The fog's going to be bad tonight, girl. A right pea-souper. You're not going out again, are you?'

'No, not tonight, Mr Green.'

'Get on home then, queen. Let's hope for a quiet night.'

She heard his footsteps echoing down the street as she did exactly that.

The smell of fried onions hit her as she opened the front door, and she divested herself of her coat and hat, then hung them up.

'That you, Lily?'

'Yes, Mam.'

She stood in the hall for a split second, listening out but couldn't hear a male voice, only Mam's and Sarah's. Then she ducked into the front room to check the fire and saw it spluttering in the grate, so she poked it. Her mam had heaped slack on it to keep it banked, but once they'd had their dinner and moved through here, where they'd while away the rest of the evening, they'd get it roaring again until bedtime.

Satisfied it wouldn't go out on her, she bustled through to the kitchen to find her mam at the stove stirring a pot and Sarah setting the table. The knot between Lily's shoulders loosened when she saw there was no sign of Mr Peterson. She smiled a greeting at Sarah then gave her mam a spontaneous hug, causing her to nearly drop the spoon in the creamy, greyish liquid.

'Lily, your hands are freezing!'

'Sorry.' She grinned. 'It's bitter out there tonight, Mam.'

Mrs Tubb put the spoon down on the breadboard and said, 'Give them to me.'

Lily held her hands out, and her mother rubbed them with her own warm ones until they'd thawed.

'Why didn't you have your gloves on?'

'I couldn't find them this morning.'

Mrs Tubb gave an exasperated sigh. It was a bone of contention that Lily left it until the last possible minute to get out of bed each morning. 'I don't know. G'won and wash your hands. I'm about to serve up. A bowl of soup will warm you right up.'

Lily, seeing homesickness for her own mam, and little brother on Sarah's face, grabbed hold of her too and gave her a fierce squeeze before going to do as she'd been told. Steaming bowls had been placed on the table by the time she returned, and Mrs Tubb said a quick grace before they tucked in.

'You can work wonders with a spud, Mrs Tubb,' Sarah declared. Lily's mam had made it clear there was to be no calling her by her first name like Sarah's friends did her own easy-going mother.

Lily murmured agreement because the soup, despite its unappealing colour, was thick, hearty and hit the spot.

They fell into their usual routine once the bowls had been scraped, whereby Mrs Tubb put the tablecloth away before giving the kitchen a general tidy, while Lily washed up and Sarah dried. Then the threesome moved through to the front room to warm their toes beside the flames and sit in companionable silence. They had an unspoken pact to leave the horrors of what was happening outside once they'd closed the front door on it all. Dissecting the sights, smells and sounds seen that day wouldn't change anything. They did, however, listen to the wireless while they knitted.

Lily must have dozed off at some point because she opened her eyes to find her mam standing over her. 'Get off to bed, Lily. You too, Sarah – you can hardly keep your eyes open either.'

Sarah yawned widely, shooting Mrs Tubb an apologetic glance as she slapped her hand over her mouth.

'What's the time?' Lily asked, rubbing her eyes and standing up to stretch.

'It's nearly eight o'clock.'

'Max might call, Mam.'

'Well, if he does, I'll wake you. So grab some sleep now, both of you, while you can.'

She was too tired to argue, and Sarah wouldn't dare. 'Night, Mam. I love you.'

'I love you too, sweetheart.'

'Good night, Mrs Tubb.'

'Sleep tight, Sarah.'

Later, Lily would wonder why her mam had her coat on, but in her drowsy state, she took herself off up the stairs to bed. Perhaps tonight, the Germans would give them a reprieve, she hoped, but still she and Sarah didn't bother getting undressed –

there was no point when they'd be sure to be up and heading down to the Anderson shelter before long.

The piercing siren woke the girls not long after they'd drifted into a deep sleep. Lily dragged herself up, feeling woolly-headed as she shoved her shoes on her feet, Sarah following suit.

'Mam,' she called out as she stepped onto the dark landing. 'C'mon, Mam.' She pushed her bedroom door open, but the bed was empty. Thinking she must still be downstairs, she trooped down the stairs, hearing Sarah's footfall behind as she wondered how bad tonight would be.

The fire had been banked, but it was empty, apart from the glow of embers beneath the heaped slack.

'Where could she have got to?' Lily wondered out loud.

'The neighbours, perhaps?' Sarah suggested.

There was no time to dwell on it further because suddenly the house lit up and the windows shattered. Both girls shrieked, running out the back door and clambering inside the shelter on instinct.

Lily caught a glimpse of the sky – lit orange now – as Sarah pulled the door shut behind her. Her heart was thudding, but all she could do was sit there in the darkness, clutching Sarah's hand and wondering where her mam was.

# 17

## 1982

'Ahright there, Fred? If I'd known you were down here already, I'd have brought you a Horlicks,' Sabrina called out as she glanced down the street to the mound in the shop doorway. She pulled the door to the bridal shop shut.

'Sabrina, my love, is that you?' Fred sang back.

'It's me ahright.' Sabrina thrust her hand in her coat pocket and fished her keys out from amongst the assortment of coins she'd tipped out from Aunt Evie's money jar. Her aunt had kept an assortment of shillings, farthings, half-crowns, sixpence, threepence, a florin or two, ha'pennies and a handful of pennies for prosperity when the decimal system was introduced in 1971, and Sabrina had felt guilty helping herself, but needs must. She'd scribbled out an IOU and popped it in the jar. She also felt guilty for not sharing her plans with Aunt Evie, but she'd only worry. This way she'd only have to worry if she and Adam managed to step through the portal.

She felt most peculiar in her antwacky clobber, like she was going to a fancy dress party with a wartime theme. With Flo's help, she and Adam had scoured the charity shops last Saturday for suitable 1940s gear – or close enough. They didn't want to look like fish out of water if they did wind up in 1945 this evening. It was nice to have some warning this time around, thanks to Alice's photograph and Mystic Lou's prediction as to where they'd wind up, and Sabrina was determined they be prepared. She knew only too well what it was like to find yourself in a time where you stood out like a sore thumb and were penniless to boot. It wasn't a comfortable place to be.

Adam had been fitted out with a great coat, cuffed wool trousers and a knitted vest worn with a shirt underneath. He'd borrowed a pair of his dad's polished leather lace-ups, and he'd taken things a step further by getting his hair cut. The short back and sides he'd asked for was taking Sabrina some getting used to, but tonight his new do was covered by a flat cap she guessed was also courtesy of Ray Taylor.

Flo had been in her element, declaring she'd missed her calling as she'd scanned the racks of second-hand clothes, and would have loved a career in costume design for film or television. She'd been the one to spot a plain A-line skirt, rayon blouse and cardigan for Sabrina, along with the belted utility-style coat, declaring the find of the day and finishing touch, however, to be a pair of Mary-Jane shoes.

Tonight, Sabrina had been keeping a close eye on the clock, knowing Adam would wait for her downstairs at their arranged time, forty minutes after Aunt Evie, who was off to Bingo, left for the evening. As soon as she'd heard Aunt Evie call, 'Ta-ra then, love,' Sabrina had launched into action, packing a bag with a few changes of underwear, a toothbrush and a nighty. Then with the curling iron borrowed from Flo she'd coaxed her hair into the gentle waves of the day, draping a scarf over her head and knotting it to stop the curls from dropping in the evening air.

'Who's Fred?'

Sabrina realised Adam was asking her a question and saw

him scanning the pavement ahead, where there was nothing to see except a pile of blankets and old coats in a shop doorway.

'Oh, Fred. He's Bold Street's nightly visitor. His favourite spot is the doorway of what used to be the Christian bookstore up there. I bring him down a bowl of porridge of a morning.'

'You're a soft touch you are.' Adam shook his head, his hands tucked away inside his great coat.

His new look was growing on her.

'No need to worry about me, girl. I've man's best friend to keep me warm.' Fred's throaty voice floated toward them.

Adam nudged Sabrina. 'Has he gorra dog under those blankets then?'

'No.' She laughed. 'He's on about his whisky bottle. His one true love.'

'Who's that you've got with you on this fine evening, Sabrina?'

'Adam, Fred. You know the fella I told you about?' She pocked the keys.

'All good I hope.' Adam's ebony eyes danced.

Sabrina tapped the side of her nose. 'That's for me to know.' She took hold of his outstretched hand, savouring its warmth in hers. Whatever happened tonight, they were in this together. The thought reassured her as she pulled Adam along in the direction of Fred's voice, both of them jumping as a pigeon feasting on the remnants of a discarded sandwich flew up in front of them.

'Bloody things,' Adam said, shooing it away with his free hand. He'd gone off the entire species after one had taken aim and fired at his leather jacket.

'Come, come, don't be shy, young man. Introduce yourself. I must see for myself if you're worthy of the affections of the lovely Sabrina.'

'Jesus,' Adam muttered, side-eyeing Sabrina. 'What planet's he from?'

'He's a sweet old fella. I think he must have been on the stage at some point in his life. I'm fond of him.'

'Soft touch,' Adam repeated quietly, though Sabrina knew he wouldn't have her any other way.

They drew level with the blankets, under which they could just make out Fred's grizzly whiskers and red nose. He had a woolly hat pulled down low on his forehead, and he grinned up at them, revealing a missing front tooth. Then, clocking what they were dressed in, he blinked. 'Am I seeing things?'

'No, Fred, Adam and I are in fancy dress.' She didn't want to fib so she said nothing further while Adam held his hand out toward the old man.

Fred genteelly shook with his fingerless mittened hand, seemingly content with Sabrina's vague answer. 'I'm happy to make your acquaintance, young Aaron. Shall we drink to this salubrious occasion?'

'It's Adam, and no. Erm, cheers though.'

'Adam. Don't mind if I do.' He produced a bottle from beneath the blankets, unscrewed the lid, then raised the molten liquid to his mouth and glugged at it as though it were a glass of milk. When he was done, he wiped his mouth with the back of his hand before giving a satisfied, 'Aaah. Elixir of the gods that is.'

'It will kill you that stuff, you know,' Sabrina said.

'Sabrina, you aren't the first person to say that, and I doubt you'll be the last, but tell me, my girl. Would you deprive a fellow of the one thing on this earth that gives him pleasure above all else?'

'Well, would you?' Adam echoed, amused.

Sabrina sighed; she knew she was wasting her time delivering a lecture on the perils of hard liquor. The God botherer, determined to get Fred off the sauce and into the church, had been trying forever. 'No, I wouldn't.'

'Glad to hear it, my girl, glad to hear it. Now then, where

would you two Liver lovebirds be off to on this fine spring evening all in fancy dress?'

She hadn't got away with it then, and Sabrina exchanged a glance with Adam. Both of them knew how it would sound if they were to tell him their plan. There was nothing for it but to fib. 'A party with a 1940s theme. It's such a lovely evening we thought we'd walk.' That much was true – the air was crisp with a springy bite to it. It was a good night for a stroll.

'A moonlit stroll.' Fred clapped his hands delightedly before tossing back more of the whisky. And as though it had heard him, the moon chose that moment to come out from behind the clouds, and Fred promptly burst into song. His off-key version of 'Moon River' garnered him strange looks from a couple wandering past with their arms linked. Or perhaps it was Sabrina and Adam, who looked like they'd walked straight out of a wartime television drama series.

Fred raised the bottle to them. 'Cheers.'

Then he carried on with his song.

'We'll leave you to it then, Fred. Aunt Evie will bring you your porridge in the morning if I'm not about,' Sabrina said, signalling to Adam with her eyes that they should be on their way.

A window above them was wrenched open. 'Oi! Put a flamin' sock in it.'

Fred sang louder as he reached the chorus.

Adam and Sabrina looked at one another and laughed.

'Good night then, Fred,' Sabrina said as they turned away, and his not-so-dulcet tones wafted down the street after them.

'Want one?' She produced her ever present packet of Opal Fruits and waved the sweets at Adam, who helped himself to the top one.

'Strawberry.' He sounded pleased as he unwrapped the sweet.

Sabrina took the orange one beneath it. The streetlights cast shadows on the pavement, and the shops were all in darkness as they turned away from Fred to make their way back past the bridal shop toward Hudson's. The traffic was sporadic now, rush hour a memory, and only a few souls were wandering about. Suddenly, the picture Sabrina had tucked away in the inside pocket of her coat felt like it was burning a hole in her pocket. How could she have forgotten it? She pulled it out and thrust it under Adam's nose. 'Look – here's the photograph that started all this.'

He took it from her, holding the cardboard frame carefully by the corners as he moved under the streetlight to examine it while Sabrina explained how she'd come to have it.

'I telephoned Alice Waters and asked her if I could borrow the photograph because we planned on going back in time, and it would help me recognise her nan. She dropped it in today. I had to promise her I'd guard it with my life.' Alice might have thought the timeslip story was completely mad, but she'd still loaned her the picture and given Sabrina a note to pass on to her nan, just in case there was any truth to it. That, too, was tucked away in Sabrina's pocket.

Adam was focused on the evidence he was holding in his hands, and Sabrina could see it was making him feel as strange as she had. It wasn't every day you saw yourself caught on camera in 1945 when you hadn't even been born.

'Adam?'

'Sorry, I was listening. It's just it's—'

'Weird. I know.'

'I told me dad I'm going away for a couple of nights with some of the lads. He weren't best pleased with the short notice, but he'll survive.' Adam handed the photograph back to Sabrina, and she put it safely away once more.

'I didn't tell Aunt Evie anything.' Sabrina would have liked to have shared Mystic Lou's prophecy with her that this time she'd find her mother, but the words wouldn't come. Her loyalties felt divided. She felt terrible putting her aunt through this on each occasion she stepped back through the timeslip, but she had high hopes this would be the last time. This time she'd finally find her mother and the answers she needed.

Hudson's Bookshop came into sight. Adam's step faltered. 'So what do we do now?'

'We walk back and forth. It doesn't always happen on the first attempt, and I don't know if it will tonight. Which will be disappointing given all the trouble we've gone to.'

Sabrina thought back to those dark days of being stuck in 1928 when she'd paced until her feet ached here on Bold Street and nothing had changed. She'd been frightened she wouldn't get back to her own time. There was no rhyme or reason to it. The strange forces at work here decided of their own mysterious accord when she would step back or forward in time.

Adam squeezed her hand, and she squeezed back, clasping it tightly so they didn't get separated. 'Ready?' She held Adam's gaze.

'Ready.'

They began to pace.

# PART TWO
LIVERPOOL, MAY 1945

# 18

Adam's hand tightened around Sabrina's as he tried to get his bearings. Where it had been night a few minutes earlier, now it was day. It had happened! He and Sabrina had stepped back in time.

His gaze swung about madly as he tried to put the pieces as to what had happened together. They'd been pacing back and forth in front of Hudson's Bookshop hand in hand. The novel *North and South* had been visible in the shop window thanks to the streetlights reflecting off the glass. He'd caught sight of the pair of them in it too and had begun to feel foolish dressed as they were in such old-fashioned get-up. Nothing was happening, and he was worried the bobby who'd passed by five minutes earlier might return and demand to know if they were casing the business.

Finally, he'd had enough and had been about to tell Sabrina that they should call it a night when the air had thickened about them.

It had made him feel strange – as if he'd stepped off a plane into the tropics. The sounds around them had faded as though someone had turned the volume down on the radio. He'd shut his eyes for a split second, and when he'd opened them, Hudson's wasn't there. In its place was Cripps, the dressmaker's. It was completely disorientating, and he wasn't sure if he was holding Sabrina's hand to reassure her or himself.

The sights and sounds of Bold Street he took for granted were different. It looked in parts as if a bomb had gone off, destroying buildings seemingly randomly while other businesses in the shopping hub remained untouched, like the dressmaker's they were standing outside of. St Luke's at the top of the street was a blackened husk, filled with rubble, not the skeletal monument to World War Two he was familiar with. Then there were the people. Where were the women in bright saris or the groups of teens with teased hair? Where were the women with shoulder pads jutting out of their blazers? There were no punks with safety pins protruding from parts of their body no safety pin should ever touch, or young men like him with longish hair wearing jeans and leather jackets.

In their place were women of all ages in dresses and cardigans, clutching handbags, their hair neatly styled similar to Sabrina's, and men in suits with trilby hats. Clusters of young men no older than Adam and in military uniform ribbed one another and laughed as they strode past, flicking cigarette butts with careless abandon and whistling at the younger women. The cars, too, were different. He recognised a 1939 Vauxhall 12 puttering up the street along with a Hillman Minx, and while the pavements were as busy here on Bold Street as they always were, with business carrying on amongst the devastation, the road was decidedly quieter.

Adam's step faltered. He felt dizzy and, unaware he was doing so, squeezed Sabrina's hand even harder.

~

'We're here,' Sabrina whispered, allowing the scene around them to soak in. She swallowed hard, trying to get her bearings because this Bold Street was a badly bruised version of the street on which she lived – recognisable but broken. The building outside which Fred had set up camp, where they'd stood chatting not half an hour ago, was gone, and in its wake was a yawning space littered with debris, while across the street a few doors down, the roof had collapsed in on a shop, yet the frontage remained undamaged. The more her gaze swept up and down the street, the more damage became apparent. Was Brides of Bold Street unscathed?

Before she could elbow her way up the busy street, however, she needed Adam to loosen his grip on her hand. It was beginning to hurt.

'It's OK, Adam. We'll be OK. I promise.' He needed reassurance, but even as she said the words, Sabrina knew she shouldn't make promises she couldn't keep.

Adam blinked. 'Will it?'

'Trust me.'

'I do, but you promise me we'll stick together whatever happens.'

'I promise,' Sabrina replied with no qualms this time, feeling Adam's tight grasp of her hand relax under her gentle reassurance.

The door to the dressmaker's burst open, and two giggling women around Sabrina's age in smart belted jackets with slimline skirts wandered out with their arms linked. They were chattering on about the dresses they'd ordered, and Sabrina wondered how they could be carrying on so normally when everything on Bold Street was anything but.

'Excuse me,' Sabrina interrupted, not thinking only needing answers as she stepped in front of them and blocked their way. 'Could you tell me what the date today is, please?'

They exchanged a glance, and the shorter of the two gave a slight shrug. 'The seventh of May, queen.'

'Ta very much, but what year is it?' Sabrina persisted.

Both women took a wary backward step, clocking the intense look on Sabrina's face as she waited for an answer.

'Please, it's important.'

'What planet have you dropped in from? It's 1945, of course,' the taller girl said, yanking her friend away from the strange woman. The pair hurried off.

'We made it,' Adam said, shaking his head as though he had water in his ears.

'It's the day before VE Day – that explains this,' Sabrina murmured, gesturing toward the buildings that had collapsed or were now only hollowed shells. 'The Blitz is responsible for all the damage.'

She closed her eyes for a moment then opened them. She mustn't let Adam see she was upset or frightened by seeing first-hand what she'd previously only glimpsed grainy black-and-white photos of in history books. It was up to her to be strong because she was the one who'd dragged him into her mysterious past.

Mystic Lou's prophecy replayed through her mind, and suddenly it became crystal clear. She turned to Adam, who was still watching the goings-on around him with his mouth slightly agape. 'Adam, did you hear me?'

'Sorry, what?'

'It's May seventh, 1945,' she said with an excited urgency. 'Tomorrow, victory's declared for Europe, and the war is officially over. Mystic Lou mentioned a celebration when I went to see her. She said it was a momentous occasion, and she saw fire, dancing flames... Don't you see? It must have been Victory Day, and the flames belong to the bonfires that were lit that night.'

Sabrina couldn't claim to have been a scholar, but learning

about the war and the effect it had on her home city had sparked and held her interest during history class. She'd tried to imagine what it would have been like – the street parties, the bonfires, all of it. Now here she was about to experience it all for herself and so close to finding the answers she needed so badly. The blood thundered in Sabrina's ears at the thought of it.

Sabrina must have seen the doubt in his face because she said more firmly than was usual, 'I will find her this time, Adam. I have to. You've not come back with me for nothing.'

Sabrina could tell he believed her, but he still looked like he could use a stiff drink. They didn't have time for that right now though.

'Let's see if Brides of Bold Street is unscathed.' Aunt Evie had never mentioned the shop having suffered under the Luftwaffe's airstrikes, but still, seeing all this, she needed confirmation with her own two eyes. 'And I want to see Aunt Evie.'

'But she won't know who you are?'

'No, you're right. She won't. She'll think I'm mad, but given she knew we travelled back to 1945 together when Alice came into the shop and started all this with her grandmother's wedding photograph, we must have gone to see her.'

'It's bloody madness,' Adam mumbled, not letting go of Sabrina's hand as she took the lead.

Sabrina and Adam weaved their way around the pedestrians toward the bridal shop.

'Adam,' Sabrina, said eyeing him, 'stop swivelling your head all over the place. You look demented.'

'I can't help it,' he said, reaching up to run his fingers through his hair but finding the unfamiliar flat cap instead. 'I feel like a fish out of water even if we do blend in, and I can't get over the destruction. Can you imagine what it was like when those bombs fell?'

Their steps faltered. Sabrina could almost smell the thick air filled with smoke, dust and the odour of burned wood.

Could almost feel the broken glass crunching underfoot as shocked and bewildered residents and shopkeepers picked their way through the debris. The memories for these people passing them by and inside the shops and businesses would still be raw.

Sabrina shuddered. She felt the same on both counts, and it was a relief to see Brides of Bold Street with a shimmering satin-and-lace gown in the window. There wasn't so much as a scorched brick to be seen on the smartly painted frontage. Her hand reached out for the door handle, but she snatched it away as the door was flung open.

## 19

Lily pushed open the door of Brides of Bold Street with a heavy heart and stepped inside the shop. She wished she'd accepted Sarah's offer to come with her, once she'd finished trying to talk her out of what she was about to do. She could have done with her best friend's support. It was too late now though. She'd told Sarah there was no need; she'd made her mind up and she'd be fine. As the door closed, her eyes swept the space. How was it possible that less than a fortnight before, she'd been twirling in her mam's wedding dress before having it pinned by Evelyn Flooks?

They'd whiled away a lovely hour catching up on each other's lives, and now here she was, back for an entirely different reason.

She'd known Evelyn from their brief time at Littlewoods making parachutes. Evelyn had taken her under her wing upon hearing her mam had been killed in the Durning Road bombing. She'd been one of over 160 others who'd lost their lives on that fateful night in November 1940. The tragedy had been so raw – it still was – and Evelyn's kindness to her gratefully received. She'd seen her as a mother figure of sorts. But when

Littlewoods had been destroyed in the Blitz, they'd gone their separate ways – until Lily had called into the shop clutching her mam's wedding dress. There was no other seamstress in all of Liverpool whom she'd trust to lay so much as a finger on the precious gown.

The dress and wearing it on her own wedding day would make Lily feel like her mam was there with her. All she had left of her was the house, the headstone next to her dad's engraved with the name Sylvie Tubb, beloved wife and mother, and the dress.

It was all by the by now, though, and she wished she could talk to her just one last time and ask her to explain why she and Dad had never told her the truth. But, instead, she'd been left feeling cheated, as though her whole life had been built on a lie.

Lily had found out later that the night her mam had died, she'd been on her way to Mr Peterson's when the siren had sounded. She'd headed to the closest shelter beneath the Ernest Brown Junior Instruction College, packing in there along with three hundred others. Lily imagined she must have been hoping the raid would be over quickly so she could carry on her way. It wasn't to be, though, because the bombs had rained down for eight hours solid, and the college had been hit by a parachute with a landmine attached to it in the early hours of 29 November. The Germans aiming for the railway station had miscalculated, dropping their load on Durning Road instead.

The college furnaces had burst, and hot water and steam had scorched many of those trapped inside. Others were killed by the falling debris, and all the while, fires had raged.

Lily couldn't bring herself to think about her mother's fate.

It was a terrible, terrible thing, and all of Edge Hill – all of Liverpool for that matter – had been in shock for days, weeks, even months after. Everybody seemed to know somebody who'd been in that shelter. Life as their tight-knit community knew it had been picked up and spun around on its axis, and when it had stopped spinning, it was altered forever.

That period of Lily's life was all a blur. She'd known in her gut her mam was gone by first light when she still hadn't returned home, but she'd searched for her nevertheless. There was a vague memory of gossipy Mrs Dixon making her a cup of sweet tea. She'd sat with her after delivering the news that her mam was one of the Durning Road casualties.

Winnie — as they called Winston Churchill — had said it was the single worst incident of the war.

For Lily, being orphaned when once she'd been so cherished was incomprehensible.

She'd been grateful for the support Sarah and her mam, and even her little brother, who had given her regular hugs, had offered, returning from Wales immediately upon hearing of Lily's loss. Fern Carter had comforted her by telling her she wasn't to think of herself as being alone — she'd always been and always would be a part of their family. Lily had been touched, but it was Max's strong shoulder she'd leaned the heaviest on in the immediate aftermath. He'd begun calling her his little Viking, knowing the story behind the name, and it had stuck.

Sylvie Tubb's younger sister, whom she'd fallen out with years ago, had appeared out of the woodwork in the days following Sylvie's death. Lily had known her mam had a sister, but all she'd ever said about her was she'd been wild and had chosen her own path. She'd introduced herself to Lily as her aunt Pat, insisting Lily come and live with her and her uncle Gordon at their house in Vauxhall. She was too young to fend for herself, and it was the least she could do for poor Sylvie, she'd said.

Lily had found it hard to imagine Pat, with her smiley face, freckles across her nose and well-padded frame, ever having been wild. It was also strange to think her mam had a younger sister she'd stopped talking to. A sister that hadn't lived far away from them but one whom Lily couldn't remember meeting. Whatever they'd fallen out about must have been significant to cause such a rift.

Despite being unable to recall ever having met her aunt, Lily had immediately felt she knew her. She'd also been certain she'd seen her before somewhere. It had teased at the edge of her weary mind, but where and when she'd seen her aunt wouldn't come, so in the end she'd put the uncanny feeling down to familial ties.

Lily had packed her bags without hesitation, eager for someone else to take charge. Still, it had been another wrench to leave Needham Road. Mrs Dixon had seen her off with a tear in her eye, promising to keep an eye on the house. It would stand empty until Lily was of an age to decide what to do with it.

She'd soon settled in with her aunt Pat and uncle Gordon, who'd made room for her in the tiny box room upstairs. At first, she'd worried their three boys – Donny, twelve; Gerald, ten; and Charlie, seven, who shared a bed in the room next door – would resent her presence, but they'd taken their cousin's arrival in their stride and treated her like a big sister. As for her aunt and uncle, they'd been kindness itself to her. So she'd slotted in, and she was grateful to them for having come for her.

Whatever bad blood had passed between her mam and her sister, Lily didn't care. It was nothing to do with her. She'd asked Aunt Pat about it, but all she'd say on the subject was how inconsequential it was in light of all the suffering the war had wrought. 'There's nowt stranger than family, Lily,' she'd said, smiling sadly.

For the longest time, things just seemed to happen around her, and Lily had felt as though she were wading through her days. Without Max, she didn't know how she'd have survived her grief, but survive it she had.

The war was all but over now, and Lily had been determined to embrace her future. She was training as a nurse at long last. Max, who'd enlisted with the Liverpool Irish Battalion as soon as he'd turned eighteen, had returned from active service barely a year later. He'd been discharged after suffering blast injuries, which, thankfully, he was now mostly healed from, but the mental scars would stay with him a long time. Lily knew he dreamed of what he'd seen and done, but she hoped the nightmares would ease with time like hers of Skem had. He'd been stationed in Southampton before shipping out as part of the D-Day invasion.

Lily had missed him every single minute he was gone. At night, she'd dig out her worry book to write in before getting down on her knees to pray he'd come back to her.

God had answered her prayers.

He'd been different when he returned, that devil-may-care attitude of his tempered by things he'd seen and done, but he was still her Max. At least the stutter he'd mentioned to her the first time they'd met hadn't returned. He hadn't been bothered by it since he'd left Skem, and upon coming home, he'd started back at Ogden's. He'd enrolled in night school too, where he was studying technical drawing. Draughtsmen would be needed to get their country back on its feet, he said, and he owed it to the boys who didn't make it back to do something with his life.

Max had popped the question a week after he'd come home as they'd jitterbugged enthusiastically on the crowded floor of the Grafton Rooms, shortly after her eighteenth birthday. He'd shouted over the top of the lively beat, 'Lily, will you marry me?' and she'd shouted back, 'I thought you'd never ask!'

At that moment, Lily had felt free, lighter than she ever had before. With Max by her side, she could tuck her worry book away forever. Her beam had lit up her face. It had been unencumbered and reflected the joy inside her, and she'd known the nervous smile that had plagued her throughout her childhood wouldn't bother her again. Marrying Max meant she'd always be his little Viking, and Vikings were fearless.

A well-groomed airman with a parting straighter than a ruler who'd overheard the exchange had nudged his pals, and the next thing, she and Max had been airborne over the crowd as a cheer went up.

Aunt Pat and Uncle Gordon had hosted a small party to celebrate the good news.

She'd chosen an antique gold band with a pear-shaped emerald surrounded by a floral platinum halo for her engagement ring. And each time the light caught the precious stone Max had said brought out the green in her eyes, she'd feel the sorrow of the last few years dissolve a little more.

She'd felt her mam's absence keenly, but she was up there in heaven with her dad, and one day soon, Lily had hoped she and Max would have a family of their own.

Now here she was, standing on the shop floor of Brides of Bold Street as afternoon sunlight pooled in through the front window, dead inside.

Her life had been built on a lie, and she'd no need of the dress now. She wouldn't be wearing it. Her reason for calling into the bridal shop was to pay Evelyn what she owed her. After that, she could do what she liked with the dress. She picked the bell up off the counter and rang it.

She wouldn't wear her mam's dress. Not after the lie her mother had told.

~

Evelyn Flooks heard the tinkling bell that signalled she had a customer out front and took her foot off the Singer's treadle. She left the cuff she was sewing on the doeskin, suit-jacket sleeve – inspired by Rita Hayworth's wedding to Orson Welles – where it was and stood up. A suit for a wedding? Whoever heard of such a thing? She gave the jacket sleeve a disparaging glance and yearned for the thirties' long sweeping lines and moulded shapes. This war had a lot to answer for.

She patted her hair, recently set in the latest side-sweep craze, then pushed her glasses – which always slipped down her nose when she was at the machine – back up before smoothing her shop coat. The coat, like the suit, was dull. The plain navy fabric was the only material she'd been able to spare. Oh, how she longed for the end of rationing. She'd vowed when there was no longer a shortage of material, she'd sew herself a shop coat in a different colour for each day of the week. She'd be a rainbow.

Since she'd reopened a few short months earlier, her business had mainly involved repurposing previously worn old bridesmaids' dresses or heirloom wedding gowns.

Lily Tubb's poor mam's dress was hanging on the rail, and she eyed it now. All it needed was a nip and tuck for Lily to make it her own. *And speak of the devil...* she thought as she stepped into the shop and saw Lily herself at the counter.

Evelyn beamed, but her tone was questioning. 'Hello, Lily?' She was sure they'd organised for her to collect her dress next Thursday. These young brides could be so eager, but she'd yet to make the necessary alterations.

As she moved behind the counter, she took stock of the younger woman. She was pasty, and her hip bones were jutting out of her skirt. By the looks of her, she'd have to re-pin the wedding dress or it would hang off her. And there was a look in her eyes... 'Is everything ahright, luv? You're looking peaky on it, if you don't mind me saying, and you've lost weight.'

The concern on Evelyn's face seemed to tip her over the edge she'd been skirting, and she burst into sobs.

Evelyn came out from behind the counter and steered her out the back. 'There, there, Lily, sweetheart. It can't be as bad as all that. You settle down there while I put the kettle on, and then you can tell me all about it.'

~

Lily sagged down on the chair Evelyn had dragged over for her before the other woman disappeared upstairs. It was as bad as all that. She'd barely eaten these last two weeks – the thought of food turned her stomach – and since stumbling across the slip of paper that had upended everything she'd thought she knew, she'd struggled to sleep.

She dabbed at her eyes with a handkerchief in an attempt to pull her emotions into check, hoping nobody called into the shop in Evelyn's absence. She'd frighten them off with her red nose and leaking eyes.

Once she'd got herself under control, Lily took stock of the workroom where she sat. The shelves were laden with jars filled with everything from buttons to pearls. There were rolls of lace, reams of ribbons, a measuring tape, a row of thimbles and a fat pincushion. On the worktable was a pattern ready for cutting out, and she could see a half-finished jacket being cobbled together over by the sewing machine.

The style reminded her of the suit Rita Hayworth had worn for her wedding to Orson Welles. The pictures had been in all the magazines, and she'd found it a little disappointing that a film star had opted for such an everyday outfit for her wedding. But, on the other hand, she'd felt a little smug thinking of her mam's beautiful dress she planned on having altered for her big day.

The shop remained empty, and Evelyn returned carrying a tray with their tea things on it. Lily watched as she set them out and nodded when she held up the milk jug. It did have therapeutic properties, she thought, sipping the hot, sweet liquid and feeling it calm her. She didn't usually have sugar, but Evelyn had dolloped a spoonful of the precious sweetener in her cup anyway. Her breath had steadied.

They drank in silence for a few minutes before Evelyn spoke up. 'Now then, Lily, luv, why don't you tell me what's been going on?'

Lily raised her watery eyes. 'I can't wear my mam's dress, Evelyn. And I'm sorry to have troubled you with it and for the work you've done. I'll pay you, of course.' She sniffed loudly. 'I don't want it back. You could sell it in your shop if you like.'

Evelyn frowned. 'I don't understand. It's such a beautiful gown, and you'll be hard-pressed to find anything else as lovely with the rationing.'

'I've gorra suit I can wear. It will do.' She blew her nose again and made to get up. 'Thank you for the tea. I'm sorry to have carried on so. I've gorra go. Let me fix up what I owe.'

Evelyn shook her head. 'No. I've not done any work. I'll hold the dress for you, Lily. It will be here when you come to your senses.'

'Please don't. I won't need it. Thank you for listening.' Lily remembered her manners as she made her way from the workroom, feeling Evelyn's eyes on her back.

She pushed the door of the shop open and nearly collided with a dazed-looking young couple. Through the haze of tears she thought there was something familiar about the woman, but she was in no mood to see anyone she knew. 'Oh, I beg your pardon,' she said before hurrying off up the street.

# 20

Sabrina and Adam took a step back as a young woman with fierce red hair exited the shop. She mumbled an apology and hurried off up the street.

Sabrina only caught a glimpse of her but instantly realised she knew her. The picture was black and white, so it didn't offer any clue as to the vividness of her hair, and she'd been wearing a wedding dress too, of course, but it was Lily, Alice's nan – Sabrina was certain of it. Her mouth formed an O as she stared after her, catching a flash of red hair now and again bobbing between the sea of heads.

She couldn't believe their timing. What were the odds that Lily should be leaving the bridal shop as they were about to enter it? But she was losing sight of her now. Sabrina blinked and told herself to snap to. There would be time to see Aunt Evie later.

'That's her, Adam! Look – up there with the red hair, see? It's Lily from the photograph I showed you. C'mon – we have to speak to her!' Sabrina hared off, desperate not to lose her, with Adam hanging on to her hand for dear life.

'Sorry,' she apologised, pushing past a dawdling couple

looking in the shop windows, her eyes trained on Lily's hair. She ducked and dived her way forward until she could reach out and tap the other girl on the shoulder.

Lily spun round, startled, affixing her hazel eyes on the sweating girl.

'Lily,' Sabrina panted, her face hot. 'I was worried I wouldn't catch up to you.'

Lily stared at the strange woman uncertainly. 'Do I know you?' she asked.

'No – well, yes, sort of.'

Lily frowned. 'Sorry, but I'm in a hurry. I've gorra a bus to catch.' She made to move away, but Sabrina reached out and took hold of her forearm. She wasn't about to let her slip away.

Lily stared at the girl's hand in alarm before trying to shake her off. 'Let go of me!'

'Please, Lily, it's important.' Sabrina loosened her grip but kept hold of her. Is there somewhere we could talk? I can explain then.'

Lily frowned and bit her lip as people sidestepped around them. 'Sorry, I've got to go,' she repeated, making to walk away again.

Sabrina grasped for something to make her stop and listen. 'I know Max,' she blurted after her.

Lily stopped and turned around once more. 'How do you know him?' she demanded.

'I've gorra a photograph. Look.' Sabrina pulled the picture from her pocket.

Lily took the cardboard frame from her and studied the photo, a frown settling between her eyebrows. Then she looked up and stared at Sabrina, not understanding. 'What is this? Some sort of trick?'

'I can explain if you'll let me,' Sabrina said.

Lily hesitated, clearly warring between curiosity and common sense. Curiosity won.

'There's a tearoom not far from here,' she said then began to walk, and Sabrina and Adam hurried after her.

~

The door to the tearooms tinkled as Lily pushed it open, the other two still following behind her.

Lily glanced around at the full tables. The place was heaving. She'd be safe as houses here if these two turned out to be unsavoury types. It had crossed her mind that they could have heard she'd been left a house and thought she was well off, but she'd dismissed this as silly. A terrace house that was always in need of something fixing hardly warranted being well off. And the only other item of value she possessed was her engagement ring, which wasn't currently in her possession either. She'd lost weight these last few weeks and had been frightened she'd lose her precious ring. As such, she'd dropped it back to the jeweller's where she and Max had bought it to get it resized yesterday.

'I'll order a pot of tea for three if you get a table,' Lily said, eager to maintain control of the situation as she tagged on the end of the queue of people waiting to be served.

A young girl with a shock of black curls and wearing a full white apron was clearing the table in the far corner of the room, and the couple made their way over to it.

Lily took advantage of the time alone to weigh up the two strangers as she waited to order. The man looked worried – he was fiddling with the sugar pot and seemed unable to sit still – but the woman remained calm when she responded to whatever he'd said, reaching over to rub his arm reassuringly.

They didn't look like con artists, but then what did she know? A con artist wouldn't get about looking like one. And there was that photograph...

There was no time to dwell on that any further, though, as

she'd reached the front of the line. She placed her order then, deciding it was better to be safe than sorry, she put her purse away, being sure to tuck it right down the bottom of her bag before closing it.

She made her way over to the table and sat down across from the couple. Her knuckles were white, so tight was the grip she had on her handbag. There was no point in dancing around why she was here with them, she decided, and launched straight in.

'How did you come by that photograph?'

She watched as the woman tucked her hair behind her ears and licked her bottom lip. Her earlier sentiment of there being something familiar about her returned, but if they'd met before, she couldn't think where.

'Listen, Lily, this is going to sound far-fetched, but I promise you every word I'm about to tell you is true.'

Lily cast an annoyed glance at the table on her right as a teacup clattered down in its saucer. It was followed by the scrape of a knife and fork, both of which sounded unbearably loud. She leaned forward in her seat, wanting to be sure to hear every word this woman was about to say.

'My name's Sabrina Flooks, and this is Adam Taylor. Erm, the thing is, Lily, we're from the future – 1982 to be precise, and I've met your granddaughter, Alice.'

## 21

Lily's head flicked back as though she'd been slapped. She hadn't expected to be told she was sitting in a perfectly respectable tearoom with time travellers. It was ridiculous – the very idea of it was preposterous. This woman was certifiable, and the lad nodding along with her, he was no better.

Lily pushed her seat back, nearly colliding with the waitress carrying their tea things on it, wishing she'd followed her first instinct and refused to hear them out. She was too flustered to apologise, and as the waitress, oblivious to the drama, set the cups and saucers, teapot and milk jug down on the table, she stood up. 'I've gorra go.' She wanted to put distance between herself and the pair. The photograph must have been doctored. There was no other explanation.

'You've got an engagement ring, Lily,' Sabrina fired across the table at her. 'It's a pear-shaped emerald set in platinum. I don't know why you're not wearing it.'

Lily stood stock-still and glanced down at her ring finger. It felt naked. How could this Sabrina have known she'd chosen a pear-shaped emerald? She waited until the waitress hurried off to serve another diner.

'It's true what I said, Lily.' Sabrina's voice was soft.

Like she was in a trance, Lily sat back down. She needed a cup of tea, but first, she wanted to see the photograph again.

As if she'd read her mind, Sabrina got the picture out once more and slid it across the table to her.

Lily stared down at it. There she and Max were plain as day. Sarah was next to her in the dress she was also having altered; Fern had been cut off at the edge of the picture, but it was definitely her. Evelyn was in the mix with this certifiable pair, and her aunt – she couldn't bring herself to call her *mam* – and uncle were standing on her left. They both looked proud as punch. Her stomach tightened as she tried to make sense of it. She'd only just called into Brides of Bold Street to tell Evelyn she wouldn't be wearing the dress after all, and yet here in front of her was a picture that told a different story. What on earth was going on? She pinched the tender flesh inside her arm in the hope this was a dream.

It wasn't. Whatever was going on was horribly real.

Sabrina set about pouring the tea, putting milk and sugar into each cup. 'Here, drink that,' she said to Lily, who usually took her tea black, a habit she'd fallen into with rationing. Today, however, Lily needed the sweet milky drink, and she didn't look at either of them as she sipped away at it.

'Tell me more,' she said.

By the time they'd drained the pot of tea, Lily had heard a fantastical story about time travel, an abandoned child and a missing mam. It was so far-fetched it couldn't possibly be true, could it? And yet there was a sincerity to the pair that had grabbed hold of her and changed her initial opinion. It was why she'd stayed and listened to what Sabrina had to say.

She'd also been informed that she was connected with this mysterious Sabrina through her mam's wedding dress. The same dress she'd left a little over an hour ago at Brides of Bold Street with instructions for it to be given away or sold.

It was all too much; her head was throbbing as she processed everything she'd been told, and the photograph taunted her.

'It's a lot to take in, I know,' Sabrina said gently.

'You say the dress connects us?'

Sabrina nodded.

'Well, I'm not going to wear it.' Lily's tone was clipped.

'But why? You're getting married, aren't you?'

Lily nodded and then hesitated. She didn't know these two. Was it wise to share her family secrets? She wrestled with herself for a moment before deciding she had nothing to lose.

'Me mam and dad have both passed on now.'

Adam nodded sympathetically. 'I lost me mam a couple of years back. It's hard.'

'And I lost mine in a round-about fashion when I was three,' Sabrina reminded her. 'We understand what you must be going through.'

'You can't possibly understand.' Lily dipped her head, not wanting them to see the tears that had sprung to her eyes despite her festering anger. Her mind drifted back to the fateful day when everything she thought she'd known to be true had been upended.


Lily went back to the terraced house on Needham Road where she'd grown up now and again. The visits were always bittersweet because she felt closest to her parents there but was achingly aware that neither of them would ever walk in through the front door again. She'd never again hear their voices filling the spaces she'd called home.

The windows had been boarded up initially, and Uncle Gordon had helped her sweep up all the broken glass. Everything inside was as it had been, as though her mam had merely stepped out – which, of course, was what she had done. Only, she'd never returned. The jumper she'd been knitting for the war orphans was still in the basket by her chair. Lily had vowed to finish it one day but had been unable to bring herself to pick it up. She'd take it back that night and give it to Aunt Pat. She was a skilled knitter who'd have it finished in no time.

Things were slowly changing inside the old place with the house getting ready for its new occupants.

That afternoon, once Lily had managed to disentangle herself from Mrs White, who'd wanted all the details of Lily and Max's upcoming nuptials, she'd smelled fresh paint as she'd stepped inside the front door. Uncle Gordon and Aunt Pat had worked miracles. The windowpanes had been replaced, a fresh coat of paint covered the walls in the absence of wallpaper, and Aunt Pat had managed to source fabric from goodness knows where which she'd made into curtains.

Lily stood there in the front room with her eyes flitting about. The old memories would linger, but the sadness would be chased away as she and Max put their stamp on the house and created happy new ones. For a moment, she imagined what it would be like when the sound of a child's laughter filled the room and felt a surge of happiness.

They'd move in straight after their wedding, and Lily couldn't wait. She wanted to be Max's wife in every way. What would it be like to lie next to him each night in bed and finally be able to give in to the desires they'd both kept at bay with increasing difficulty?

She hadn't come here today to daydream though. She needed her birth certificate to take to the registry office. Her mam had kept a shoebox under the bed filled with important papers and the like, though Lily had been told it was out of bounds.

'Mam, that doesn't count anymore now you're not here,' she said out loud as she took to the stairs and ventured into her parents' old room. This would soon be her and Max's room. She smiled at the thought, visualising the new quilt spread out on the bed. Aunt Pat was patching it together with scraps of material she'd had tucked away. It would look lovely, she decided, venturing over to the bed and getting down on her hands and knees.

She sneezed as she lifted the bed skirt, disturbing the dust that had gathered under it, and resolved to give upstairs a good going-over after church on Sunday. The box had been pushed right under the bed, and she had to flatten herself out and stretch long to retrieve it.

'Mam, I'm going to be covered in dust,' she muttered, dragging it out and then sitting back on her haunches to open it.

She placed the lid to one side and sifted through the papers. There weren't many, and they were dry to the touch. Some were yellowed by age, and she plucked out an envelope, turning it over to see who it was from. The address of a solicitor's on Bold Street was stamped on the back, and when she pulled the contents out, she saw it was her grandparents' will. She scanned the wordy text briefly and then gave up, putting it back where she'd found it.

Her fingers alighted on her parents' wedding certificate next, and hot tears stung her eyes. She blinked them away. They'd been luckier than most, her mam and dad. Their time together might have been cut short, but it had been happy. She swallowed the lump that formed in her throat, and as she shifted an insurance policy to one side, she saw the plain white envelope with her name neatly handwritten on it.

'Aha, there you are,' she said, unhooking the envelope flap and sliding what had to be her birth certificate out. She scanned the typed text and frowned. Why was there no entry next to 'Father'? Something was wrong.

She read the brief document once more – slowly this time – to ensure she hadn't made a mistake because next to 'Mother' was Patricia May Rigby's name.

Her name was there: Lily Jean. There was no mistake; it was her birth certificate, and the truth was staring up at her plain as day.

Lily switched into automatic pilot as she scrambled to her feet and kicked the box back under the bed. She shoved the certificate back in its envelope and into the pocket of her dress, then fled the house. Mrs Dixon called out, asking what her hurry was from her front doorstep, but Lily ignored her. All she could think about was getting home to confront Aunt Pat with what she'd found. Adrenaline made her shake as she rode the bus, unaware of her surroundings as it carried her back to Vauxhall.

'Aunt Pat!' she yelled, bursting through the front door as though the hound of the Baskervilles were snapping at her heels a short while later. She pushed the door shut behind her with unnecessary force.

'Good God, Lily, I'm not deaf! What's happened, girl?' Aunt Pat appeared in the kitchen doorway, wiping her hands on her pinny.

Lily stared at her, feeling as though the carpet had been wrenched from beneath her feet. How had she not seen it before? They were peas in a pod.


'Me mam's younger sister is me mother.' Lily finally raised her gaze, looking from Sabrina to Adam. 'I was lied to all my life.'

'It would have been a terrible shock finding out like that,' Sabrina said.

'It wor, and I don't understand why they didn't tell me. I would have understood if Mam and Dad had told me the truth. Patricia was young; she wasn't married. My parents were desperate for a child but were unable to have a baby of their own.'

'Ah, Lily. Life's never black and white. People have reasons for doing what they do, but that doesn't mean they're always right. So don't be hard on them.'

'Me not be hard on them?' Her eyes flashed across the table at Sabrina – she'd gone too far. 'Me mam wouldn't let Aunt Pat have anything to do with me. It was one of the conditions for her and Dad bringing me up. I was to be theirs.'

Adam jumped in, defending Sabrina's sentiment. 'Things are slowly changing in the eighties, Lily, but I'd imagine the stigma of being an unmarried mother would have been hard to bear in the forties. Your aunt – or mam – she did what she thought was best for you and your parents, and from what you've told us, they loved you. That's what you need to hold on to. Dwelling on the past doesn't do any good.'

'Max said the same thing.' Lily remembered how he'd tried to calm her down, wanting her to meet with her aunt and iron the past out, but Lily had refused. Instead, she'd packed her bags the very afternoon she'd confronted Aunt Pat, who'd turned whiter than a ghost as the birth certificate was flapped in her face. The last words she'd said to her aunt were, 'You're a liar, me mam and dad were liars, and I don't want to see you ever again.'

Revisiting the recent and still raw memories had made Lily angry. What frightened her was what would happen when she stopped being angry; she was scared of the hurt that lay beneath her bubbling rage.

'Lily, I told you I wasn't raised by me mother either, but it doesn't make Aunt Evie any less my mam. Same as your mam's still your mam. The circumstances of your birth don't change that.'

Lily's mouth set in a stubborn line.

Sabrina didn't push further. Instead, she pulled an envelope from her jacket. 'Your granddaughter gave me this.' She slid the envelope – upon which the words *For my nan, Lily Waters* were neatly written – across the table. 'I don't know what it says,' she added.

Lily picked it up, reluctant to open it. She'd heard enough for one day, and she waged a silent war with herself. But her natural-born curiosity finally won out, and she slid the piece of paper contained inside it out. There was something else in the envelope though. Another photograph.

The colours grabbed her first; the picture looked so real. A young man and woman, arms wrapped around each other, stared back at her. She bit her lip. The woman had red hair the same hue as her own and could have been her sister, but the haircut, the clothes... they were bizarre. She bit her lip and stared at it a few moments longer before sliding it back into the envelope and turning her attention to the letter.

Sabrina and Adam watched as she unfolded the paper and held it up to read, obviously curious about what it said, but Lily made sure her face gave nothing away.

She scanned the few paragraphs, realising this Alice, who the letter was from, looped her Gs the same way she did. No matter how many times her teacher had tried to correct Lily on this, she'd persisted in her own overtly flamboyant loop as Alice had. Then she reread it, slower this time to absorb the message.

*10 April 1982*

*Dear Nan,*

*How strange it is even to be writing this letter. I expect if you're reading this, you're thinking the story Sabrina's told you is ridiculous, just as I did.*

*If you are reading it, though, then you'll know it's true. Sabrina and Adam have travelled back in time from 1982 to 1945 when you married Granddad.*

*I'm going to pretend for a moment that you will get this letter, and I'm not going to think long and hard about what I'm going to write. This is because I don't know if I believe Sabrina, and I don't want to tie myself up in knots thinking about what I should say if you're never going to read it. It's also because I believe a letter is always better written straight from the heart.*

*I don't want to reveal too many things because you've still got your life to live, but I want you to know I'm happy. I'm training to be a chef. Food's my passion, and one day I'd like to open a restaurant. In under two weeks, I'm marrying a man who makes me laugh and feel like the only woman in the world, and I can't wait to be his wife. His name's Mark Edwards, and he's in the army like Granddad was.*

*The day he asked me to marry him was the happiest of my life because I knew the moment I met him that I wanted to be his wife one day. Granddad told me that you always said you knew the first time you saw him that he was the one for you even though you were only kids.*

*I wear your emerald engagement ring as my own now because I know how happy you and Granddad were. I'm also going to wear the wedding dress you and your mam wore on my day, and one day I'll pass it on to my daughter if I'm blessed with one.*

*It's the dress that's brought this letter to you. I took it into Brides of Bold Street just as you did to have it altered and met Evelyn Flooks and Sabrina. Who knows, Nan, perhaps it was fate?*

*I do know, though, I love you, and I especially want you to know that.*

*Your Alice*

*PS: Granddad called you his little Viking. That's something only I would know.*

Lily blinked. Was it true? It was too much to comprehend. How was she supposed to believe she was holding a letter from her future granddaughter? She folded it up feeling most peculiar and placed it back in the envelope with the picture before tucking it away in her handbag.

She could feel Sabrina and Adam looking at her expectantly.

'Where are you staying?' she asked after a beat.

'We've nowhere to go,' Sabrina stated simply.

Lily met Sabrina's umber-eyed gaze across the table. What was it about her? It was there – tantalisingly out of reach on her mind's periphery. She didn't understand any of this, but she did know what it was like to be alone. The scars left mentally by Mrs Cox still tingled from time to time, and the wound of the woman she'd called her mam's death throbbed despite what she'd since learned.

Max wouldn't believe them if they relayed their far-fetched tale, and he'd tell her she shouldn't either. He'd convince himself the letter and photograph were trickery, being far too practical to take any of what she'd listened to this afternoon on board. Of course, he'd be angry she'd heard them out in the first place, but he didn't need to know, did he?

Her mind raced ahead. She could hardly believe she was entertaining taking them in. She didn't want to lie to Max either. She could tell him a half-truth – something along the lines of how she'd met Sabrina and Adam in a tearoom today and got chatting. They'd lost their home and had been billeted with a local family, but it was less than ideal given how crowded it was, and she'd asked them to stay because, well, because she had a spare room and it was the charitable thing to do. She should have done it before now given how many were suffering in overcrowded makeshift accommodation. And he wouldn't pry once he'd heard what happened. He knew some stories were too painful to share; he'd never mentioned his childhood, not since the day he'd left it behind in Skelmersdale.

'I need to get home.' Lily got up from her seat and before she could change her mind said, 'C'mon. You can come with me.'

∽

Lily chattered inconsequentially on as they made their way to the bus stop. Now she'd made her mind up that Sabrina and Adam could stay, she seemed keen to regain some sense of normalcy.

The bus whined to a halt a few minutes after they'd reached the stop, and they clambered aboard, Lily paying their fares. Sabrina squeezed in by the window, and Adam slid in next to her. The bus wasn't full, and Lily sat in front of them, twisting in her seat. 'Will you promise me something?'

Sabrina and Adam waited to hear what she was going to ask them.

'Don't breathe a word of what you told me to my Max. He wouldn't believe any of it anyway. So I think it's best to tell him you're homeless because you've fallen on hard times. Which isn't exactly a lie. I'll say we got talking at the tearoom, and given there's a spare room at mine, I invited you to stay. He doesn't need to know all the rest.'

'We won't say a thing,' Sabrina assured her, and Adam nodded his agreement. 'But won't he want to know more about who we are?'

Lily shook her head. 'Max takes things at face value. He won't pry. It's not his way.'

The trio lapsed into silence, and Sabrina, her nose pressed to the window, stared out in disbelief as the bus took them down streets where the Luftwaffe had done their worst, leaving behind shells of buildings that now stood like empty carcasses. Rubble was piled high on the pavement, so pedestrians had to step out onto the road to walk around it. She felt Adam's breath on her neck as he too leaned over to look.

These sights were the norm for Lily and the rest of Liverpool, Sabrina thought, her throat tightening at the destruction the Blitz had caused. She'd seen photographs, of course, but they were nothing compared to seeing it first-hand.

'Awful, in't it? So much loss,' Lily said, her eyes filling. Perhaps it felt like she was seeing it all again for the first time, like these two were.

Sabrina didn't know what to say, so she said the first thing that came to mind. 'It won't always be like this, Lily. Liverpool will be rebuilt.' She knew it was trite, especially for people like Lily, who'd lost their nearest and dearest, because buildings could be fixed, but people couldn't be replaced. She chewed her bottom lip to stop herself from crying.

∼

Lily stared at Sabrina. Her eyes were an unusual shade, Lily's attention drawn to them by the unshed tears that shone there. Brandy sprang to mind as she tried to name the iridescent shade of brown. She knew someone else with eyes that colour – Sarah's mam, Fern. It struck her then that Fern had said the exact same thing to her about it not always being like this, as if she too had known what the future held.

Her heart began to bang against her chest. It was a preposterous idea, and she tried to shoo it away. It wouldn't disappear though, the question slowly crystalizing in her mind.

Could Fern Carter be the woman Sabrina had come to find?

## 22

Lily grew more convinced as the bus rattled along that she'd just solved a piece of Sabrina's mystery. Fern Carter – her dear friend's mam, the woman whom she thought of as a second mother since losing her own – had to be Sabrina's mother too. The similarities now she'd placed them were impossible to ignore: they had the same slightly uptilted noses, and although Fern now had grey streaks at her temples, their hair was a similar shade of reddish-gold. The more she stared, the more she could see Sabrina took after Fern more than Sarah and Alfie, who had their dad's darker colouring. It was inconceivable though and so out of the realms of possibility, but truth could be stranger than fiction, so did that mean she was right? Could it also be true? Could any of this be true?

She fidgeted in her seat, taking a surreptitious glance at the couple she'd taken under her wing for reasons that were still unclear to her – although now she wondered if she'd unconsciously picked up on Sabrina's resemblance to Fern, whom she adored.

As people clambered on board or jumped off the doubledecker, Lily thought about Fern's funny ways and the feeling she'd had that Sarah's mam was privy to knowing what lay ahead for them all sometimes. Sarah had often wondered out loud whether her mam had been gifted with second sight, and her being from the future would make sense of Fern's funny ways – there were those who said she was eccentric, while others sniffed that she was far too modern in her ideas of how things should be done. Perhaps it truly was the latter.

Their stop loomed, and Lily was aware of a prickling at the back of her neck as she recalled Sarah laughingly telling her more than once that her dad often said her mam belonged in another time.

'Penny for them?' Sabrina asked, but Lily wasn't ready to share her swirling thoughts – not yet. Maybe she never would be. She simply couldn't wrap her head around it all.

What she did know, however, was that her loyalties lay with the Carters, and if Fern had never shared any of what Lily suspected about where she came from with her family, then it certainly wasn't her place to do so – not without talking to Fern first. Say Sabrina really was Fern's daughter, separated from her as a small child by a time portal, and she blustered in announcing this to the family. The truth could blow the Carters apart, doing every bit as much damage as the Luftwaffe's bombs. Lily wouldn't be responsible for that. Her hand reached for the cord, and she pulled it.

'This is us.'

She'd barely had a chance to slot the key in the front door when Mrs Dixon popped her head out next door. 'You've visitors I see, Lily.'

Lily sighed. She was fond of her neighbour, but she was a terrible curtain twitcher. 'I have yes. Not much gets past you, does it?'

'I pride myself on keeping an eye on the comings and goings along Needham Road. You know that, Lily.'

'Yes, and I'm grateful to you.'

Mrs Dixon had ensured her house didn't become home to squatters or a playground for naughty children during her time staying with her aunt and uncle. It would take a brave soul to take the woman on when she was wielding her wooden spoon, that was certain!

'As it happens, I was watching out for you because I made you this.' She held out a cloth-covered dish. 'Potato and onion hotpot. I thought you needed fattening up. It will stretch to three if you've some bread and jam for afters.'

'That's very kind of you, Mrs Dixon. And this is Adam and his wife, Sabrina.'

She noticed Sabrina's face pinken – likely at the mention of being Adam's wife – as she gave her nosy neighbour the story she planned on telling Max later, and when she'd finished, she added what she thought was a nice touch. 'We have to help those less fortunate than ourselves, don't we, Mrs Dixon? And poor Sabrina and Adam here have nowhere else to go,' Lily said, opening her door.

'Yes, that's true.' Mrs Dixon smiled warmly at the couple. 'Are you putting the kettle on then, Lily?' she asked, thrusting the dish at Sabrina so she could close her front door.

Sabrina and Adam were upstairs in Lily's old room resting, worn out from their day. Lily had reheated Mrs Dixon's tasty dinner and, as she'd suggested, filled them up on jam and bread for afters. It had been a busy afternoon, with everything that had happened since meeting them outside Brides of Bold Street, and Lily stifled a yawn as – having refused the couple's offer of help – she tidied the remainder of their meal away.

The price exacted in return for the hotpot had been the Spanish Inquisition. There'd been no stopping Mrs Dixon once she had her brew in front of her. Her mam had been a fan of Agatha Christie mystery novels, and Mrs Dixon was like a chubby Miss Marple, Lily had thought, only half listening to the rapid-fire questions being shot across the table. It was just as well Adam and Sabrina had been quick off the mark with their replies or the woman would have smelled a rat, and then she'd have been like a dog with a bone until she got to the truth of what had brought them to Lily's home. What would her gossipy neighbour have made of their fantastical time-travel tale? The thought had made her smile, despite her racing mind.

Now she wrung the dishcloth out, leaving the dishes to drain on the worktop. It was time to put her feet up in the sitting room. She planned on pulling the letter from her future granddaughter – which was plain spooky – out from where she'd stashed it in her pocket and taking her time rereading it. Then she would call round to the Carters' to see Sarah – but would get Fern alone so she could have a word. If she tossed back her head and laughed in that big-hearted manner of hers, then Lily would know for certain she'd got it wrong and was seeing things that didn't exist. That was the first step in unravelling the mystery of the couple upstairs.

No sooner had she sat down in the armchair where once her mam had sat of an evening knitting, however, than the front door burst open.

'Lily! The Nazis have surrendered. Turn the wireless on. Winnie's going to speak at some point. We don't want to miss his speech.'

The Nazis had surrendered! This news swept away the strangeness of the afternoon and her plans to call round to the Carters' house.

But before she could reach the wireless, she found herself being swung in the air by a jubilant Max.

'Can you believe it? It's over, me little Viking. We beat the bastards!' He was grinning from ear to ear. 'I left my dinner half eaten on the table, I was so desperate to get here.' Max still lived with his brother and his family.

She giggled with a mix of surprise and excitement at the news and at being picked up like so. Of course, the whole country had known it was coming, but it was a different matter altogether for it to be made official.

He kissed both her cheeks, his lips making loud smacking sounds in the quiet room.

Then he twirled her again, and she laughed, feeling giddy. 'Put me down; you're making me dizzy!' She wanted to hear the news with her own ears, and once her feet were back on the ground, she caught her breath and switched the radio on. The droll BBC announcer's voice filled the room, informing them that the Nazis had indeed surrendered.

Lily flopped back down in her seat. She couldn't stop smiling. 'There'll be a holiday tomorrow for sure.' It occurred to her then that as momentous as the news was, babies would still be born, people would still pass away, and the tide of the Mersey would ebb and flow. Life, as it had during the war, would go on, just as Fern had said it would.

Max shrugged. 'I heard talk the dockworkers might even get two days off after the official announcement's made. We won't know, though, until Winnie's said his piece. But, of course, no one knows when that will be.'

Lily wasn't a drinker, and neither of her parents had been either. A sherry decanter three-quarters full of the rich golden liquid was tucked away in the cabinet upon which the wireless sat though, brought out for celebratory moments like birthdays and Christmas. And this was definitely an occasion worthy of a tot!

She retrieved two glasses, wiping the dust from them with the hem of her skirt before setting them down on the sideboard. The decanter's stopper was sticky, and she jiggled it, breathing in the foreign, spicy, almost woody aroma once she'd released it. Then she poured two small measures and handed a glass to Max.

'It's got to be a good omen for us,' she said as he clinked his glass with hers. 'Not starting married life under the shadow of war.'

Max nodded, and as Lily raised the glass to her lips, he said, 'I think I should make a toast.'

Lily paused and studied his face from under her lashes, unable to read his expression.

He stared at the amber liquid in his schooner for a moment and then looked up, raising his glass once more to Lily's. 'To absent friends and family. May God be with them.'

'May God be with them,' Lily repeated woodenly. She understood as she knocked her glass against his that while they were right to be triumphant, others, like herself, would still be mourning loved ones whose futures had been cut short. Europe's victory over the Germans was bittersweet.

'Lily, I know you've been struggling with all that you've learned about your aunt, and your mum and dad, but life's short, sweetheart. Surely if this war's taught us nothing else, it's taught us that.'

Lily felt the hard kernel that had settled inside her where her mam and aunt were concerned soften a tad. All this pain and anger consuming her at what should be a joyous time was no good. She was going to marry the man she loved, after all. There should be no clouds hanging over her. It occurred to her that she couldn't change the past, but perhaps she could understand it a little better. 'You're right,' she said softly.

They drank the sweet alcohol down, and then there was a creak followed by footfall on the stairs. Max raised a questioning eyebrow at Lily. 'Is someone else here?'

Max's cheeks had reddened from the shot of alcohol, and he turned expectantly to the door to see who it was. He instantly bristled at the sight of a strange man in his fiancée's house, but the rigidity of his shoulders softened when he saw Adam wasn't alone; Sabrina was following behind him. He turned back to Lily, a question in his ice-blue eyes.

Lily smiled reassuringly. 'Max, this is Adam and Sabrina. Max is my fiancé.' Then, to Max, she said, 'I met them today.'

Adam thrust a hand out toward Max, who stared at it for a moment before taking it. Lily noted that he shook it a tad harder than was necessary before releasing his grip and looking past him to where Sabrina stood. His smile was curious as he took her in, and Lily knew he too thought she looked familiar. 'Have we met somewhere?' he asked her.

Sabrina shook her head. 'I don't think that's likely.'

He focused on Lily, waiting for her to elaborate on what the strangers had been doing upstairs.

'We got chatting in a tearoom today,' she supplied, her eyes bright from the alcohol. 'I'd gone to see Evelyn at Brides of Bold Street to tell her I no longer need my dress.' She looked down at the swirls of patterned carpet, bracing for Max's reaction.

'Ah, Lily, why'd you do that?'

She wouldn't meet his gaze. 'You know why.'

'It doesn't mean I have to agree with it. You'll regret making decisions in anger. I don't want you to look back on our wedding day with any regrets whatsoever.'

They never fought, but they'd argued over her refusal to go and see her aunt and hear her out. Admitting she might have been wrong wasn't something that came easily to Lily, but she'd begun to suspect it was the case this time.

'G'won then.' Max sighed. 'You all met in a tearoom.'

Lily carried on with the tale she'd told Mrs Dixon earlier, and when she'd finished, Max appeared to have moved on from his pique over her decision not to wear her mam's wedding dress because he was smiling.

'My Lily's got a big heart,' he said to the couple, but he wasn't done with them yet.

Lily watched as he sized Sabrina and Adam up, giving them

a slow once-over, and now it was her who smiled, touched by his protectiveness. He must have decided they looked trustworthy and that Lily wouldn't get up tomorrow morning and find the family silver gone because he showed them his glass. 'We were toasting the good news.'

'The Nazis have surrendered,' Lily supplied, relieved he'd accepted the story she'd given him. 'It's wonderful, isn't it? Would you like a sherry?'

Sabrina and Adam couldn't help but nod enthusiastically at this news, even though they must have already known it was coming.

'Lovely,' Sabrina murmured, glancing at Adam, who, Lily noted, still looked as pale as he had earlier. She supposed it made sense if this was his first experience of time travelling. 'We'd love a tot, wouldn't we, Adam?'

Adam nodded mutely.

So it was that the only person unaware of the truth about Sabrina and Adam's sudden appearance as they raised their glasses was Max.

## 23

May the eighth dawned with no broadcast from Winston Churchill having been made as yet, but that had done nothing to dampen the sense of anticipation of the day that lay ahead. Nor did the gun-metal sky blanketing Liverpool flatten its residents' spirits because the streets were soon brightened by the colourful bunting strewn across them.

Children ran about excitedly outside while mams busied themselves in the kitchen for the street parties that would surely follow. It was only a matter of time now until the ceasefire was officially declared. Dads whistled away outside as they painted the bomb shelters with colourful union jacks. The wirelesses were tuned to the BBC. Harry Leader and his band were broadcast into homes across the country before moving into the daily service.

On Needham Road, Sabrina watched the goings-on outside from the front room's window with a mix of curiosity and awe. She and Adam had made themselves scarce after their tot of sherry, not wanting to fend off awkward questions from Max, saying they were exhausted. It was true. Still, she'd tossed and turned, wondering how she would go about searching for her mother, and when the impossibility of it all had threatened to overwhelm her, she'd burrowed into Adam. He'd held her close, promising that everything would be OK.

Today, however, adrenaline at the thought of what the day might bring prevented her from feeling tired. Adam, too, was fidgety and had gone outside after breakfast to help fasten the bunting and hang the flags. He'd told Sabrina that things didn't seem any less strange in the light of a new day, but he wanted to pitch in and feel part of the festive atmosphere. It was the first time he'd left her side since they'd stepped through the portal.

Sabrina wondered what Aunt Evie was doing to celebrate with Bold Street's residents and business owners and, for a moment, yearned to be there with her. She shook the thoughts away because they were futile. Aunt Evie wouldn't know her; she was here in 1945 for a reason. To find her mother. Today was the day that might finally happen.

~

Lily was busy putting away last night's dishes. She'd tucked the letter Sabrina had given her yesterday away inside an old coat pocket in her wardrobe. There'd been no chance to reread it last night as it had been late by the time Max went home.

Today, she needed to call in on Fern before she did anything else and tell her the story of the strange couple she'd met the previous day. If Fern laughed and said it was a fun story she was after telling, there'd be no need to mention Sabrina's search for her mother and she could stop dwelling on the unsettling business of her time-travelling guests. At least for today, at any rate. She wasn't rostered at the hospital, but she knew her fellow nurses would be celebrating, and she didn't want to miss out because today was history in the making. She was desperate to share the day with her best friend but wouldn't be able to relax in her company until she'd seen her mam first. It wouldn't take long – the Carters' house was only around the corner.

Later, she'd meet up with Max. He'd already be in his khaki uniform, out on the streets with the other lads who'd served and made it home. She hoped today would be the last day he ever had to wear it.

'I'm going to head to the Royal,' Lily said, using the name locals called the hospital as she sought Sabrina out. The other woman was still where she'd left her, staring out the window. 'You and Adam should go to the town hall. The mayor's going to announce the ceasefire from there.' She hesitated, not knowing for certain yet whether she was leading them on a wild goose chase as she added, 'It's as good a place as any to start your search.'

Sabrina nodded and let the curtain fall.

'Good luck today. I hope you find what you're looking for.' Whether she believed Sabrina's story or not, it didn't take away from the fact that Sabrina clearly did, and she liked the woman, even though part of her wished they'd never met.

'Ta, but you know, Lily, now I'm so close to finding answers, I'm frightened.'

'Of what?'

'I've never thought further than finding her. It's what's spurred me on. Of course, I assumed she wanted to be found, but what if she doesn't?'

Lily felt the hairs on the back of her neck stand up. Yes – what if she didn't want to be found? The look on Sabrina's face made her seem very young and vulnerable, even though she had to be a few years older than her, and Lily gave her a spontaneous hug despite her own misgivings. 'Then at least you'll know. I think it must be the not knowing that's the hardest.'

The same could be said of her own circumstances, she thought. Not knowing why her mam had chosen to keep the circumstances of her birth secret was eating away at her. She had to know the truth too.

Sabrina squeezed her back before Lily released her, finding it difficult to look her in the eye. She needed to change into her nurse's uniform before heading out, and with that in mind, she was glad of the excuse to race upstairs to change.

∼

Adam moseyed back inside, shaking his head and looking at her; Sabrina wondered when she'd stop being surprised upon seeing his short back and sides haircut.

'It's the weirdest thing,' he said, scratching the near bald side of his head.

'Your hair?'

He laughed. 'No. Although it is taking some getting used to. I'm talking about us being here in 1945. I've just been talking with people who don't know what happens over the next thirty-seven years. I mean there're cold wars, assassinations, AIDS, Thatcher—'

'I get the idea.'

'It's weird though, in't it? I mean right now, today, them out there don't even know about the atomic bombs on Japan.'

Sabrina wasn't arguing with him. It *was* weird. 'There are good things too though.'

'Yeah.'

Sabrina was suddenly desperate to find the good things. 'Like man walking on the moon, the Concorde and – and...' She thought hard. 'And Woodstock.'

'Woodstock? Where'd you pull that from?' Adam stared at her, and the look on her face made her giggle. Then he began to laugh too. 'If anyone could hear our conversation...' he began.

'They'd think we were raving lunatics.'

'Barmy,' he agreed, pulling her to him, and she rested her head on his chest, feeling his heart beating beneath his shirt.

'I'm glad I'm here experiencing this with you,' he said softly, his breath ruffling her hair.

'I'm glad you are too.'

Lily bowled back into the room then, and they sprang apart.

'Lily, I wouldn't have recognised you,' Sabrina exclaimed. She had been transformed into a nurse.

Lily grinned. 'The hair would have given it away.'

It was true, Sabrina thought, noting the copper tendrils escaping from beneath her nurse's cap.

'Did Sabrina tell you I suggested you should head to the town hall? There'll be loads of people gathering there to hear the Lord Mayor's speech.' Lily directed her question to Adam.

He, in turn, looked to Sabrina, who repeated Lily's earlier sentiment. 'It's as good a place as any to start.'

The heavens had opened by the time the trio left Needham Road, but nobody cared. They wouldn't melt. Tables were being dragged out onto the street – a hint of the parties to come regardless of what the weather decided to do. Adam and Sabrina waved Lily off then joined the wet, bedraggled throng bunched up on a tram to rattle through streets where parades of people were already singing and dancing, undeterred by the rain.

The noise was stupendous, with the bells pealing from churches and municipal buildings across the city to mingle in with laughter and shouts from the celebrating thousands.

Adam nudged Sabrina. They grinned at the sight of a woman banging a petrol drum she'd slung around her neck with sticks as she led an enthusiastic crowd in 'It's a Long Way to Tipperary'.

This would be a day no one experiencing it would ever forget.

Sabrina felt a tap on her shoulder and twisted round to be informed by the young woman squeezed in behind her that she had paper stuck to her shoe. A glance down revealed some sort of flyer caught under her heel, and she retrieved it, giving it a cursory glance.

It was a bright and bawdy advertisement for a performance of *Lady Here's a Laugh*. The text boldly stated there'd be glamourous dresses and beautiful scenery and two performances at the Shakespeare Theatre on Fraser Street that very day. The picture of the cast held her attention though. The fellow peering around the lead actors had a twinkle in his eyes she recognised. She scanned the names of the performers, and her heart began to thump.

Fred Markham. It was him! Her Fred. She'd been right. He had been on the stage. She hoped she had time to see the play and to speak to him. She'd dearly love to know his story. She wanted to call in on Aunt Evie today too, though she had to find her mother first. Her eyes darted everywhere, scanning faces as she searched for something familiar in the features of the strangers surrounding her.

They jumped off the tram and joined the sea of bodies flooding onto Castle Street; they were all gathering to hear the Lord Mayor of Liverpool's ceasefire speech. The sight of so many people was disheartening, but Sabrina swallowed the feeling down. They'd come this far. Fate would lead her to her mam somehow. Mystic Lou had prophesied it would happen, and that was what she had to hold on to – though as they were jostled along, she decided that her priority needed to be holding on to Adam for now. She was terrified of losing him in the melee.

The rain was short-lived, and the clouds had been swept away to make way for sunshine by the time Lord Sefton stepped out onto the town hall balcony. From there, overlooking Castle Street, he announced to the waiting crowd the cessation of hostilities. Patriotic music blared, and the crowd erupted, with hats being thrown into the air and strangers turning to hug strangers. The city was united in shared joy.

The music eventually quietened, and a hush descended over the revelry. Then, shortly after three p.m., Winston Churchill's speech was broadcast through loudspeakers. He reminded the British people that while they could allow themselves a brief period of rejoicing, they must not forget for a moment the toils and efforts that lay ahead. He spoke too of Japan as yet being undefeated. And Sabrina and Adam clutched each other a little tighter. But, for now though, celebrating was the only thing on the British people's minds. The victory bells began to ring out again as their prime minister's speech drew to a close, and a cheer went up over the city, the likes of which had never been heard before or since.

On the Mersey, a ship's hooter rang out.

It was official: the war was over. Sabrina stood on her tiptoes and kissed Adam firmly on the lips.

## 24

Sabrina and Adam had skimmed over faces in the crowds around the town hall for hours to no avail. So finally, as the noise and volume of people began to take their toll they decided to make their way back to Lily's house.

They were weary, and the thought of battling the crowd to get to Bold Street to see Aunt Evie or elbowing their way through the throngs to the theatre where Fred was performing was too much, even though Sabrina was curious to see him trotting the boards in his heyday. Besides, the theatre might not even be open with everything happening in the streets. She decided today was a day 'when the show must go on' didn't apply.

A group of young lads already three sheets to the wind struggled to stay upright on the tram. They clutched on to one another, slurring, laughing and not giving a toss as to the spectacle they were making of themselves. A woman beside them tutted under her breath.

'I wonder what the scene's like in the Swan,' Adam said to Sabrina as their stop approached.

'Probably full of lads like that.' She grinned over her

shoulder before jumping nimbly down onto the pavement.

They arrived back at Needham Road to a busy tableau. Tables now lined the best part of the road. Sheets were draped over them, serving as tablecloths, and plates upon plates of food had been ferried out from the houses either side. Children wearing rosettes pinned to their chests and party hats on their heads enjoyed sandwiches and home-made lemonade, making the most of being allowed to help themselves. At the same time, parents dressed in their finery milled about, beaming and keeping a loose eye on proceedings.

A woman with dark curls wearing a string of creamy pearls and a slash of red lippy along with a pinny over her dress approached them as they drew nearer to Lily's house. 'You're young Lily Tubb's guests, aren't you?'

'Yes, we are,' Sabrina affirmed.

'Well, here you are then.' She retrieved two plates from a pile on the table and said, 'Don't be shy. Fill your boots. There's enough food there to feed an army.' She surveyed her community's effort with pride.

'Ta.' Adam didn't need to be asked twice, and he reached over to pluck a sandwich from a plate, quickly moving on to a pasty and the scones with jam and mock cream. Sabrina realised she was starving too. They hadn't eaten since breakfast, so the spread would serve as lunch and dinner.

It wasn't long before they'd taken the woman at her word, and the plates they carried in the direction of Lily's house were piled high.

They perched on the front steps and ate lustily while watching the celebrations on the busy road as dusk deepened.

At the top of the road, Sabrina saw a girl in a nurse's uniform making her way down the hectic street and, thinking it was Lily, waved. It was only as the young woman drew nearer that she realised her hair was dark. It wasn't Lily heading toward them but Sarah, whom Sabrina recognised from Alice's precious photograph. She'd made a beautiful bridesmaid, and she looked like the sort of nurse you'd want to see administering your medicine because her eyes – the colour of sable as they crinkled in greeting – were kind. Sabrina liked her on the spot.

She smiled up at her, abandoning her food and getting to her feet. 'Hello, I'm Sabrina, and this is my, erm, husband, Adam.'

Adam held up a hand in acknowledgement though it was clear he had no idea who Sarah was. *You're not supposed to know who she is either*, Sabrina reminded herself.

'Hello, I'm Sarah. Lily's friend. Is she in? I didn't see her out on the street. Only we were supposed to meet earlier today at the Royal, but she didn't show.' Her brow furrowed. 'She could have got caught up in all the mayhem with the celebrations on her way there, of course.'

'No. She's not home. We haven't seen her since she left this morning. She did say she was on her way to the hospital though.'

Seeing Sarah's puzzled expression – she was obviously trying to work out who they were in relation to her best friend – Sabrina explained they were staying with Lily and how the situation had come about.

Sarah took the explanation at face value then scanned the street in case she'd somehow missed Lily in the melee.

'We've not long come back from the town hall,' Sabrina told her, 'and it was bedlam, so I think you're right and it's likely she got caught up in all the celebrations on her way to the Royal. She's bound to show up here soon. Have you eaten?'

'I have, far too much, but I will join you if you don't mind. I fancy a glass of squash. Can I fetch you both one?'

'Yes, please,' Sabrina said, and Adam echoed her.

'Right, back in a jiffy. Oh, there's Mrs Dixon. I better say hello to her first.' Sarah made her way over to Lily's neighbour.

When she was out of earshot, Sabrina sank back onto the

doorstep. 'I wonder if Mrs Dixon will press Sarah for more information about us.'

'Probably. That or ask for advice on how to treat nosyitis.' Adam grinned, making Sabrina laugh, before taking a bite of the triangle sandwich and mumbling through his mouthful, 'This potted meat is tasty.'

'I liked the egg mayonnaise ones.'

Sarah returned a while later, balancing three enamel mugs full of orange squash. 'Sorry I took so long. Mrs Dixon bent me ear off,' she said, smiling as she passed out the drinks. 'Still no sign of her then?'

'No. Bunch up,' Sabrina said to Adam and shuffled along to make room on the doorstep. Sarah sat down next to her.

'We've to return these cups to Mrs Reid's table across the way when we've finished with them,' she said, taking a sip from the mug. 'Have you seen the size of the bonfire they're busy building on the green at the end of the road? All the children from the streets around here are involved.'

'No, but I did see some kids carting a load of stuff down the road earlier. So that's what it would have been for,' Adam said, half to himself.

'You probably saw our Alfie, me younger brother, then – he's in the thick of it. A proper firebug that one. They'll be lighting it once it's dark. We should go down and watch,' Sarah suggested.

Sabrina was instantly on high alert, and any weariness from the hecticness of the day was banished. Mystic Lou's words about dancing flames galvanised her.

An excited shout went up then as the streetlights flickered on for the first time in what felt like a very long while.

～

The bonfire's flames were leaping high, consuming the effigy on top of the pyre. Young lads fed the fire with glee while mothers did their best to keep their little ones away from the showering sparks. The faces of the people gathered to celebrate glowed orange as Lily charged toward Fern breathlessly.

'I've been looking for you all day!' Lily was so relieved to have at last located Sarah's mam she felt tears spring forth. Nor was there any sign of Sabrina and Adam – a good thing, she thought, her heel throbbing with a threatened blister. The day hadn't panned out as she'd planned at all, and as the hours had ticked by in a fruitless search, she'd become increasingly panicked by the idea that Sabrina and Adam might somehow catch sight of Fern and instantly pick up on the resemblance she'd seen between her dear friend's mam and Sabrina. After her initial feeling of having met Sabrina, or at least seen her before, once she'd made the connection, it had become plain as day, so there was every chance someone else could jump to the same conclusion, and that could be disastrous if she didn't forewarn Fern.

As the fear that she'd be too late had grown, Lily had tried to keep things in perspective. Sabrina and Adam simply spotting Fern through the sea of people was hardly a likely scenario – though being part of their story in the first place was the farthest thing from a likely scenario imaginable, which meant it wasn't out of the realms of possibility.

She'd gone straight to the Carters' house as planned after leaving home that morning, but no one had been in, and her neighbour – tarred with the same brush as Mrs Dixon – had said Fern and the younger children had gone to join the festivities outside St George's Hall – or was it the town hall? She couldn't recall for certain which. Lily had decided to start with St George's Hall, not anticipating how long it would take to fight her way through the crowds milling in and out of Lime Street Station.

It wasn't long before she'd decided she hadn't just sent Sabrina and Adam off on a fool's errand – she was on one herself. How on earth did she expect to find Fern amongst so many people? It was like searching for a particular grain of sand on the beach. And she didn't know for certain she was even there. There'd been a moment where she'd thought to heck with it – she would forget all about Fern, Sabrina and Adam and go to the Royal as planned before it was too late. Then, thinking of Sarah and how she'd feel facing her but unable to share what was on her mind, she'd steeled her resolve, giving up on St George's to head for the town hall.

Now here she was. Her tears spilled over. She'd finally made it back but was dead on her feet from elbowing her way through the hordes, scanning faces all day and into the evening to no avail. She hadn't eaten since breakfast either, and instead of feeling jubilant, she's spent the day detached from the city's celebrations, unable to give in to the festive atmosphere until she located Fern.

'Isn't it wonderful, Lily!' Fern fetched a hanky tucked into the cuff of her blouse.

She must have mistaken her tears for ones of joy at the momentous occasion, Lily thought, nodding mutely as she took the hanky and dabbed them away. Then, finding her voice, she said, 'I must speak with you about something. It's important, Fern.'

'Now? What is it? Has something happened?' Fern had picked up on the urgency in Lily's tone and was panicked by it.

'Everybody's alright. Sorry, I don't mean to frighten you, and to be frank you might think what I have to tell you is completely ridiculous. I'll hold my hand up to jumping to conclusions that aren't there if that's the case.'

*Please let it be the case*, Lily silently prayed, suddenly wishing it wasn't her who was going to have to open this can of worms.

'Lily, you're frightening me. Would you just come out with it?'

'Not here. Somewhere quieter.' Lily took Fern by the elbow, intending to steer her away from the bonfire so she didn't have to shout over the top of the excited shrieks as children continued to toss sticks on the fire.

∼

'Oh, look, that's our Alfie over there. The lad poking at the fire with that big stick. I told you he's a firebug. Look how close he's getting.' Sarah tutted as they entered the circle of people fanning out around the bonfire. 'I shall have to pull him away if he keeps that up, or he'll fall into it if he's not careful.'

Sabrina and Adam looked at the lad in short pants having a glorious time with his stick.

'I would have been exactly the same at his age,' Adam said, laughing as he gave Sabrina's hand a squeeze.

Sabrina squeezed back, knowing what it meant. Like her, he couldn't believe they were here amongst this party that would go down in the history books.

Sarah, still keeping one eye on her younger brother, said, 'Dad's in France still; he's hoping to be demobbed and back home soon. He'll take Alfie in hand when he gets back. Mam does her best, but he's been running wild of late.' Sarah's dark eyes looked enormous in the firelight and glistened as she said, 'Oh, I wish Dad was here to see all of this.'

'I'm sure the atmosphere in France is equally joyous,' Sabrina said soothingly.

'Yes, I'm sure you're right, but France isn't home, is it?'

'No. Of course not.' Before Sabrina could think of something comforting to add, Adam suddenly pointed through the haze of smoke and spitting sparks.

'Lily's over there.'

The two women tracked his finger to where Lily, still in her nurse's uniform, was leading another woman away from the fray surrounding the bonfire.

'That's me mam with her,' Sarah said, her eyes flitting between Lily and her mam and Alfie, who was still dancing dangerously close to the flames.

'Alfie!' she shouted over the din. 'Stand back a bit.'

The little boy heard his name and did as he was told.

'Well, that's a first,' Sarah said, grinning. 'Come on. I want to know where Lily's been all day.'

She weaved her way eagerly through her immediate neighbours and those from surrounding streets, shouting greetings, with Sabrina and Adam in her wake.

'Lily, Mam!' Sarah called out as they drew closer. 'Where are they going?' Sabrina caught her muttering before she called out again, louder this time.

Fern stopped in her tracks upon hearing her daughter's voice and shook Lily – who was now trying to drag her away – off. 'Stop it, Lily. Sarah's wanting to catch us up. There's nothing you can say to me you can't say in front of her too. You know that.'

Sabrina frowned. What on earth was Lily up to? Why was she trying to run away from them like so?

A kerfuffle by the fire caught the attention of the small group before anyone could ask Lily where she'd been all day.

'Where's Alfie?' Fern asked, concern creasing her face.

'He was by the bonfire, Mam,' Sarah said, squinting into the melee.

All eyes scanned the area as the sound of a crying child grew louder.

'That's Alfie!' Fern cried, but before she could move off to look for her son, a large woman elbowed past Sabrina and Adam, and there, trailing behind her, was a wailing lad clutching his wrist. He ran to his mam and buried his face in her skirt.

'There you are, Fern. Your Alfie's only gone and burned himself. You'll want to get some cold water on it quick as you can.'

'Alfie, I told you not to get so close to the fire,' Sarah admonished, fright making her sharp. Her words only served to make her brother howl even louder.

'It's too late for tellings-off now. There, there, son. You'll live. Come with me, my brave soldier. Lily, your house is closer – do you mind if we pop in there?'

Lily's eyes were swinging wildly from Sabrina and Adam back to Sarah and Fern. 'Of course. I'll come with you.'

'Me, too,' Sarah chimed in.

'There's no need for you two to miss out on the fun,' Lily was quick to toss back at Sabrina and Adam before hurrying away with Fern, a wailing Alfie and Sarah. 'I'll be back later.'

∼

Adam stared after them. He'd only caught a few glimpses of Sarah's mam's worried face in the firelight, but her eyes had transfixed him. They were the same curious amber as Sabrina's, and there was something more... He had the strangest feeling they'd inadvertently stumbled into the woman they'd travelled back thirty-seven years to find.

Sabrina's mother.

'*I see fire, flames dancing. Look for the woman you seek amidst the celebrations,*' Sabrina said softly.

Adam turned toward Sabrina, who was staring, mesmerised, at the group of three women and one young lad. She didn't so much as blink until they'd disappeared from sight. Then she turned those brandy-coloured eyes on him.

'Adam, it was her.' Her body had begun to tremble.

Adam put a protective arm around her shoulder, and she leaned into him.

'She's got other children. Not just me.' The shock was evident in Sabrina's voice, and when she next spoke, her voice was a strangled rasp. 'I never once thought I might have brothers or sisters. I have to speak to her.'

'Of course you do.' Adam stroked her hair, as shocked as she was, but then he didn't know what he'd thought they might find. A woman in eighties clobber wandering about lost in time, like in his uncle's favourite anecdote? He certainly hadn't expected to meet a mother of two children who was clearly settled into her life in an era that wasn't her own. His role now was to be strong for Sabrina. It was why he'd come. 'We'll go back to Lily's. There's a chance we could be wrong.'

'We're not wrong,' Sabrina said, already pulling free as she began to walk away from the flames.

## 25

Lily's front door was unlocked, and Sabrina and Adam didn't knock as they let themselves in, following the voice through to the kitchen. Alfie was sitting on the worktop beside the sink, legs – with the scabby knees and scuffed shoes of a young lad – dangling while his mother held his hand under the tap's running water. His tears had dried up, and he was eating a piece of jam on bread.

Lily was making a cup of tea, and Sarah was sitting at the table, quizzing her friend. Her questions petered off upon seeing the couple enter the space, and Sabrina knew by the way the colour drained from Lily's face that she'd put two and two together. She knew. When had she figured it out? she wondered.

Sarah, meanwhile, picking up on her friend's strange reaction, looked perplexed. How could she not see it? Sabrina wondered when Fern was right there. She stared at the older woman, who was still concerned with her son, willing her to look at her and see who she was.

'Oh, hello. I didn't hear you come in,' Fern said, finally registering their arrival, apparently oblivious to the odd atmosphere.

She glanced toward a white-faced Lily, expecting her to make the introductions. 'You look like you've seen a ghost, Lily. Alfie's going to be fine, you know.'

Lily shook her head but stayed mute.

Sarah scraped her chair back and shot an apologetic glance at Sabrina and Adam. 'Lily?'

Finally, she spoke up. 'Alfie, I think that hand's been under there long enough. Why don't you and Sarah come with me to the bathroom and I'll see if we can't find a dressing?'

'Lily, you've forgotten your manners.' Sarah frowned. 'Mam, this is Sabrina and Adam – they're staying with Lily – and this is my mam, Fern. Mam!' Sarah exclaimed as her mother swooned.

Lily was swift to take action, racing to Fern's side. 'Steady on there.'

All the while, Sabrina was unable to do anything other than cling to Adam.

The older woman gathered herself and mustered a reassuring smile for her daughter and Lily. 'I think it must have been the shock of thinking about what could have happened to Alfie. A sip of water and I'll be fine, girls.' She looked everywhere but at Sabrina as Lily led her to the table and sat her down while Sarah fetched her a drink of water.

Alfie jumped down from the worktop.

'Come on, Alfie,' Lily said. 'Sabrina, Adam, you'll keep an eye on Fern?'

'Of course,' Adam replied.

Sarah looked at her mam. 'You're sure you're all right?'

'Fine, Sarah. Go and keep an eye on your brother and make sure he doesn't fuss for Lily while she dresses his hand.'

Sarah did as she was told, and footfall could quickly be heard going up the stairs.

'It's you, isn't it? You're me mother,' tumbled forth from Sabrina's lips.

Fern jolted as though being startled out of a dream, and she shook her head. 'I don't believe this is happening.' Her hand snaked out unbidden, as if to touch Sabrina's cheek. 'You're real. I'm not dreaming.'

Adam steered Sabrina over to the table.

'I tried to find you. I tried so hard,' Fern was saying as Sabrina and Adam sat down.

'I've tried to find you too.' Sabrina swallowed down all the questions she wanted to ask, not wanting to bombard Fern, who, by the searching look on her face as she studied Sabrina's, felt the same.

'Lily.' Fern straightened. 'She's been trying to tell me about you.'

Sabrina merely nodded confirmation, and Adam held Sabrina's hand tightly under the table.

'Sarah and Alfie don't know.' Fern raised her eyes to the ceiling; movement could be heard upstairs. 'That's why Lily wanted to warn me – for their sake.'

Sabrina wished Lily had given her some forewarning of her suspicions. That way perhaps she wouldn't be feeling as shell-shocked as she did right now. She gazed at this woman whom she felt as if she'd always known yet was a stranger pull a crumpled packet of cigarettes from her pocket. She felt like she was observing her in slow motion as Fern tapped a smoke out and lit it, sucking on it hard before exhaling slowly.

'Please tell me what happened? How we became separated, erm...?' What should she call her? Sabrina wondered.

Fern sat smoking for an infuriating moment longer before speaking. 'I've thought long and hard about what I'd say to you if I ever saw you again, Sabrina, and now the moment's here, I don't know where to start apart from to say I don't expect you to call me mam. That's who I am though. I'm your mother.' She fixed her gaze steadily on Sabrina's.

'Not just *my* mother.'

'No.'

They all jumped at the sudden spluttering crack of fireworks. It was followed by raucous cheering.

'What happened?' Sabrina asked.

Sarah ducked her head around the door. 'Alfie's good as new. Lily's due to meet Max by the bonfire, and I said I'd take Alfie back.' She studied her mother. 'Is everything alright, Mam?'

Fern's head snapped toward her daughter. 'Yes, you three go on to the bonfire. I think Alfie's learned his lesson. I'll join you shortly. We're just enjoying a cup of tea and getting to know one another.' Her reassuring smile didn't quite reach her eyes, however.

The front door banged shut a moment later, and the house fell into silence until Fern took them back to that fateful day in 1983.

∾

It was a normal summer's day, albeit too hot. There'd been no hint of what was to come as Fern pushed Sabrina in the fold-out umbrella pram up Bold Street. At that moment in time, her main worry in life was her hair. She was worried the ridiculous heat would cause the hair she'd spent an age getting oomph into earlier that morning to flop. It wasn't even midday yet, but the day was set to be a scorcher.

'Is he my daddy?' Sabrina demanded as she twisted in her seat, trying to see her mam behind her.

The plump, decidedly middle-class man her daughter was referencing shot Fern a panicked glance before hurrying on his way.

*No chance*, Fern thought as she leaned down toward Sabrina. 'I've told you, Sabby, your daddy is away.' It was true, but she dreaded the day she'd have to tell Sabrina this was a permanent arrangement and not just a holiday.

Sabrina slumped back in her seat and shoved her thumb in her mouth.

Her hair was sticking to her forehead, Fern noticed, relieved the heat meant she would be spared the usual tumble of demands to know more. She blamed the animated woman at the story-time session she'd taken Sabrina to for having read *Are You My Mother?* to her toddler audience. Sabrina had replaced 'mother' with 'daddy' and had been questioning strange men ever since.

Pete, her dad, had buggered off when Sabrina was six weeks old. Fatherhood wasn't for him apparently. Moreover, it was *negatively impacting his music vibes*, he'd said.

Fern hadn't known if motherhood was for her either, but she hadn't had a choice in the matter. There was no walking away from her daughter, nor had she wanted to once she was born. Fern loved her girl with a fierce might that had taken her by surprise. What had surprised her most, though, was the love she received in return. It was unconditional. She'd never experienced a love like that before. Certainly not from her mam, who'd preferred the drugs to her. They'd killed her in the end.

As for Pete, unfortunately, he was more in love with himself than he was with her or Sabrina. He fancied himself Liverpool's answer to Phil Oakey from Human League. He'd even had his hair cut in the same lopsided fashion, and she'd had to hide her lipstick from him.

As he'd swung his duffle bag over his shoulder and headed out the door, Fern had tossed after him that he couldn't play his stupid Yamaha synthesiser to save himself, and his voice sounded like Marianne Faithfull's, only *she* could hold a tune. Her parting shot had been a belter. 'You'd crack the tele screen if you ever make it on *Top of the Pops!*'

She'd met him on a night out with a lass from the hostel

she'd moved into once she'd turned eighteen and was officially too old for the system. It had been an interim fix until a flat could be found. She'd been in and out of foster care all her life, the arrangement becoming permanent when her mam overdosed. Fern had been eleven years old.

She'd thought Pete had a look of Adam Ant about him in his leather trousers, and she'd quite fancied being a musician's girlfriend. Who knew? She might even make the pages of *Teen Beat* if he got one of the gigs he reckoned was in the bag.

So she'd packed her bags and moved into his grotty little flat over a butcher's one month later, glad to see the back of the hostel.

She'd enjoyed playing house, even if the flat was small enough to be a doll's house. It was nice to have a place to call home.

However, Pete's habit of not putting his clean washing away when she left it in a pile on the bed for him had soon become irritating. So had his aversion to doing dishes. Then there was the way he'd leave wet towels wherever they fell on the bathroom floor, so it smelled even damper in there. The gloss had worn off their living arrangement smartly. Worst of all, though, was how he flat-out refused to air his leather trousers on the communal washing line out back for fear of someone nicking them. She'd fully expected them to get up and walk out of the door of their own accord.

Nobody was perfect, though, and had he opted to stick around, she'd have been prepared to let his not-so-attractive traits go by the by.

Pete's leaving had meant two things. The first was that she now had a deep and abiding dislike of the synthesiser as a musical instrument. The second was that, like her, it was doubtful her daughter would ever know her father, which made her sad. Fern had wanted Sabrina to have the sort of family she'd missed out on. The kind of family with a mam, dad and a little brother or sister. A proper family. Now Sabrina just had her, and she wasn't sure if she'd be enough. It was a lot to live up to being everything to someone.

As Fern carried on pushing the pram, she noticed Sabrina had undone the straps again.

'What have I told you?' she huffed, veering out of the way of a woman in a pink sari with a sweater overtop despite the sweltering temperature.

'Don't like it, Mummy.' Sabrina wriggled to avoid being buckled back in, but Fern was having none of it.

'Stop that right now, do you hear me? Or there'll be no chocolate bar when we get to the station.'

The wriggling stopped.

The shop beside them had a 'To Let' sign in the grimy window, and an empty lager can along with a collection of cigarette butts littered the doorway. Fern wrinkled her nose because she was sure she could smell wee.

She bent over the pushchair to click the strap back in, jumping as a piercing wolf whistle sounded. The culprit was a fella with longish hair leaning out the passenger window of a white van as it sailed past.

Pulling a face and pretending to be annoyed, she tugged the hem of her skirt down. Then, ignoring a group of lads with Mohicans in every shade of the rainbow, studded dog collars wrapped around their necks, and scrawny white arms protruding from Union Jack singlets, her eyes cut to the familiar striped awning framing Tabac across the street.

The café was a source of fascination because it was a great spot for celebrity spotting, and the food was good. Unfortunately, she was too skint to call in for coffee or a bite to eat, but she could veer past and see if anyone of note was dining in there today.

She waited for a break in the stream of cars. When it came, she bounced the pram across the road, coming to a halt under the awning to gawp in the window. But, unfortunately, there were no diners whose lunch was worth interrupting to ask for an autograph, and so, with a disappointed sigh, she hurried on.

The sign for the wedding shop, tucked between two larger buildings a short distance ahead, caught her eye.

It was the boutique where one of the girls she'd been in care with had had her wedding and bridesmaids' dresses made. Brides of Bold Street. She'd done all right for herself had Diane, marrying a fella who worked for the bank. Her mouth tightened. She hadn't been asked to be a bridesmaid.

The irritation that still rankled at the snub disappeared, however, as she saw the newsagent where she'd called in to buy her monthly magazine treat just a week before had gone. In its place was a shop with posed mannequins in the antwacky gear she had vague memories of her mam poncing about in. Retro was all the rage these days. Not that she'd be caught dead in clobber like that.

Her eyes swung out to the road. *How strange.* There were nowhere near as many cars as there'd been a moment ago, and the ones tootling up the street were similar to the old banger her miserly granddad had refused to part with.

The air had changed too. It felt thick, almost as if Fern were wading through tepid soup. She came to a halt. The sensation wasn't dissimilar to the time she'd stood at the top of the Blackpool Tower and her legs had threatened to give out on her.

'I'll just close my eyes for a second,' she mumbled, having decided she must be having a funny turn of sorts.

The whoosh of people carrying on about their business as they passed her by continued. Nobody seemed to find anything odd about her standing in the middle of the pavement with her eyes squeezed shut, clutching the pram for support.

She cautiously opened them once more and blinked rapidly to assure herself things were as they should be.

Only they weren't.

The blood turned to ice in her veins as she realised the pushchair was empty.

∼

'I didn't understand what had happened. All I knew was one minute you were there sitting in the pram, the next you'd gone, and I tried to stay calm. You were forever running away and hiding, you see. You'd done it to me before when we were out. So I told myself I'd find you giggling in one of the nearby shops. I'd give you a smack on your bottom, and we'd go home and have egg and chips for our dinner. Only, you weren't in any of the shops, and that's when I began to panic. I grabbed hold of this fella's arm and asked him to tell me what street I was on because even though the buildings were the same, the shops were different. He said what I already knew — I was still on Bold Street.'

Sabrina had to remember to breathe, as dizziness threatened to overwhelm her.

'Then I asked if he'd seen my daughter, and he looked at me like I were two pennies short of a shilling. He offered to buy me a cuppa so I could have a bit of a sit-down, but I asked him what year it was. When he told me it was 1963, I panicked and ran off.'

'It was my uncle you met that day. Uncle Eddie,' Adam interjected.

Fern looked at him, startled, coming out of the almost trancelike state she'd gone into as she told her tale. 'Who are you?'

'Sabrina's boyfriend, Adam. Me uncle always talked about this strange encounter he had in 1963 on Bold Street with a young woman who was looking for her child. He'd say she was adamant it was 1983, and how he'd put her right, but she was having none of it. Me uncle said you ran off. He said you vanished, and it was like you disappeared into thin air right before his eyes.'

'I did run off to find Sabrina, but there was that shift in the air again, and then just like that, everything was as it had been before. The punks I'd seen earlier were hanging about outside a record shop; the woman in the sari had stopped to talk to another woman. It was all the same, but Sabrina was gone.' Her eyes filled with tears, and she swiped them away with the back of her hand. 'None of it made sense. It never has.'

Fern nipped at her bottom lip, listening as Sabrina told her how her search for answers as to what had happened that fateful day had begun in earnest when Adam had relayed his uncle's story. 'I began to wonder whether I hadn't been abandoned after all.'

'I would never willingly have left you, Sabrina.'

'What did you do once you realised I was gone? Properly gone, I mean.'

The threatened tears welled over, and Fern's voice had a tremor in it as she said, 'I wanted to understand, to try and make some sense out of what was going on, and the only thing I could think of doing was going to the library.'

Sabrina screwed up her face. The library. Her child had gone missing and she'd gone to the library? What kind of a mother was she? It was too much. Exhaustion or shock – both maybe – overwhelmed her, and she stood up, clasping the table to steady herself. How her mother had managed to wind up here in 1945 was still a mystery, but what was blatantly obvious was that she'd given up her search for her missing daughter and started a new family. She'd been replaced. Hadn't she seen that with her own two eyes here tonight? Her eyes flashed with pain.

'I don't want to hear any more!' she sobbed, running from the room and, because she had nowhere else to go, heading upstairs.

~

Adam and Fern stared at one another. The only sound was a door swinging shut upstairs and then the loud ticking of the wall clock.

'I should go.' Fern stood up after a few seconds.

Adam nodded. 'I'll talk to her. She just needs a chance to sort everything in her head. I'm sure you do too.'

Fern nodded. 'It's a lot to take in. Lily knows where she can find me when Sabrina's ready to talk some more. I've waited this long. I can wait some more.'

Adam hesitated and then blurted, 'Please don't hurt her. She's been hurt enough.'

'I never intended to hurt her, Adam. It was out of my control, and believe me not a single day has passed since we were separated where I haven't yearned for her.'

Adam nodded. It was late; they were all beyond tired. He got up from the table himself, manners automatically prevailing as he said he'd see Fern to the door, even though it wasn't his house.

~

Upstairs, Sabrina had buried her face in a pillow to muffle her sobs. She'd found her mother, but she hadn't found the answers she'd wanted to hear. She should have left things well alone, but even as she thumped the pillow, she knew she'd not had a choice because everything that had happened was governed by fate and by time, both of which she and Fern had no control over.

She heard the door close downstairs and Adam's steps approaching.

Thank goodness she had Adam because without him she would be truly lost.

## 26

Sabrina had expected to toss and turn all night, but wrapped in Adam's arms she'd slept soundly. Her body knew what her mind needed, she supposed, or maybe it was the other way round. Adam must have woken early because when Sabrina opened her eyes to discover a new day had dawned, she found his side of the bed was empty. She lay there slowly coming to the surface, gradually becoming aware of the sounds outside: the clink of bottles, the rumble of a car, a mother calling her child in while inside the murmur of voices drifted up through the floorboards.

What she'd learned the night before came crowding back in on her, and she squeezed her eyes shut at the bolt of pain as her mother's face danced before her. She couldn't leave things as they were. Besides, parts of Fern's journey were still murky, like how she'd wound up here, and with that in mind, she got up and stretched. Her limbs felt sluggish and her head foggy with having slept too heavily, and she padded over to the dressing table to peer in the mirror. The dishevelled apparition reflected at her made her grimace, and she went through the motions of washing, dressing and making the bed before going downstairs to find tea and toast waiting for her.

Adam and Lily were sitting at the table.

'Morning,' Lily greeted her, dressed in her uniform once more. 'We heard you moving about.'

She sipped her own tea as Sabrina joined them. She and Adam were chatting about the bonfire and how she'd met up with Max. 'We said good night or good morning or worever it was around three o'clock. It was some party. I don't think I'll be seeing him until later. He'll be sound asleep about now.'

Sabrina got the distinct impression she was avoiding the topic of Fern and her relationship to Sabrina, and before she'd even finished her toast, Lily sprang up from her seat.

'I don't want to be late for my shift at the Royal!'

She was out the door before Sabrina could swallow her mouthful. She'd intended to ask where they'd find Fern, but Adam, reading her mind, said, 'I have her address.'

The Carters' home was a carbon copy of Lily's terrace house. It was only a short walk from where the bonfire ashes smouldered. Alfie was kicking a ball about with some other boys in the street and, recognising them from last night, waved out. Lily had told Adam that Sarah was also working a shift at the hospital. This was good, Sabrina thought, because the conversation that needed to be had was between her and Fern. And Adam because she wanted him there to hear it all with her.

Fern seemed unsurprised to find them there when she opened her door and ushered them in. 'Make yourselves at home. After all, this is your home too, Sabrina,' she said, unaware Sabrina had stiffened as she saw them into the sitting room.

'I'll put the kettle on.'

Adam settled himself on the sofa while Sabrina hovered anxiously, ignoring his pat of the seat next to him.

It was a cosy room with a painting depicting a farmer in a field of haystacks hanging a little crookedly against the striped wallpaper. The carpet was busy and beginning to wear thin in places, and the furnishings looked lived in. It was the art deco sideboard that immediately drew Sabrina over though. A wireless along with some china knick-knacks and a trio of silver-framed photographs were arranged on it. She picked up one of the frames. Her eyes grazed over the handsome man in uniform staring out at her. Mr Carter. Sarah had said her dad was still away and was hoping to be demobbed soon. It was from him that Sarah and Alfie got their dark good looks, she realised, peering intently into his unreadable eyes. What was he was like?

She put the frame down carefully, hearing the creak of the floorboards beneath the carpet as Adam joined her, equally curious. She picked up another photograph. It was of the family clustered out the front of the house here, and seeing them gathered made her feel peculiar – as if she'd been cut from the frame. Sarah was younger, with her hair clipped back from her face, and Alfie just a babe. She absorbed the image of their mother – *her* mother – young and pretty in a flowery dress with a shy smile for the camera. She looked to be in her later twenties. Her husband, in uniform, stood a head taller than her with his arm wrapped protectively around her shoulder.

'You're the spit of her, Sabrina,' Adam said gently.

The last picture showed the Carters on their wedding day. The fashion was of the late twenties, and Sabrina wondered idly if she'd had her dress made at Brides of Bold Street. The couple had shied away from the stern-lipped fashion of the day and were smiling broadly at the camera. She made a beautiful bride, her dress exquisite, Sabrina thought. For an eerie second, it was like seeing herself on her wedding day.

They heard the rattle of china approach, and she fumbled the photograph in her haste to put it down as Fern appeared with a tea tray.

'I'd be curious too.' Her smile was gentle as she set the tray down on a table with fold-down wings and began pouring the tea.

'I wondered if you'd had your dress made at Brides of Bold Street?'

'No. I don't go anywhere near Bold Street anymore.' Fern's tone was sharp, and Sabrina noticed Fern's hand was shaking. She was just as tightly coiled inside with all the things they needed to say to one another.

'Milk and sugar?' Fern asked, not making eye contact with either of them.

'Yes, please – we both have our tea with milk and a teaspoon of sugar,' Adam answered, sitting down on the sofa once more.

Sabrina joined him, sitting closer to him than was necessary, with her leg pressing against his.

The cups Fern offered them were like clacking false teeth in their saucers, and Adam took them quickly lest she drop them altogether. He put Sabrina's down on the side table tucked in alongside the sofa, perhaps doubting her ability to hold one steady either.

Fern flopped into a sunken armchair, placing a tapestry cushion behind her back and ignoring her tea. 'Shall I pick up where I left off?'

'Please,' Sabrina replied, determined to hear Fern out today as she clasped her hands in her lap so tightly her nails dug into her palms. She felt as if every nerve ending in her body was jangling with anticipation.

'I searched and searched for you that afternoon, Sabrina, and I was going to go to the police, but what would I have told them? That this weird moment of something I didn't understand had made me lose my daughter? If I'd told them that, they'd have thought me barmy, and I was frightened they'd think I'd done something to you. A single mother, struggling. I know how they think. When you've grown up in the system like I did, you don't hold much faith in it.'

Sabrina felt a pang of sadness for the girl her mother had once been. 'So you went to the library?'

'I did because it dawned on me that perhaps I wasn't the only person this – whatever this was – had happened to. And I was right. I asked the librarian if they had any newspaper stories on file about anything odd happening on Bold Street. There was, of course, and I leaped on the tales of other people's experiences of being pulled back to another era only to wander out into their own again. If this was what had happened, then it meant you hadn't been snatched but that we'd become separated by some strange force at work on Bold Street. I wasn't going mad, and there was no point trying to get a search underway to find you because I was twenty years too late for that.'

'I must have got out of the pushchair and found my way down to Cripps *after* we went through the timeslip to 1963.' Sabrina was thinking out loud. 'It's where I was found. I stayed in 1963, but you were taken back through to 1983.'

'Cripps?' Fern mumbled, dipping her head and rubbing her temples. When she looked up, Sabrina could see the anguish stamped in her eyes. 'I was so close, but I was pulled back to where we'd come from before I got as far as the dressmaker's.'

'What did you do when you twigged about the time portal?'

'I wouldn't say I've ever understood what that pocket is on Bold Street, but I did realise the only chance I had of getting you back was to try and make it take me back to 1963 because I thought that's where you must be.'

'And I was. So you stepped through the portal?' Sabrina stated.

'Yes, I went back,' Fern confirmed, and something unreadable flickered across her face. 'Only I found myself in 1924, and no matter how many times I traipsed up and down that weird pocket on Bold Street hoping against hope to step into 1963, nothing changed. It was so disorientating – terrifying actually – to be stuck somewhere familiar yet so different. I slept rough for the first few nights.' She winced at the memory. It was obviously still raw.

Sabrina recalled her own evening spent huddled down an alleyway with only rats for company. It was an experience she'd no wish to repeat, and she shuddered.

'I was hungry and thirsty, and I stood out in my sweater and jeans, so I resorted to thieving. I stole an apple and a dress. I'm not proud of that.'

'You did what you had to do,' Adam said.

Fern nodded. 'Doesn't make it right though. I'm not a thief. Kenneth saw me huddled in a doorway and took pity on me, offering to take me for something to eat. He wor so kind; I didn't want him thinking I wasn't right in the head, so I told him I'd come to Liverpool after losing me mam and dad to find me aunt, only to learn she'd died too.' Her smile was rueful. 'Whatever he thought, he accepted what I said and took me home to his mam. God rest Florrie Carter's soul – she wor a wonderful woman. The mother I never had. Kenneth's family became my family, and, well, I fell in love with my Ken the moment he held his hand out to me on Bold Street. He felt the same way, and we were married after a few months.'

'And did you keep trying to go back?' Sabrina asked, surprised by how much whatever her mother was to say next mattered to her.

'I did – at first.' She twisted the wedding band on her finger. 'But then I fell pregnant with our Sarah, and I realised something. Please don't judge me too harshly, Sabrina, but I was happy. Happiness wasn't something I'd had much of in my life – apart from when you came along, of course. And if I kept visiting Bold Street, there wor no guarantee I'd step into 1963 and find you. I could have wound up losing not just you but Kenneth and his people. They were the first proper family I'd known.'

'But I was your family too.'

'Try and understand, Sabrina. I was frightened. I couldn't keep tempting fate. It had never dealt me a fair hand until I met Kenneth.'

'So you chose to give up on me?' Sabrina's voice caught. 'I never gave up on you.'

'Sabrina, let Fern finish,' Adam cut in.

Sabrina wasn't listening though. She'd risked everything for this woman who'd chosen a fresh start over her, while Adam, in turn, had risked everything for her. She should have listened to Mystic Lou's warning.

Forgetting her promise to herself that she'd hear Fern out, she sprang to her feet, ran from the room, out the front door and sprinted away from the Carters' house, not caring if she never saw the woman who'd given birth to her again. It was over.

## 27

Lily had finished her shift at the Royal, but she hadn't gone home to Needham Road. There was nothing she could do for Fern – or Sabrina and Adam – now. They had to work their strange story out for themselves. All she could do was hope Sarah and Alfie didn't get hurt in the process, but if they did, well, she'd be there for them just as they'd been there for her when she'd needed support. Their tangled past had given her an inkling as to the fragility of the world in which they moved, and she knew it was time for her to accept her own past.

This was why she was making her way to her aunt and uncle's house, telling herself she was a Tubb. Nothing could change that, and the Tubbs were a brave bunch. They had Viking blood running through their veins. Be that as it may, she still fancied she could hear the hammering of her own heart over the din the small lads kicking a ball about in the street were making. She scanned their ruddy faces to see if her cousins – *Your half-brothers, Lily,* she corrected herself – were there in the fray but couldn't see them.

There were no signs of shadowy life behind the net curtains of the front room either, but given the time of day, she'd hazard a guess her aunt – she couldn't bring herself to call her mam – would be in the kitchen. The boys were probably hovering around underfoot with their noses twitching, waiting for dinner. She pictured the familiar scene with Aunt Pat flapping them away with a tea towel.

It wasn't too late. She could turn and walk away. *No, Lily, you've come this far*, she told herself and took a steadying breath. Her conversation with Max the night before nudged her on. She'd promised him she would listen to her aunt's side of things, and she reminded herself of this as she climbed the three steps to the front door and knocked.

Thundering footsteps sounded, and the door swung open to reveal Donny. He was nearly as tall as Lily now. How was it possible for him to have grown in the short time since she'd last seen him, or was it her mind playing tricks on her? She stared at him, thinking how odd it was knowing he wasn't her cousin after all but rather a brother. 'Hello, Donny. Is Aunt Pat about?'

'Where've you been then?' Donny demanded, filling the space between the frame as he postured. 'Mam said you'd moved back to the house where you used to live. You made her cry, Lily Tubb, and ta very much for not saying goodbye.'

His glare was accusatory as he waited to hear what she had to say. Lily would have found the seventeen-year-old acting the man of the house amusing if she hadn't been on eggshells about seeing her aunt. She knew Donny clashed with his dad at times over his behaving as if he ruled the roost. Her aunt had explained he'd got used to his dad being away during the first half of the war and had found it hard to relinquish the title of man of the house when he'd returned.

'I know I did, and I'm sorry.' Lily met his gaze steadily.

Donny didn't budge. 'She won't tell me what you did.'

'I didn't do anything, ta very much.' Lily was beginning to feel annoyed, and if Donny didn't step aside and let her in, she'd push him out the way.

'Who's at the door, Donny?' Her aunt bobbed out from the kitchen, straightening her pinny. She came to a halt as she registered who her oldest son was talking to. 'Lily!' Hope flared on her face.

'Hello, Aunt Pat.'

'Donny, let the girl in, for goodness' sake.'

Donny moved aside reluctantly, and Lily stepped inside, breathing in the familiar scents of the house that had been a home to her when she'd needed it most.

'Come on through to the kitchen, Lily luv. I've a pie in the oven, and if I don't keep an eye on it, the top will burn. You know how temperamental my cooker is. Donny, round up your brothers and take them outside for a bit, would you?'

Donny bristled but did as he was told.

Lily followed behind her aunt, and as she hovered in the kitchen doorway, she heard a whooping coming down the stairs. She received a much warmer welcome from the littler of the brothers. Charlie wrapped himself around her legs, and Gerald stood grinning up at her. She realised how much she'd missed the boys, even Donny. She knew he was only looking out for his mam. He herded the younger two toward the door.

'Don't bang the door shut,' Aunt Pat called as Gerald did precisely that. She gave a rueful smile, but it didn't reach her eyes, which shone with uncertainty. 'Those lads will be the death of me. Sit down, and I'll put the kettle on.'

Lily would have offered to make the tea. She knew where everything was, but it didn't feel right to make herself at home. So instead, she sat at the table, her stomach giving an involuntary growl at the whiff of pie as her aunt opened the cooker to check on it.

'You've lost weight,' Aunt Pat remarked once she'd righted herself, glancing over at Lily before busying herself with warming the teapot. A cake tin was produced, and she sliced a wedge of carrot cake, all the while prattling on about how Lily would have to cook proper meals once she was wed.

'I'll give you my Lord Woolton pie recipe. It's the secret ingredients I added to it that makes it tasty, luv.' She slid the cake in front of Lily. 'The war might be over, but we won't see the end of rationing for a while longer. You'll have to learn to be creative in the kitchen. I can write down a few recipes for you, if you like?'

Lily nodded absently. She hadn't come here to talk about food, as Aunt Pat knew well. However, her aunt was just as anxious as Lily was, and somehow that made her feel marginally better.

The tea things were set down on the table. 'Get that down yer, luv, before you fade away.' Pat gestured to the untouched cake.

'Aunt Pat, tell me what happened,' Lily said, ignoring the cake. 'I want to know why I was brought up by your sister and her husband.'

'Your mam and dad, Lily Tubb, and don't you forget it. You were loved as much as any child could be. What was done was for the best at the time.' She turned the teapot three times as was the custom. 'That's all any of us can do, you know. Our best.'

Lily nodded but didn't speak because she hadn't come here to butt heads. All she was after was answers.

Pat sighed and poured the tea. 'There's not a lot to tell. I was only sixteen when I found out I was expecting you. I'd met this fella at a dance, you see. Frank was his name. He never told me his last name. He swept me right off me feet, although when I look back now, I think I was more in love with the idea of the sweepin' than the actual being swept.' She gave a tinkly laugh, but Lily didn't raise a smile.

'We went out a few times. He took me to nice places. Places

I'd never been to before or since. Restaurants with fancy place settings and silver so shiny you could see your face in it. I'd wear me mam's best dress and sneak out of the house feeling so grown-up, only I wasn't, of course. I wor a silly child, Lily, whose head was easily turned. I didn't know I wor pregnant until I was nearly four months gone, and when I told Frank, well, he took fright. He arranged to meet me a few days later and then fobbed me off with a handful of notes and the name of a place he'd heard about where I could go to get rid of the baby. It wasn't the fairy-tale ending I'd hoped for, and I knew then he wor married and that I'd never see him again. I wor on me own where you were concerned.'

Lily tried to put herself in her aunt's shoes, imagining how frightened she must have been, and she watched the trembling of her hand as she raised her teacup to her mouth.

'I went there, you know, to the place he told me about. It wor down a back alley. Filthy, dirty place.' She shuddered. 'The women hanging about were a rough lot. I stood outside that door for an age. I was terrified of what would happen if I went through it and equally terrified of having to go home to tell me mam and dad if I didn't.'

Lily felt a wave of sorrow for her teenaged aunt as she waited to hear what had transpired next.

'I went home in the end, of course, and faced the music.' Her face was clouded. 'I was sent away to me mam's sister's down south, where nobody knew me, to have the baby. It wor Sylvie who suggested she and Joe bring the baby – you – up as their own. They'd not been blessed, you see, and so it was all arranged. Sylvie thought it better if I didn't see you. She wor scared—'

Lily interrupted, 'Of what? I don't understand!'

'I've thought long and hard about this, and I s'pose she thought you might love her less if you knew. I lost you and me sister.' Pat drained her tea and carried her cup and saucer over to the worktop. She stared out the back window at the fence beyond.

Lily sat there absorbing what she'd been told, and it dawned on her then. 'It wor you. All along it wor you.'

Pat didn't turn around.

'My guardian angel.' The woman she'd seen all through her childhood from afar; it was Aunt Pat. Of course it was. How had she not realised sooner?

'You're not to think badly of Sylvie. I won't have it, Lily. She wor a good mam and a good sister once.' Her back was rigid.

'She was.' Lily ached for a minute more with her mam. She wanted to tell her it didn't matter. She didn't love her any less. She could have told her, and it wouldn't have changed how she felt about her and Dad.

'We've gorra learn. Haven't we, Lily? To move forward and not dwell on the past. Surely that's something this godforsaken war has taught us?' Pat turned around then, her eyes bright with tears.

Lily got up from her seat and took the short few steps across the small space to her aunt. 'We do.' A twin set of hazel eyes stared at one another, and then Pat opened her arms and pulled Lily into her.

'I love you, girl. Always have, always will.'

## 28

Adam flicked one last glance at Fern's distraught face then made to go after Sabrina, nearly colliding with young Alfie as he barrelled in through the front door.

'What's the hurry, mister? I just saw your missus running down the street like her house were on fire.'

Fern, who'd come out to the hallway, said, 'Alfie, mind your business and let Adam pass.'

'But, Mam,' he whined, 'who are they?'

'Alfie!' Fern's tone meant business, and he reluctantly moved aside. 'Go,' she urged Adam. 'Sabrina needs you.'

Adam didn't need to be told twice and hurried off. His jog turned into a sprint upon seeing Sabrina in the distance. Her step faltered as she reached the top of the street, obviously undecided where she should go. She turned right, running again as Adam hared after her. He could feel the curtains in the houses he was pounding past twitching, and he kept his gaze straight ahead, ignoring the curious looks of passers-by until at last she was only a few houses ahead of him.

'Sabrina!'

She slowed but didn't stop, and it gave him a chance to

catch her up. His arm stretched out toward her, but she wasn't quite within reach. 'Stop!'

She stumbled to a standstill, and he grasped hold of her, panting, as he pulled her to him. Her voice when she caught her breath was small and broken, 'She didn't want me, Adam.'

'Ah, come on now. It wasn't like that. She did want you. The poor woman tried her hardest to find you, but it was out of her control.' Adam stroked her hair.

'She gave up on me, and she chose them. You heard her!' Sabrina pushed away from him, raising her anguished face, which was streaked with tears. 'I want to go to Bold Street now. I want to go home to Aunt Evie where I belong.'

Adam shook his head, his expression firm. 'No. We're not going. Not yet. This might be your only chance to make your peace with your past. She's your mother, Sabrina.'

Sabrina's chin jutted out, as if she was about to argue, but then the fight went out of her and her body slumped against his. He held her tightly.

'Whatever else Fern has to tell you, Sabrina Flooks, I'm here for you. And you are loved. Your aunt Evie loves you, Florence and her family love you, your grateful brides love you.' His lips brushed the top of her head. 'And I love you too, girl.'

∽

There in Adam's arms, Sabrina felt something warm open and unfurl inside her, like a spring flower blooming. Adam was right, and she was so very grateful he'd come on this journey with her. So long as he was by her side, she could be strong. 'I love you too.'

'You'll come back then?'

Sabrina bit her bottom lip, and after a beat of hesitation she nodded and let him lead her toward the house she'd run away from, determined to never look back.

. . .

Alfie shot them a resentful glance as his mam herded him outside to play after opening the door to Sabrina and Adam.

'No whining, Alfie Carter. Off you go.' Fern had adopted a stern tone.

Sabrina stared at the little boy who was her half-brother.

'I'm glad you came back, Sabrina.' Fern saw them inside.

The sofa, which Sabrina sank onto gratefully, was still warm.

This time, Fern, a cigarette halfway to her lips, said, 'I still have nightmares about that day, Sabrina. What happened to you after we were separated?'

Her hand shook as she struck a match and lit her smoke, and Sabrina understood she was terrified as to what the answer might be.

'I was found by Evelyn Flooks, who's the proprietor of Brides of Bold Street, outside Cripps.' Sabrina relayed how she'd tugged at Evelyn's skirt. 'I told her my name was Sabrina then asked her where my mam was. She enquired inside Cripps whether anyone's child had run off while they were in the shop. Then she spent an age stopping passers-by on the street to ask them if they'd seen a woman looking for her daughter. No one had. In the end, she took me back to Brides of Bold Street. She assumed you'd come barrelling in at some point, frantic, trying to find me. But when that didn't happen, she decided there was nothing else for it but to take me to the police station. She got as far as the station, and when she saw there was no talk of a missing child, she decided she couldn't hand me over. Aunt Evie said there were whispers rife at that time about what happened to children in care or those who were orphaned and the like. There was talk they were put on ships and sent to Canada and Australia, never to be heard of again.'

Sabrina broke off, thinking about her friend Patty. Her

brother had been sent to Australia, and she hadn't set eyes on him until she was an adult and had travelled to Australia to find him.

'Aunt Evie was worried about what would happen if you did turn up. For all she knew, you could've been in an accident and wound up in hospital. You could have lost your memory. If no one was looking for me, then I'd have been placed in care, and she couldn't risk me being shipped off to Australia.'

Fern stared at the glowing orange tip of her cigarette. The smoke spiralled past her face as Sabrina continued to talk.

'Days turned to weeks and then months with no word of a missing child, and eventually, it was like I'd always been with Aunt Evie. Nobody questioned the story that I was her niece and her me aunt. She took care of all the legalities – well, had the necessary documents for me to become Sabrina Flooks forged.'

Fern raised her chin. 'A resourceful woman. Have you been happy?'

Sabrina nodded and looked at Adam, who gave her a smile, his hand still gently squeezing her leg. 'I've had a lovely life with Aunt Evie. I've followed in her footsteps as a dressmaker, and I manage the bridal shop these days.'

Fern shut her eyes for a moment, and when she opened them, Sabrina saw the sadness marring her unusual irises – so like her own. 'I'm glad you've had a good life. I prayed for it.'

The two women lapsed into silence, and Fern sat smoking, clearly trying to absorb Sabrina's story with each deep inhale of her cigarette.

Right then, Sabrina wished she smoked too. Adam squeezed her hand, signalling she should be patient and let Fern come back to her side of the story in her own time.

The sounds of children laughing overrode the ticking carriage clock and the muffled sound of shouting next door.

Fern dipped her head toward the wall. 'Those two are

always at it since he came home from France. Between us, Mrs Smith got very friendly with one of the volunteer policemen in his absence.'

'I imagine there'll be a few couples who haven't picked up where they left off,' Adam said, while Sabrina remained quiet, waiting.

Fern ground out her cigarette and then looked at Sabrina. 'I got pregnant with our Sarah not long after Ken and I married. I'd convinced myself by then that you'd have found a good home, Sabrina. All I ever wanted me whole life wor a family of my own. I'd have given anything to have you here with me and Ken where you belonged.'

'But I didn't belong here,' Sabrina said softly.

'No. You didn't, but that didn't stop me thinking about you every day, wondering where you were and what sort of life you were leading.' Fern's sigh was weighty. 'It was the not knowing that was the hardest.'

Sabrina could understand that.

'In the end, I suppose I put my trust in fate because fate tore us apart, and I prayed it would see fit to bring us back together. And it has – just not how I imagined it.'

'Kenneth doesn't know about me?' Sabrina asked after the silence had begun to stretch long.

Fern shook her head. 'No. I could never find the words to tell him. I never changed the story I told him when we first met, and he never questioned any of what I said. We don't live in the past, do we, luv? Life propels us forward. It's the way it is.'

That was true, Sabrina thought. Then she asked herself if she would change her life. If she had the opportunity to go back and change everything, she'd have had her mother, but she wouldn't have had Aunt Evie. Nor would she have Flo and the Teesdale family – or Adam for that matter. You couldn't change what had already been. You could only make peace with it.

For whatever reason, on Bold Street in 1983, the future had

shifted and changed. Fern had vanished from 1983, as had three-year-old Sabrina, never to be seen again, but they'd both found happiness.

Sabrina knew she was standing at a crossroads. One direction would see her remaining angry with her mother, continuing to wrestle with her feelings of being rejected, or she could take the other path. The path back to Aunt Evie, Flo and her family, with Adam by her side.

She pushed up from her seat and embraced her mother, breathing in the vaguely remembered scent because she'd chosen the path back to Bold Street – home, where she belonged with the people she loved and who loved her.

∽

Adam watched the poignant scene with a lump in his throat because this was what they'd come for. He'd also figured something out, something he wasn't sure he would share, and it was making his head reel.

Fern was aware, right now, here in 1945, of where Sabrina could be found in 1963. Her three-year-old daughter would be outside Cripps, wondering where her mother was and why she hadn't come for her. There was only one reason why Fern hadn't gone to her firstborn child when time caught up to the day she'd lost her. It was because she wouldn't live to see her fifty-ninth birthday.

He observed the connection between the two women, mother and daughter separated by time but bonded together forever, and knew he'd never breathe a word of what he'd figured out to Sabrina. There was no point. You couldn't change what was written in the stars.

## 29

'I never doubted you'd be back, Lily. Not for a moment.' Evelyn Flooks smiled before fetching the wedding dress Lily had previously returned from the back of Brides of Bold Street.

'Well, I'm very glad you didn't listen to me.' Lily smiled gratefully. 'Thank you, Evelyn.'

'I'm a wise owl me. You'll be a beautiful bride.'

'You'll be there to see for yourself, won't you? It's short notice, but there's an available slot at Toxteth Town Hall this Thursday at two fifteen p.m.' Lily's aunt and uncle were coming, along with her half-brothers, who'd been told the truth of who she was and taken it in their stride, the way children did.

'Might I ask what the rush is?' Her eyes strayed to Lily's flat-as-a-pancake middle.

'Evelyn Flooks! It's certainly not what you're thinking. The war's taught us all there's no time to waste, and I don't want to wait anymore. Nor does Max.'

'Well, that sounds as good a reason as any to wed to me. I'll close the shop for an hour on Thursday afternoon then. I wouldn't miss your big day.'

'It won't be a big affair,' Lily said, quick to temper Evelyn's enthusiasm.

'Be that as it may, it will still be perfect,' Evelyn replied.

∽

It had been three days since Sabrina had made peace with Fern, and she and Adam had told Lily repeatedly how grateful they were for her hospitality. Lily had been happy to help Sabrina and Fern spend more time together, to get to know the intricacies of one another's lives, though she knew that would also make saying goodbye all the more painful when Sabrina and Adam finally went home.

Fern had taken to calling round to Needham Road each evening when Sarah returned home from her shifts at the hospital, free to keep an eye on Alfie for a few hours. And Lily, privy to Sabrina's decision not to disclose who she was to Sarah and Alfie, had gone along with the charade that Sabrina and Fern had simply hit it off as friends upon discovering they'd loads in common when Sarah commented on the intensity of the new relationship. They'd laughed away her remark of how similar they looked by saying everybody had a doppelganger. Theirs was not her secret to give away, and while there were no more secrets in her own family, some secrets were better off kept – like Sabrina and Fern's.

Now the drama of her initial encounter with the couple had been resolved, Lily had warmed to them and was pleased they'd agreed to be there on Thursday afternoon to see her wed Max. She'd also been surprised by how much it mattered to her that they attend. She wanted them to be able to tell her future granddaughter, Alice, about her grandparents' wedding day.

Of course, when she thought about it, she needn't have worried about them being there at Toxteth Hall because it was a foregone conclusion, given they were in her and Max's wedding picture. The very idea made her head whirl, and Lily didn't think she'd ever make sense of anything that had happened since Sabrina and Adam had accosted her outside Brides of Bold Street. But then again, perhaps she wasn't supposed to.

~

The temperamental clouds of the morning had been blown away by the time the newlywed Mr and Mrs Waters left the registry office. Instead of grey gloom, it was the sun that greeted the small party who'd gathered on the steps of the building where Lily and Max had just said their vows. They were waiting for their photograph to be taken.

On the pavement below, giving the bride and groom a clap, was a huddle of well-wishers. A mix of neighbours, including Mrs Dixon, and people the couple worked with.

Max's friend, a keen amateur photographer, stood centre stage, adjusting his camera. He'd been doing his best to tune out Mrs Dixon, who was bending his ear about how she'd known Lily since she was a young girl.

'Isn't it a shame her poor, dear departed mam and dad weren't here to see her in all her finery today?' she'd said just as the bride and groom appeared, dabbing at her eye with a handkerchief.

He was responsible for the photograph Alice had told Sabrina to guard with her life, Sabrina realised, positioning herself on the steps for a better view of the bride.

Lily was radiant, and the dress Aunt Evie had worked her magic on to ensure it fitted Lily perfectly was exquisite.

Sabrina had itched to hug this younger version of the aunt she knew and loved when she'd appeared at the registry office, and it was only through sheer willpower she'd kept her mouth shut and her arms by her side.

As it happened, Evelyn had been more interested in Adam.

'You're not related to Ray Taylor by chance, are you?' she'd asked, a curious expression on her wily face.

'Distantly,' Adam had replied, deliberately vague.

Sabrina brushed the tendril of hair that had come loose from the sweeping side-do she'd attempted away. Her eyes travelled past Lily to her new husband. Max was beaming from ear to ear with his brother, a burlier version of himself, proud as punch by his side. She moved her attention back to Lily and saw Sarah was taking her maid of honour role seriously as she titivated the bride's veil.

Sarah looked lovely in the dress she'd had repurposed for her best friend's big day – the lilac was stunning with her dark colouring. It was on her sister that Sabrina's gaze lingered. The sister who would never know she existed. She'd made her peace with that but was still sad at the missed chance for them to know one another. Maybe one day they'd have a second chance; she'd have to wait to find out. For now though, this was the way it had to be. She hoped Sarah found a man like Max – or like Adam, she thought, feeling the warmth of his hand in hers. She hoped she would have a happy life too, and that ragamuffin half-brother of hers, Alfie, too.

Sarah must have felt her gaze on her because her sable eyes flicked to Sabrina, and she smiled.

Sabrina smiled back.

Lily's aunt Pat fussed with the youngest of her three boys' hair, trying to smooth it down while he squirmed. Then, finally, her uncle told her to leave the poor lad be. He glowered at his other two sons, who were giving one another sly kicks.

As for Lily, she basked in the love she was surrounded by, and Sabrina knew her mam and dad would be with her in spirit as she stood proudly beside her husband on the registry office steps.

'Ahright, you lot. If you can hold still and on the count of three, say cheese.'

There was a last-minute kerfuffle as everybody took their places.

'One, two, three.'

'Cheese!'

The camera whirred and clicked, just as Fern tried to reel in Alfie, who didn't like having his photograph taken – mostly because it meant his mam attacking his cowlick, which permanently stood to attention. So it was that Fern Carter was captured neither in or out of the photograph's frame, and then the group descended the stairs.

Adam pumped Sabrina's hand gently. They would make their way to Bold Street now in the hope that today, with Lily and Max's wedding done and dusted, the inexplicable forces at work on the Liverpool street would take them home. They moved off to the periphery of the group, watching as the bride and groom were met with congratulations and pats on the back.

Fern, aware of their plans to try to go back to their own time after the wedding, made her way over to them, leaving Alfie with his sister. Both looked unimpressed at the arrangement.

She reached for Sabrina's free hand and held it in both of hers, her eyes sweeping over her like she was trying to commit every detail of her firstborn to memory. 'I'm going to come right out and say this, Sabrina.' Her gaze travelled swiftly to Adam. 'You'll have to forgive me for being selfish.'

He didn't let go of Sabrina's hand.

Fern turned to Sabrina once more, desperation lacing her tone as she said, 'I want you to stay. Please don't go.'

For the briefest moment, Sabrina felt a tug. She could stay and get to know Fern, Alfie and Sarah, be part of a family she hadn't known she had, but then she focused on Adam's hand, solid in hers, and knew what her answer had to be. He was where her future lay.

Sabrina shook her head slowly. 'I can't stay.'

'I know.' Fern's eyes glistened, and her smile was watery. 'I had to ask though.'

'I'll try to come back,' Sabrina said, not knowing if she would be brave enough to.

'No.' Fern's mouth tightened. 'You've your whole life ahead of you. Don't keep looking back over your shoulder.'

'Mam!' Sarah called, irritation spiking her voice over something her brother had done.

'Go,' Sabrina said, pulling her into a fierce embrace. 'This is where you belong.'

'I love you, girl. Always did, always will.' Fern held her close.

'I love you too,' Sabrina murmured, not wishing to cry on Lily and Max's special day.

Adam was by her side as she began to walk swiftly away. The tears were coming now, and she didn't want the curious onlookers to see them; nor did she trust herself not to change her mind.

'Sabrina, Adam, wait!' Lily had picked up her skirts and hurried after the couple.

They slowed, allowing her to catch them up while Sabrina furiously swiped her eyes with the backs of her hands.

'I wanted to give you something.' Lily unclipped the dainty pearl earrings she was wearing, 'Will you give these to Alice? From me. They were me nan's, and I want her to wear them on her day.' She glanced down. 'As well as the dress.'

'She'll look just as beautiful as you do, Lily.' Sabrina sniffed, feeling choked as she took the earrings, tucking them away before embracing the redhead. Adam gave her a quick squeeze too.

'Be happy, Lily, and have a wonderful life with your Max.'

'The same to you two,' she said, turning back toward her husband.

Sabrina and Adam walked away, and this time they didn't look back as they made their way to Bold Street.

It was time to go home.

# EPILOGUE
## LIVERPOOL, 1982

Evelyn, Sabrina and Adam were seated on chairs that could have done with a tad more cushioning. Adam shifted for the umpteenth time since he'd sat down and tugged at his shirt collar. Evelyn, her face in shadow beneath the brim of her new wedding hat – a delicate peach affair – glowered at him from behind her glasses. She'd thawed toward him since he and Sabrina had returned from their sojourn into the past, but she was yet to thoroughly defrost.

Mercifully, Sabrina had found the answers she'd so desperately needed in 1945 and still come back to her. Evelyn knew she'd have withered inside if the pull to stay in the past with her mother, a woman called Fern, had been too strong. She studied the backs of her hands, which were resting on the lap of her two-piece peach suit. They were hands that had given her so much joy with their ability to create beautiful gowns. Sabrina, though, was her most immense joy.

Sabrina deserved to be privy to her and Ray Taylor's story, she mused, twisting the small sapphire ring she wore on the middle finger of her right hand. One day soon, she'd tell her, she resolved, feeling Sabrina's arm resting against hers, but not today.

∼

It was just over a week since Sabrina and Adam had said goodbye to Lily and Fern and left the half-sister and brother Sabrina wasn't destined to grow old with.

The air had grown soupy within minutes of them beginning to traverse the pavement outside Cripps. Fate – or was it serendipity? Sabrina was starting to think it was the former which had brought them home to 1982. To where they both belonged and where, this time, she planned to stay.

Sabrina nudged Adam to sit still. The chairs, with their mean padding, had probably been bought with the intention of the backsides gracing them not being sat on them long enough to go numb.

She reached into her purse to retrieve her Opal Fruits but didn't bother offering Aunt Evie the packet. She'd only get a monologue on how false teeth and chewy sweets were a recipe for disaster. She held the tube under Adam's nose instead, and he helped himself, leaving a pink one beneath the sweet he took from her.

She unwrapped the square sweet and studied it momentarily. It was the same shade of pink as her new dress – a colour the shop assistant at Chelsea Girl had described as this season's jellybean pink. She popped the sweet in her mouth and sat up a bit straighter, smoothing the skirt of the pink belted dress with its gold buttons and shoulder pads. Aunt Evie said she'd get stuck going through doorways given the size of them, but Adam had said she looked gorgeous, and when Aunt Evie wasn't looking, he'd pinched her bum.

She chewed away and eyed the windows situated a little over to her left but out of reach with longing. She could feel the beginnings of a headache, thanks to the cloying mix of perfumes rivalling for top dog in the small space in which they'd crowded.

The registry office room could seat eighteen, and rows three seats wide and three seats deep were evenly spaced either side of the aisle Alice would soon walk down. Sabrina hoped it was sooner rather than later because her fiancé Mark was jiggling from leg to leg as though he needed a wee. Nerves, she guessed. He was handsome in his army uniform. Then her eyes swung to the plump, rosy-cheeked celebrant, who looked like she'd be more at home baking cakes than officiating a wedding. The celebrant leaned over and said something that made him smile. The jiggling stopped.

They were honoured to be here with Alice, who'd insisted they come, saying it was what her nan would have wanted. She hadn't said she believed Sabrina's long-winded story of having gone back in time to when Lily was young. Nevertheless, she'd stared at the earrings Sabrina had proffered as though they were the most precious gift she'd ever been given. Lily would have indeed been happy the three of them were here today for her granddaughter's special day, Sabrina thought, scanning the room in which every seat was taken.

'That must be Mark's mam,' she whispered to Evelyn. 'Alice said she was put-out they weren't having a big do.'

Evelyn looked to where Sabrina had indicated a stick-thin woman in an apple-green dress with a matching hat she almost needed an entire row to accommodate. Her expression was one of dissatisfaction as she glanced back to survey the small gathering.

'Good on them for sticking to their guns,' Evelyn whispered back. 'It's their day, after all. His mam obviously decided if she couldn't have a big do, she'd wear a big hat. Mind you, she needs something to distract from the size of that nose.'

Sabrina sniggered.

'What's so funny?' Adam asked.

Before she could answer, though, the doors swung open, and the wedding march sounded from an unknown source. Alice stood there poised in the doorway as all eyes swivelled toward the bride, who'd decided she didn't need anyone giving her away. An appreciative murmuring swept the room.

'She looks gorgeous,' Evelyn breathed.

'Stunning,' Sabrina said.

'She looks just like Lily,' Adam stated.

The dress, which had served three generations of Alice's family, brought out the creaminess of her skin, just as it had Lily's. Her red hair was pulled back today in a bun and threaded with apple blossoms. In her ears were the pearl earrings Lily had pressed on Sabrina. The perfect finishing touch. Her hands held a spring posy of peonies, larkspur and love-in-a-mist.

She glided forward to meet the man who would officially become her husband in a few minutes, and the service that followed was short and sweet. It might have been a no-nonsense affair, but it still saw Evelyn reach for the tissues. Sabrina too was busy dabbing her eyes when the couple were bent over the table beside the celebrant and two witnesses signing the marriage documents.

And then the jubilant newlyweds walked hand in hand from the room, their family and friends filing out after them.

'I'm starving,' Adam said in Sabrina's ear. 'Can't wait for lunch.'

'You're always thinking of your stomach.' Sabrina grinned up at him, although she was looking forward to the luncheon that was to follow at the restaurant where Alice was an apprentice. It was French, no less.

'I hope they're serving lamb. I like a nice bit of spring lamb,' Evelyn said. 'Although it does tend to get stuck in me dentures.'

'Aunt Evie!' Sabrina admonished. 'Keep your voice down.'

The group gathered on the steps of the registry office under a clear spring sky. Sunlight was dancing off the puddles from the rain that had been and gone in the time Alice and Mark had said their vows. A man in an ill-fitting suit took charge, flapping about, arranging them just so on the pavement in front of the one-storey brick building before clicking away with his camera.

'Toss your bouquet, Alice. It might gee our Terry up if I catch it,' a girl around Sabrina's age called out.

Laughter echoed about the group, and Alice took her place in front of them all.

She glanced back over her shoulder. 'Ready?'

'Ready!' a handful of eager female voices replied.

Alice tossed the posy high in the air over her shoulder. All eyes remained fixed on the gentle pinks, purples, blues and whites bunched together.

Sabrina's hand spontaneously shot up and caught the bouquet.

'You're for it now, mate,' someone jeered, but Adam just grinned, and Sabrina dipped her head to hide her pink face as she breathed in the sweet fragrance of spring.

# A LETTER FROM MICHELLE

Dear reader,

I want to say a huge thank you for choosing to read *The Dressmaker's War*. If you did enjoy it, and want to keep up to date with all my latest releases, just sign up at the following link. Your email address will never be shared, and you can unsubscribe at any time.

*www.bookouture.com/michelle-vernal*

I hope you loved *The Dressmaker's War*, and if you did, I would be very grateful if you could write a review. I'd love to hear what you think, and it makes such a difference helping new readers to discover one of my books for the first time.

I love hearing from my readers – you can get in touch through social media or my website.

Thanks,

Michelle Vernal

# KEEP IN TOUCH WITH MICHELLE

www.michellevernalbooks.com

facebook.com/michellevernalnovelist
x.com/MichelleVernal
goodreads.com/goodreadscommichellevernal

# PUBLISHING TEAM

**Turning a manuscript into a book requires the efforts of many people. The publishing team at Bookouture would like to acknowledge everyone who contributed to this publication.**

### Commercial
Lauren Morrissette
Hannah Richmond
Imogen Allport

### Cover design
Emma Graves

### Data and analysis
Mark Alder
Mohamed Bussuri

### Editorial
Natalie Edwards
Charlotte Hegley

### Copyeditor
Laura Kincaid

### Proofreader
Maddy Newquist

**Marketing**
Alex Crow
Melanie Price
Occy Carr
Cíara Rosney
Martyna Młynarska

**Operations and distribution**
Marina Valles
Stephanie Straub
Joe Morris

**Production**
Hannah Snetsinger
Mandy Kullar
Ria Clare
Nadia Michael

**Publicity**
Kim Nash
Noelle Holten
Jess Readett
Sarah Hardy

**Rights and contracts**
Peta Nightingale
Richard King
Saidah Graham

Printed in Dunstable, United Kingdom